A Time to Heal Workbook

This *Inner Work Book* is
part of a series that explores
psyche and spirit through writing,
visualization, ritual, and
imagination.

Other books in this series include:

The Adult Children of Divorce Workbook
BY MARY HIRSCHFELD, J.D., PH.D.

The Artist's Way
BY JULIA CAMERON

At a Journal Workshop
BY IRA PROGOFF, PH.D.

The Family Patterns Workbook
BY CAROLYN FOSTER

Following Your Path
BY ALEXANDRA COLLINS DICKERMAN, M.F.C.C.

The Inner Child Workbook
BY CATHRYN L. TAYLOR, M.A., M.F.C.C.

A Journey Through Your Childhood
BY CHRISTOPHER BIFFLE

The Path of the Everyday Hero
BY LORNA CATFORD, PH.D., AND MICHAEL RAY, PH.D.

Personal Mythology
BY DAVID FEINSTEIN, PH.D., AND STANLEY KRIPPNER, PH.D

The Possible Human
BY JEAN HOUSTON

The Search for the Beloved
BY JEAN HOUSTON

Smart Love
BY JODY HAYES

True Partners
BY TINA TESSINA, PH.D., AND RILEY K. SMITH, M.A.

Your Mythic Journey
BY SAM KEEN AND ANNE VALLEY-FOX

A Time to Heal Workbook

Stepping-stones to Recovery for Adult Children of Alcoholics

Timmen L. Cermak, M.D.
and Jacques Rutzky, M.F.C.C.

A Jeremy P. Tarcher/Putnam Book
published by
G. P. PUTNAM'S SONS
New York

I dedicate this book to all the alcoholics, other drug addicts, and their families who are not yet being reached by the help they need.

T. L. CERMAK, M.D.

This book is dedicated to those individuals who have shared their journey, their hope, their pain, and their healing.
And to the mamafish . . .

JACQUES RUTZKY, M.F.C.C.

A Jeremy P. Tarcher Book
Published by G. P. Putnam's Sons
Publishers Since 1838
200 Madison Avenue
New York, NY 10016

Jeremy P. Tarcher, Inc.
5858 Wilshire Blvd., Suite 200
Los Angeles, CA 90036

Library of Congress Cataloging-in-Publication Data

Cermak, Timmen L.
    A time to heal workbook : stepping-stones to recovery for adult children of alcoholics / Timmen L. Cemak and Jacques Rutzky.
        p.   cm.
    "A Jeremy P. Tarcher/Putnam book."
    Includes bibliographical references.
    ISBN 0-87477-745-3 (pbk.)
    1. Adult children of alcoholics—Rehabilitation.   2. Self-help techniques.
I. Rutzky, Jacques.   II. Cermak, Timmen L. Time to heal.   III. Title.
HV5132.C452   1994
362.29 ' 24—dc20   94-2179 CIP

Design by Mauna Eichner
Cover design by Susan Shankin
Cover photograph © Sorensen/Bohmer Olse/Tony Stone Worldwide

Printed in the United States of America
1   2   3   4   5   6   7   8   9   10

This book is printed on acid-free paper.

Contents

Preface

In 1945 I was born to an alcoholic father. But it was not until thirty-three years later that I began understanding how my father's alcoholism had affected me. Some effects were so obvious that only my willingness to be blind had kept them out of sight. But most effects were subtle mixtures of benefits and burdens. I took pride in the strengths they gave me, even as I ignored the toll they extracted. They gained most of their power by their pervasiveness rather than their intensity. They had woven themselves into the very fabric of my life, and I had little knowledge of the individual threads that had come together to form my identity. In 1978, during my residency in psychiatry, I finally began picking apart and examining these threads. To my surprise, this self-examination repeatedly revived memories of my father's drinking.

That same year I co-led the first psychotherapy group ever run for adult children of alcoholics, at the Stanford Alcoholism Clinic. This experience intertwined the personal and professional aspects of my life in ways that continue to benefit me. In 1983 I helped found the National Association for Children of Alcoholics (NACoA). A year later I founded the Genesis Psychotherapy and Training Center with my wife, Mary Brand Cermak, M.F.C.C., and together we developed a treatment program for Adult Children of Alcoholics (ACoAs), which continues to this day. As our experience accumulated, we gradually revised and refined our approach. In 1986 we worked with my coauthor, Jacques Rutzky, to further develop the Genesis groups and added a workbook that greatly increased their effectiveness. Now it is time to expand, revise, and make the workbook available to a wider audience.

Genesis recovery groups have one goal—*to help people personalize information about children of alcoholics. . . .* It is not sufficient to know, for example, that alcoholic families keep secrets. Self-knowledge requires more than theory; it requires honesty about concrete details. Personalizing information means being able to say, "The secrets *my* family kept are . . ." This workbook provides information and exercises to help people from alcoholic families in the struggle to know themselves. It is through such *self*-knowledge that you will find new freedom.

The more I work with adults recovering from their experiences growing up with parents who were alcoholic/drug addicted, the more I understand three important paradoxes:

1. Every adult child of an alcoholic/addict is unique, yet important commonalities thread through his or her experience.

2. Recovery takes place in an infinite variety of ways, yet each is consistent with all the others.

3. The words *adult* and *child* are of equal importance, but recovery involves their integration into a sense of self, that transcends both.

Let's take these one at a time.

First, with over thirty-five million Americans of all ages having at least one parent who is addicted to alcohol or other drugs,* it would be very superficial to assume that our experience has all been the same or that each has the same recovery needs. We were born with different temperaments, into different social and

---

*Throughout this book, alcohol is considered to be as much a drug as any other psychoactive substance that is swallowed (in liquid, pill, or other form), inhaled, snorted, or injected. Readers are reminded to translate the word *alcohol* into "and other drugs" whenever "alcohol" is used alone. Although there are a few differences, primarily revolving around the legality or illegality of a parent's drug of choice, the effects on children are roughly the same, whether a parent is chronically intoxicated by alcohol, marijuana, prescription tranquilizers, cocaine, heroin, etc.

economic classes, with different family constellations, ethnic, and religious backgrounds, and each of our parents had very different personalities and varying levels of severity in their addiction. Our experience with an alcoholic/drug-addicted parent affected us in very different ways.

First, although attention to individuality is necessary, the early stages of recovery frequently do involve exploring the common threads that wind their way through each of us. Because we were all children, we all had the same needs for truth and safety from our moms and dads. We all misinterpreted our parents' intoxicated behavior. We all tried to make a bad situation work. Most of us survived; some did not.

This workbook is designed to help you explore these common threads weaving through your life and to sort out the specific ways they have made an impact on you.

Second, just as religions travel up different faces of the same mountain, coming closer to one another as they approach the peak, so do the different paths of recovery converge toward the same point within each of us. At the base of the mountain, these paths may appear to be going in opposite directions. One begins with a strong spiritual base; the other avoids spiritual concerns. One begins with an individual psychotherapist; the other quits therapy and does ninety self-help meetings in ninety days. There is no one way that all must follow.

This workbook is designed not to prescribe the way you must take to recover but to illustrate the steps that many others have successfully taken, and to facilitate those steps that fit for you.

The concept of a "child within" has been helpful to many ACoAs. Some critics have denigrated this concept because it seems to infantilize people and to prevent them from accessing the adult skills that they do have. It is blamed for much of the fluff created by the pop psychology of recovery. What these criticisms fail to understand is that most ACoAs aborted their childhood and never grieved for what was lost. Unless this is understood, one will never be able to comprehend the power that the "child within" holds for many ACoAs.

On the other hand, the goal for most people is not simply to recover the child within but to integrate it into the realities of being an adult as well. Although this integration often must begin with an unconditional acceptance of one's inner child, it must eventually include the gradual and effective maturation of that child as well. Effective maturation does not mean aborting childhood prematurely and becoming unaware of one's childlike needs. For maturation to occur, the inner child has to be found and accepted; but it must also be coaxed into further growth. Perpetual indulgence of one's inner child does not serve recovery. Such indulgence stems from the child's having gained the upper hand and dictated to the "inner parent" how it wants to be treated. The problem is that children do not always know what is best for them. They must be guided into growth, not subjugated. When this guidance occurs, the "inner child" and the "inner parent" blend into a mature sense of self in which both adult and child needs live together.

This workbook is designed for *adults* who have, or had, a parent addicted to alcohol or other drugs and who may continue to suffer during their adult lives because of childhood needs that were never met, acknowledged, and respected. We believe that giving credence to these childhood needs and breathing life back into them is often the first step in leading to their maturing into more effective parts of our current lives.

But a workbook is deceptive. It looks as though it's easy for readers to complete and easy for authors to write. Neither is true.

Most books are monologues, which you can turn on and off with a flip of your hand. A workbook, however, is closer to a dialogue, which calls upon you to act, to experience, and to answer honestly.

This book is in your hands because something within is calling to you. You may feel troubled, incomplete, or dissatisfied. You may be hopeful, or in despair. Whatever is moving you, it comes from a deep place. Changes on such a deep level take time and effort. This workbook is only one set of tools, each serving as a stepping-stone along your path.

I wrote *A Time to Heal: The Road to Recovery for Adult Children of Alcoholics* in 1988 to help people respond to this calling within themselves. In it, I gave personal expression to much of my own experience, both as someone who grew up in an alcoholic family and as a practicing psychotherapist with special interest in the issue. The book probably did more for me than for its readers. I say this because healing comes from telling your own story—honestly, realistically, and to the right people. Much of the therapy I practice involves helping people find their own voice, to tell their own story.

The *A Time to Heal Workbook* is organized to guide both your head and your heart through some potentially painful and difficult material. Each chapter begins with the feelings stimulated by the content of previous chapters. This creates the same ebb and flow that we observe in ACoA groups at Genesis as people come to *feel* the facts of their lives as well as to *know* them.

As you turn to the Introduction, it will be like entering a Genesis Time to Heal group. We illustrate important points throughout the workbook with experience from our groups. We describe how people in our groups have often responded to the material you are struggling with. And we lead you through many of the same experiences that our members have had in the groups.

Of course, there is no substitute for the real thing—and the real thing involves other people. Although the workbook will be valuable even if you complete it alone, it will never have the healing power of sharing your story with other recovering people. I encourage each of you to multiply the value of completing this workbook by finding a forum in which to discuss it with others. For some of you, this may mean asking a few friends to complete the book with you; and we will give suggestions in Appendix I for how this can be done. Others may want to attend at least one self-help meeting a week to hear ACoAs tell their stories and to have the opportunity to tell portions of their own. Still others may find it helpful to use reactions to the workbook in their therapy.

However you use this workbook, we hope that you do *use* it. Mark it up. Dog-ear the pages. Write comments and thoughts wherever they fit. Work through these pages as slowly as you like, for that will give you the time you need for information and experiences to percolate through both your heart and your brain. Although some of you may be tempted to race through the chapters, be aware that there is no value in turning this book into one more "self-help trophy" that you have bagged, only to display on your bookshelf gathering dust.

Best wishes as you embark on this important work.

Timmen L. Cermak, M.D.

Introduction

To help bring our workbook alive, we introduce you to ten people from one of our groups at Genesis. Throughout the workbook, you'll listen to their questions, their stories, and their insights. This particular group had six women (Denise, Marion, Sharon, Susan, Gail, and Estella) and four men (Brian, Mark, Bill, and Bob). Although their economic, ethnic, and social backgrounds varied dramatically, each had at least one alcoholic or drug-addicted parent. Their ages ranged from Susan at fifty-five to Gail, the youngest group member at eighteen. Except for Gail, who was unemployed, the group included a nurse, a mechanic, an architect, a writer, a mother and homemaker, an office manager for a large corporation, a secretary, a day-care worker, and a shipping clerk.

Let's look at some of the questions the group members had about the workbook.

"What can I expect from the workbook?"

This workbook helps you regain access to many memories and feelings from your childhood and uses this information to identify and understand the common problems and characteristics that come from growing up in a chemically dependent family. We also point you toward a number of tools for dealing with your past in healthy ways. *This workbook will:*

- help you develop a deeper understanding of how some of your current life problems *and strengths* are related to the experience of growing up in an alcoholic family, without blaming everything on the past or yourself.

- give you new tools to explore a past that may have been hidden or unavailable to you since becoming an adult.

- help you with the grieving that is essential for recovery.

- help you replace unrelenting self-criticism with a more compassionate attitude toward your recovery.

- provide guidelines for using the workbook in a group setting.

"What's not going to happen with this workbook?"

Although many self-help books prescribe specific answers (for example, "Here are the five ways to heal your inner child . . ."), we've tried to avoid panaceas. Even after a decade of work with people who grew up in chemically dependent families, we don't have any easy answers.

Our concern is that "cookie cutter" approaches fail to comprehend the unique details of *your* life. For this reason, we have steered clear of offering easy solutions and answers. This book can be very beneficial, but it also has limitations. *This book will not:*

- answer all your questions, though it may help clarify them and point to where the answers can be found.

- take away feelings of pain, loneliness, and fear. In fact, you may experience these feelings more deeply.

- replace being in therapy or Twelve-Step Programs.

"How long should I take to complete the workbook?"

There is no set time for using this workbook. Whereas many people may complete one chapter per week, others will take a more leisurely approach. For example, Gail was only able to start most of the exercises from week to week and needed to keep coming back to certain chapters over and over again until she felt that she had completed them to her satisfaction. If you find yourself rushing through the book, avoiding certain exercises or chapters, take the time to ask yourself the following questions:

- Why am I rushing through this particular section?
- What feelings am I protecting myself from?
- What feelings are just beneath the surface that I'm trying to rush past?

If you rush through the workbook, you'll get to the end more quickly; but it may be at the expense of deeper awareness and healing. Give yourself permission to respond to each question with a relaxed attitude rather than complying with an obligation. Remember, getting to the end of the book is not the goal. Take your time. You deserve it.

"Should I do the workbook from cover to cover?"

Not necessarily. Although the workbook is designed to flow from one topic to the next, you may be more comfortable skipping around. Our intent has been to facilitate a gradual unfolding of awareness rather than have you plunge in so deeply that you feel disoriented or overwhelmed. We encourage you to

- pay careful attention to your feelings as you work on a given topic, question, or exercise.
- give yourself permission to go slowly enough that you can tolerate whatever emotions arise.
- "take a break," if you need to. It may be important to set the workbook down for an hour, a day, or a week, in order to focus on the feelings and memories that are coming up for you.
- remain alcohol and drug free while using this workbook.

"Can I do this alone?"

If by *this* you mean the workbook, the answer is yes.

If by *this* you mean recovery, the answer is no. Recovery is not truly possible in isolation. Although you may have needed to keep silent in your childhood, continuing such isolation is antithetical to the process of recovery.

"What does it mean if I can't relate to some of the topics or stories in the workbook?"

Individual experiences in alcoholic families vary. Some people grew up in families where dramatic outbursts were daily events, whereas others came from an environment where the alcoholic retreated into silence. If details of the stories we present do not fit your life, consider whether the *emotional realities* are the same.

> In my family no one was drunk, no one was violent or abusive, no one threw things across the room, and no one got arrested. My father just drank before dinner, during dinner, and after dinner. Then he fell asleep in his chair.
> Gail

Although for a few weeks Gail had some difficulty identifying with the other people in the group, she eventually realized that she felt just as abandoned as those in the group whose parents lived at the bar. Her awareness of *the emotional realities* allowed her to connect with other group members.

"What if I can't remember what happened in my childhood?"

Be patient. Painful events are often kept from conscious recall in order to keep you from being overwhelmed. This form of self-protection helped you to survive. Events will reveal themselves when you are ready, when you have the strength and support to integrate them. We caution against indiscriminately opening old wounds without providing the support you need to cope with the powerful feelings that are released.

"Should I talk with my family to help me remember?"

When asking family members about past events, take time to evaluate the risk with each individual. Think about your past experience with the person and ask yourself two important questions:

- Will this person violate my confidence?
- Will this person blame, shame, or humiliate me for inquiring about my alcoholic family?

If the answer is "no" to these questions, you may have a safe foundation to discuss your family. Keep in mind that, even though an older sibling's perception may fill in blanks in your family history, your brothers and sisters may also have a different perspective, especially if they left home before the drinking reached its worst stages. When in doubt, think about what you are going to say, talk with someone else, and wait a little while before acting.

"Should I share my workbook experience with my family?"

Especially in early recovery, there is a common impulse to share hard-won insights with other family members and friends. We encourage the same caution as above. Indiscriminate sharing, without attention to the safety of the relationship, may result in a rewounding when the people you approach are not able to hear what you have to say. This rewounding can easily reinforce a basic rule of isolation: "Don't say anything; you'll only get hurt."

"What kinds of groups can use the A Time to Heal Workbook?"

The workbook can be used by individuals, but it is especially powerful when used by peer groups or professionally led therapy groups.*

Peer groups generally form among Twelve-Step Program members, churches, schools, or simply among a group of friends. If there is no therapist to organize and guide the group, the role of the facilitator is usually rotated among the members and a consensus is relied upon for decision making. *To help peer groups use this workbook, we've provided special guidelines in Appendix I.* These guidelines and the exercises in each chapter will structure the group's work from week to week.

How to Use the Workbook

As you flip through the workbook, you'll notice that each chapter is divided into four sections: a **Topic** section, an **Exercise** section, a **Journal** section, and a **Recommendations** section. *We*

---

* Using the *A Time to Heal Workbook* does not give the right to use the Genesis name, the title "A Time to Heal," or promote oneself as having obtained training through Genesis without expressed written authorization of Timmen Cermak, M.D. A *Therapist Manual* for the *A Time to Heal Workbook* is available through Genesis; 1325 Columbus Avenue, San Francisco, CA 94133.

encourage you to purchase a blank journal to use in conjunction with the Exercise and Journal sections of the workbook.

The Topic section in each chapter contains information on issues of key importance to ACoAs. Included are the how, what, where, and why of each issue, plus personal accounts of group members illustrating how the topic relates to both the past and the present. The Topic section helps you

- understand issues commonly faced by ACoAs.
- develop a perspective on how these issues arise for people growing up in an alcoholic family, and how they can have an impact on adult life.

The Exercise section uses a variety of contemplative questions, drawings, visualization, and structured experiences to stimulate childhood memories and to amplify issues introduced by the topic section. This section engages you in activities designed to

- deepen your self-exploration.
- determine whether the issues introduced by each topic are relevant to you.
- personalize information about ACoAs beyond the intellectual level.
- *integrate information presented in the topic section into your present-day life.*

The Exercise Section of each chapter contains an exercise labeled **Feelings.** *We strongly encourage you to use this exercise for at least ten minutes a day.* This will help you develop a consistent awareness of your feelings throughout the day, and from day to day. Instructions for the Feeling Exercise are in chapter 1, and your responses will be used in chapter 4.

The Journal section helps you reflect further on the chapter's topic and your experience with the exercises. This section is especially useful because it both gives you the freedom to explore whatever arises while using the workbook and gradually increases your ability to look carefully at day-to-day experiences and relate them to the past. *In order for this journaling process to best meet your needs and not be restricted by any space limitations of the* *workbook, we encourage you to purchase a separate book in which to record your thoughts.*

Group members typically raise a number of questions about journaling, such as the following:

"What kind of book should I buy?"

We recommend a blank writing journal/diary, which you can find at your local stationery or bookstore. Some people like smaller books that can be carried around easily; others prefer larger, full-page ones. Some like blank pages; others go for lined pages. Suit yourself.

Because many ACoAs grew up in families plagued by a sense of financial and emotional scarcity, pay close attention to how you go about choosing a journal. Notice whether you buy something appealing, plain, or just cheap. If you tend toward the cheap, ask yourself what this is about. Is this another example of how you try to get by with as little as possible, even when you were more attracted to other choices? Take time to ask whether you could buy yourself something special. Rather than using something that's merely functional, or pieces of paper you were about to discard, see if you can give yourself something nice—something that does justice to the important work it will hold.

"Does it matter if I'm not a good writer?"

Absolutely not! You are the only one who will read your journal. Do not obsess about grammar, spelling, or finding the perfect words to describe your thoughts and feelings. Just write down the first responses that jump out of your heart and mind—without editing them. If you want to add more later, you can. Try to let your thoughts flow naturally, as though you were simply talking to yourself, while a scribe wrote down your words. Remember that this workbook is yours alone, and you don't need to share it with anyone. It doesn't even matter whether you write in whole sentences or jot down random ideas. You can doodle in your journal, draw in it, or color in it. It doesn't need to be great literature to be valuable. The workbook is a diary of your thoughts, feelings, and responses to the exercises. It's a testament and remembrance of your life growing up in an alcoholic family. It is simple, personal, and just for you.

"When should I write in the journal?"

Whenever you have the time. Some people set aside a half hour at the end of the day and find that this regularity helps. Others write when the energy feels right; they may work in spurts with great passion and then cool down for a while.

"What if I have a hard time journaling?"

You're not alone. Many ACoAs have hidden their thoughts and feelings for so long that they can write only a few words at a time. If you find yourself in this situation, try asking yourself very gently, "Can I elaborate on that just a bit?" and see if anything more comes up. See if you can discover one more small facet of each feeling or event that you are recording. You might ask yourself, "If I were feeling something else, what might it be?" Or ask yourself, "If I were to see someone that same age, in that same situation, what would I imagine he/she'd be thinking and feeling?"

"What should I do with the journal when I'm finished?"

Anything you want. Many people find it helpful to review their journal entries week by week to gauge their progress, where they are having difficulties, and when things are going well. Some save their journals and review them year after year as a point of reference. Others set them aside for some important ceremony by themselves, or to use in a group, with a therapist, or with their family.

The Recommendations section suggests additional resources for exploring the topic of each chapter.

Note: For peer groups, we recommend that everyone read the workbook and complete the exercises through the first chapter, as well as familiarizing themselves with the guidelines for peer groups in Appendix I, before the first meeting.

Chapter One

Breaking the Silence

Many adults who grew up with a parent addicted to alcohol or other drugs have an experience that we call "Breaking the Silence"—the moment when truth is spoken for the first time. Silence exists on many levels. You may recognize the silence in your family in the following descriptions.

For some, whether for reasons of shame, fear, or denial, your family may literally have said *nothing* of importance about the alcohol/drug usage for years. Despite the obvious presence of an alcoholic family member, this topic may have been avoided like the "emperor's new clothes." Conversations may have stayed at such a superficial level that nothing of importance about *any-thing* has been discussed for years. Such superficiality can cause divisions between people to run so deeply that the family is eventually destroyed. In such cases, members may even have said *nothing at all* to each other for years. Silence can be so maddeningly oppressive that it begins to obscure the truth even within your own mind. Eventually it is even deafening, when every member of the family has retreated from the pain of trying to communicate, and no one would be heard if he or she did speak.

Or you may come from a family in which endless complaining about the alcoholic/drug-addicted parent is the accepted way of relating to him or her. In these families, people often acknowledge the alcoholic's problems but remain silent about their own feelings and shortcomings. What is *not* talked about is the pain and emptiness that family members feel. What is also *not* talked about is the crazy or painful ways that the rest of the family is acting, because all the blame is laid at the feet of the addict.

Unfortunately, the family's silence is a deception; it denies the most important emotions that lie beneath the surface, such as pain, loneliness, and anger. Because deception is most effective when it includes self-deception, the best way to keep our feelings hidden from others is to deny to ourselves as well that we have them. Once we have done this, the feelings seem to become less important. Their immediate intensity is lessened. But they lurk underground, buried, until some unforeseen time in the future when they resurface unexpectedly.

Denial is a normal, even a necessary, psychological defense that all healthy people use every day. Just as we become increasingly sensitive to the smells of foods when we are hungry, so we can become desensitized to events that are continuously present. This is akin to getting used to wearing a ring that initially irritated our finger.

Denial is also a valuable tool whenever life deals us a blow that we cannot react to all at once. When feelings threaten to overwhelm us, denial allows us temporarily to put most of our reactions on the back burner. Then, bit by bit, we can bite off pieces of the experience, chew, swallow, and digest them, before going back for more. This process enables us gradually to find meaning in the stressful events of life and to deal with them without being overwhelmed and incapacitated by our emotional reactions.

Unless we have the ability to use denial to desensitize ourselves to persistent events or to give us time to respond to traumatic ones, we are in trouble. Unfortunately, this capacity to tune out events can also be used to cope with the constant tension and pain that people in chemically dependent families experience. Denial is not the enemy; the problem comes when we fall into self-deception—when we become unaware that we are using denial. It is then that we become so disconnected from our immediate experience that we begin losing sensitivity even to everyday events. And it is then that we mistake our ability to keep traumatic events at bay for proof that the events are not important—or that they did not really happen at all.

Alcoholism is often called a "disease of denial," because drinkers deny the pain that their drinking is causing themselves and others. It should be no surprise that denial also begins to permeate their families, as everyone begins accommodating themselves to the alcoholism in order to hold the family together. In its many forms, denial plays a central role in the life of people who are harmfully involved with alcoholics and other substance abusers. If you have reluctance talking about your parents' alcoholism, or letting yourself react emotionally to their drinking, you may still be struggling with the veil of silence that your family threw over itself.

There are typically four levels of denial that ACoAs may find within themselves:

1. Denial of the basic fact that a parent is an alcoholic

2. Acknowledging that a parent is alcoholic but insisting that the alcoholism has had little effect on the rest of the family

3. Acknowledging both that your parent is alcoholic and that the alcoholism also affected the rest of the family, but feeling that through force of will it did not affect you

4. Potential problems arising from your own alcohol and drug use

Although excessive denial begins to create problems of its own, these problems can be denied as well. A process takes over that resembles the debtor who borrows from credit cards to pay the mortgage, then gets a line of credit to pay the credit cards. On the surface, matters appear normal. Below the surface, a hole is being dug deeper and deeper. Denial becomes a trap door that we are standing on above that hole. As long as it stays shut, nothing seems to be wrong. But, as soon as it cracks open, we are in danger of plummeting into the depths. Although the tension of standing on such a trap door may seem unbearable, increasing our denial keeps us unaware of the toll this tension takes on our lives.

Breaking the silence means dismantling the denial you have used to protect yourself. It means looking down at the trap door and acknowledging your fear that it will open at any moment. Denise's story illustrates the terror that can rise up when confronting denial. She came late to the first meeting. The first thing she said

was "I don't know why I'm here. I don't think my dad is really alcoholic." When I asked her what it felt like to be in the group,
Denise said, "I feel like a delicate glass. I'm afraid I'll crack at the
slightest touch. . . . I really don't know if my dad is alcoholic." I
asked what it would mean to her if her dad were alcoholic, and
she burst into tears. Shaking with sobs she said, "I just don't want
it to be true." I said I understood. We all understood. When denial diminishes, we finally have to deal with the realities of our
lives.

Your picking up this workbook, even to look at it in the bookstore, is an act of breaking the silence. You are acting coura-
geously.

Our experience with Time to Heal groups is that most members are affected by their decision to join the group for a few days,
even a few weeks, *before* the first meeting convenes. The impact
of being close to breaking the silence has already begun. Some
have intense dreams, or restless nights. Others feel increasing
anxiety throughout the day. And others find that the resolve to
join the group begins to waver. "Maybe things weren't so bad. . . .
Maybe I'm blowing it all out of proportion. . . . Maybe my parent was not really alcoholic."

We have seen ACoAs about to begin with a group doubt that
a parent was alcoholic even when the parent had been treated
several times in chemical-dependence hospitals, or had passed
out at every child's wedding and recently been arrested for the
third time for drunk driving. When people have forgotten many
portions of their past, they often begin to deny the significance of
the incidents that they do remember. But, once you begin understanding the insidious way that denial pervades our lives, your
world will be changed forever. That is the risk of breaking the silence.

Breaking the silence means different things to each person,
because there is both an inner and an outer silence created by denial. For some, ending denial means breaking the inner silence,
listening to yourself, and taking yourself seriously—for the first
time. For others, ending denial means breaking the outer silence
and mentioning the unspoken for the first time, perhaps to another family member.

The goal of recovery is to speak out to others about your own
experience. In this speaking out, we make our experience real

again. Denial creates unreality in your life by diverting your attention from whatever causes pain. In the process, denial also drains the vitality from life. Breaking that denial lets in the sound of truth and revitalizes our experience, just as the clear sound of a bell can awaken our senses.

Breaking the silence also often means experiencing the pangs of betrayal. The lesson that your family must be protected from the truth can run so deeply within your spirit that simply entertaining different thoughts feels like an attack on the family. And, because many families would respond to your thoughts once you have dismantled your denial by feeling betrayed, attacked, and unjustly mistreated, you may have good reason to keep your use of this workbook your own secret for the time being.

It is critical to understand that, although our feelings must be listened to, properly labeled, and taken seriously, they do not always give us accurate information about the outside world. Our feelings deserve our respect; they never lie about how we are relating to the world. But they do not always tell us the truth about ourselves. We can fear things that present us with no real danger. We can feel to the center of our bones that we are betraying our family, and they can agree with every fiber of their beings, when we are not actually betraying them. We can feel shame when we have done nothing wrong, because we have been taught to misguide our loyalty, or because we have inherited shame that the generation before us never resolved.

When you break the silence, a whole set of feelings will be activated. Some people feel fear; others experience shame. Some people feel relief; others experience deep sadness. Look at these feelings. Do not try to push them aside as irrelevant. Do not try to minimize them. Instead, let them come to the surface and announce who they are. These feelings are in you for good reasons. They are not there because feelings randomly appear on the horizon. They are not there because you are overreacting. If the feelings present today seem to be more intense than circumstances at hand warrant, then they may be telling us about the intensity of past events.

Until we understand the full significance of these past events, the intensity of feelings connected to them hangs on, contaminating our current life. For example, I may be confused by a child's fear of the small fire in my fireplace until I learn that his house burned to the ground only a few years ago. Obviously, the meaning of that fire in my fireplace is different for him than it is for me. So, if you have anxiety, and a sense that you are betraying your parents by exploring whether your parents were alcoholic or addicted to other drugs, look at these feelings as the smoke that lingers long after a fire has raged. You may find that this smoke can finally be cleared from your life if it is just attended to directly.

· · · · · · · **EXERCISES** · · · · · · ·

> I wasn't sure I was ever going to get here. I canceled the first interview for the group, took several weeks to call back, and had thought about not showing up tonight. My stomach's been in a knot all day. I've been really petrified about opening this whole subject up. I've never talked with anyone about what happened in my family, not even my husband. I don't know if I'll be able to stay here. I feel so trapped. I've gotta do something. (sighing) I guess I might as well be here.
>
> Denise

In the first chapter we invite you to participate in several exercises to help personalize the experience of breaking the silence, exploring your relationship to denial, and taking a first step in reaching out.

Exercise 1:
Breaking the Silence

The first step is breaking the silence within yourself. The fact that you've bought this book and gotten this far means that you *have begun* to break that silence. The following exercise will help you deepen the process by teaching you to become more aware of your thoughts, feelings, intuitions, judgments, and physical responses to beginning this journey.

We encourage you to answer the questions as you would write in a diary, rather than as you would if you were taking a test. When you write in a diary, the style and grammar mean little. Try not to edit your thoughts and feelings for fear that someone *might* read it. *You are the only person to decide who has access to this information.* When taking a test, most people tend to be concise, to the point, and write in short sentences without allowing room for open expression and the natural stream of consciousness. Give yourself the freedom to let your words flow unimpeded.

Be sure to take enough time to respond openly and with patience to the questions. Allow your answers to come in the form of images from the past, as well as the feelings that arise with the images. If you find yourself rushing through any of the text or exercises, limiting your responses to one-word sentences, or thinking the answers to yourself without "needing to write them down," you may be cheating yourself. Take the time you need.

We often find that group members think about these questions and respond to them bit by bit for several weeks. Feel free to go back to any chapter or exercise as often as you want to and take as much time as you need. This should release you from having to be "complete" with your initial responses.

Use the journal you've purchased to respond in writing to the following inquiries:

1. When you take the time to let it sink in, what does it feel like emotionally (you can consult the Feelings List in the back of the workbook) and physically (Is your stomach tightening . . . your heart pounding? Are your palms sweating?) to begin writing in this workbook at this very moment?

2. Think back to when you were a child. What memories do you have about the times when your mom or dad, siblings or relatives explicitly or implicitly warned you *not to talk* about the alcoholism in the family?

3. What incident do you remember that you wanted to tell someone about but didn't?

4. What happened when you tried to talk to someone?

5. Allow yourself to think back on when you were a small child. What were your secret prayers or fantasies about someone finding out about the problems in your family and saving you?

6. Did you fantasize about having secret or special powers and, if so, what were they?

7. What was *your special fantasy* that you kept alive?

8. Now that you have given it some thought as an adult, what do you hope for in terms of breaking the silence for yourself and your recovery in general?

9. What are your fantasies about the impact this workbook will have on your life and your family? Be honest; we all have fantasies, hopes, and dreams.

10. What is the most important result you hope for if nothing else happens?

One group member responded to these questions with the following:

> I have to admit that I've been procrastinating starting the workbook for at least two weeks now. Every day I wake up knowing that I haven't started the first chapter and get down on myself for being such a chicken. I can't help it. Even sitting here, alone at my desk at two in the morning I feel guilty for telling the truth about my family. I know I'm the only one who's going to read this, but I can't get the thought out of my head that someone's going to burst into my room, hold this up, and say, "Ah hah! Now see what you've done." I have to stop for now. My heart is racing so hard, I can barely hold the pen to write. I'm so wired with fear. I feel so ashamed to even write this that I'll probably binge with food tonight.
>
> Denise

Exercise 2: Acknowledging Your Denial

The second step in breaking the silence is taken by acknowledging to others that you grew up in an alcoholic family. Eventually, breaking the silence involves dismantling the denial that you carry about the severity of your parents' drinking problem, the ways in which the alcohol affected your family, your current life, and perhaps even your own relationship to alcohol and drugs.

Bob was amazed at how hard it was for him to admit that his parents were alcoholics. In a clearly subdued tone, he told the group how his parents neglected his most basic needs for regular meals and clean clothing even when they weren't drunk, which was rare. They would *forget* to buy groceries and were too busy to wash his clothes and wondered why he didn't learn to wash them himself—"You're already six years old." In order to make sure he and his brothers had something to eat, Bob would use his paper-route money to buy food at the corner store. One night, after he brought home the food, his mother actually returned the groceries and bought beer. "I know they had a drinking problem," he said, "but I don't think they were alcoholics."

Bob slowly looked around the room at the shocked faces of the group members and said, "Well, maybe they were."

Take the time to read the warning signs of the four levels of denial below. Record in your journal how each applies to you.

Level-I Denial: Your Parents' Alcoholism

- Defending your parents when other people bring their alcoholism to your attention. Lying when asked directly about their drinking by friends, family, the doctor, a schoolteacher, priest, or rabbi

- Rationalizing your parents' drinking with:

    "They work hard and deserve a chance to unwind."

    "They're retired now so what does it matter."

    "It doesn't hurt anybody."

- Hiding your parents' drinking from others. Covering up for their problems by calling in sick, canceling appointments for them . . .

- Minimizing the amount they drink and its effect

    "They only drink _____ (beer, wine, etc.).

    "They only drink on weekends."

    "He's never had an accident."

    "She's only hit me a couple of times when she's been drinking."

- Speaking in euphemisms

    "Social drinkers"

    "Heavy drinkers"

    "They like to have a good time."

    "It's his hobby."

Level-II Denial: The Effect of Parental Alcoholism on You

- Refusing to acknowledge that your parents' alcoholism has had a major influence on your life
- Defending your parents by taking sole responsibility for any problems stemming from your childhood

  "I was a problem kid. I was always in trouble."

  "I just needed more than they could give."

  "My mother raised me as a single parent and did her best. It should've been enough."

- Not having any feelings about your parents' alcoholism

  "It never really affected me much. I managed pretty much on my own."

  "I'm not sure what you mean by how I feel about their drinking. What's the question?"

  "I didn't have any feelings about it, it just was."

Level-III Denial: The Excessive Use of Willpower

- Not letting yourself feel angry
- Trying to rise above it all
- Feeling superior to your parents
- Taking full control of your own life, as though the alcoholism never existed

Level-IV Denial: Your relationship to alcohol and other drugs

- Comparing yourself to your parents and thinking "I'm not an alcoholic; I don't drink the way they do," and minimizing your drinking without looking closer at the effect drinking may be having on your life.
- Rationalizing your drug use as nonproblematic because, after all, "It's not booze."

- Being defensive when someone expresses concern about your alcohol/drug use. Getting angry when the issue of your alcohol/drug use is brought up. Refusing to discuss the issue.

1. After you have read the list, look at it again and see if any additional memories, images, or feelings come up about any or all the items. What did you learn about yourself from your responses? You might find yourself wondering about your relationship to alcohol, as Denise did. Or you, like Marion, might remember the ways in which you participated and embraced being a "good girl" and became fiercely independent.

2. Choose the image or memory that is the clearest and write a one-page autobiographical story (in your journal) recalling more of the details of the event.

3. Recall what happened, how you felt at the time, and how you feel about it now.

4. If you give it some thought, what would you do differently today?

Here is how Denise responded to Exercise 2:

I thought this exercise would be easy. I was all ready to acknowledge my denial about the drinking in the family (I didn't figure it out until my father died and the doctor told me he had cirrhosis), but I didn't expect to look at my own drinking. I always figured that I didn't have a problem because I didn't drink before noon, I never drink at the office, and never get drunk. But now that I think about it, I do have at least two or three glasses of wine every night when I come home from work. I get anxious when I don't have any wine at home and am the first one to suggest at the office that we go out for a drink on Fridays. Maybe I do need to look at this a little closer. Gosh, I hope I don't end up like them. I just couldn't handle that.

Denise

Denise's comments reveal how ACoAs often compare their own drinking to their parents', and thereby minimize their own use of alcohol. It is easy to compare yourself to parents with years of addiction and conclude that you have "no problem." It took Denise an entire year of individual therapy, exploring whether or not she was a "social drinker," to realize that she had come to be psychologically dependent on alcohol. Given her family history, she decided to stop drinking.

Exercise 3: Reaching Out

This exercise helps you explore feelings about reaching out to others. As we mentioned in the Introduction, reaching out during early recovery *always* implies reaching out to trustworthy people who will keep your confidence and respect your sharing without judgment or criticism.

If one member of your family was an ally, you may already know how important it was when your brother, sister, relative, or a family friend acknowledged what was going on in your family. Even if it didn't change a thing, you know what it was like to have someone on your side. This is one of the many benefits of attending Twelve-Step meetings for ACoAs.

For those of you who have never been to a meeting, this is what you are likely to see when you go:

Many meetings are held in churches, hospitals, or special meeting houses. If you arrive a few minutes early, you'll notice people setting up tables, putting out Al-Anon literature, or preparing coffee or tea. You are welcome to browse through any of the material or literature on hand. When the meeting comes to order, a secretary is likely to introduce him- or herself by first name only: i.e., "Hi! I'm Barb, and I'm the secretary at this meeting." The group will respond with a resounding, "Hi, Barb!" The secretary is someone who has regularly taken the time to facilitate the meeting's opening, closing, and choice of chairpersons and guest speakers.

Next, the secretary will probably read the guiding principles for the meeting, which will be followed by the opportunity for each member to introduce himself/herself as Barb did. You are free to respond or not. If you want to introduce yourself you can say, "My name is

_____; I'm an ACoA" or "My name is _____; I'm a visitor," or "This is my first meeting."

After the introductions, the secretary may introduce the person chairing the meeting. The chairperson may share something about his/her life, recovery, past experiences or a topic of personal significance. While the chairperson is sharing, no one is likely to interrupt or jump in. To do so would constitute "cross-talk." Cross-talk is not part of the meeting's process and the rule against it ensures a safe environment where each member can share without fear of personal confrontation.

At some point, the chairperson usually invites other people to "share." The next person will introduce himself in a similar manner and the group will respond welcomingly. The person sharing is not required to maintain the same topic or follow up with any continuous thread of the previous speaker (although this often happens). The person sharing may talk about whatever she or he feels a need to say.

You are not required to speak at all. We encourage you to watch and listen for the first few meetings and become familiar with the process and your feelings as they arise. If someone does happen to invite you to speak (though this is rare except in meetings when very few people attend) and you do not feel ready, it is completely appropriate for you to say "I pass."

At some time in the meeting, a piece of paper may be circulated with first names and phone numbers on it. If you would like your number available for people to call you, place yours on the list. If not, just pass it on. At some point a contribution plate will be passed. You are not required to contribute, and the speaker may even suggest that first-timers not give anything.

When the meeting adjourns, people may talk informally in little groups for a few minutes before leaving. You might even find one or more of those present introducing themselves, welcoming you to the meeting, or inviting you to coffee afterward.

Task #1—Planning

If you do not regularly attend Al-Anon or ACoA/Al-Anon meetings, within the next week call the local chapter of Al-Anon to find out the times of local ACoA meetings. Twelve-step groups are listed in the yellow pages under *alcoholism*.

Task #2—Action

In the next week we'd like you to go to at least one meeting to observe how many thousands of other ACoAs are reaching out to one another. If you do go to regular meetings, try a different one for the sake of exploration. If you've never been to a meeting, consider attending an *open meeting* (one without restrictions and open to newcomers) or a *beginner's meeting*. When you call for information, ask for these two types of meetings.

If you have a hard time going to your first Al-Anon meeting, at least pass by one when it's in progress. That's all. Don't go in. Just walk or ride by and see what that's like.

After attending a meeting, use your journal to respond to the following questions:

Task #3—Reflecting

1. Describe your feelings when you read through the chapter and got to the point where we suggested that you go to an Al-Anon meeting.

2. Record the details of your response. How did your stomach feel? Did your forehead tense up in a familiar way?

3. Did you feel anxious, nauseated, relieved? (You might flip through the Feeling Dictionary for reference words at the end of the book.)

4. How did you feel as you were getting ready to go to the meeting?

5. Did you think about or actually decide not to go several times?

6. What was the conversation in your head like about this one?

7. Describe how you felt throughout the process of planning to go, arriving, listening, leaving.

8. If you had never been to a meeting before, what was it like for the first time?

Feeling Exercise

In order to cultivate awareness and explore the length and breadth of your emotional life, we'd like you to spend a few minutes each day reviewing the feelings you've had. Many group members find ten minutes in the evening is a good time to sit down and reflect. Be sure to find a quiet place where you won't be disturbed. It could be helpful to be consistent with the Feelings section from day to day as you will be using it in later chapters.

Instructions for the Feelings Section

1. Take a *deeeeeep* breath.
   Let it out *slooowly.*
   Relax for a full minute.

2. Remember how you felt the moment you awoke this morning, the first moment of consciousness as you opened your eyes. Do you remember your dreams and the residue of feelings left by the dreams?

3. Now, follow your activities throughout the day from the moment you got out of bed, step by step, and remember the feelings that occurred as you took a shower, had breakfast, went to work, met people, came home, etc., until the moment you found yourself writing in the journal. Record each of these feelings in your journal, like the example below. When you've finished, draw a line under the last word on the list (see the example that follows).

4. Then look at the Feelings List in the back of the workbook. Circle the words in the dictionary that you've just listed.

5. Look over the Feelings List again. If you recognize any more feelings that you forgot to write down but experienced today, write them down now under the line you

drew. This will help you notice how your ability to label your feelings increases over time.

If you were to take the time to do this each day you might have seven lists like these by Denise.

Monday	Tuesday	Wednesday	Thursday
tired	excited	sad	annoyed
frustrated	alive	supported	vulnerable
bored	afraid	_____	careful
alone	concerned	anxious	_____
_____	_____	tender	bored
sad	happy	wishful	left out
embarrassed	satisfied	needed	abandoned

Friday	Saturday	Sunday
lucky	bored	scared
important	distant	pleased
cared for	resentful	comfortable
_____	_____	eager
trusted	unloved	_____
talented	worthless	honest
_____	_____	sure

Denise's entries in the Feelings section made it more obvious to her how unhappy she felt. Although this was quite painful for her to acknowledge, it helped her face how she *actually felt* compared with how she thought of herself, as "a happy person."

This was easy for me to do, but it was also somewhat painful. I kept noticing how often I'd use words like *anxious, scared, intimidated, upset, frightened,* to describe how I felt. It made me realize how much of my life I have spent being afraid of people. Although there were a couple of days when I felt better, on those days I hesitated to write down the good feelings. I was afraid (again) that if I put it down in writing, somehow the feeling would go away.

Denise

Marion, the group's busy overachiever and most ardent Al-Anon member, had a hard time identifying her feelings. In the beginning, she relied heavily on the Feelings List in appendix II.

I had a completely different experience from Denise. I had the hardest time coming up with more than a word or two to describe how I felt. I'd sit and look at the page for ten minutes and just feel a blank. I got upset that I wasn't able to do it and then realized I was getting upset so I wrote "upset." I felt like it was a waste of time for the first few days, and then I actually decided it was okay to look in the Feeling Dictionary—I always try to do things without help—and found three or four more words to describe how I felt. Most of them were like *tense, stiff, uptight.* I wonder what this says about me?

Marion

Journal 📖

This next section adds yet one more layer of reflecting on your experience with the exercises. It will deepen your awareness of what the exercises have to teach you. These questions will identify which exercises have been hard for you and help you explore the reasons for the difficulty. The questions will also reinforce the exercises that came more easily for you.

Write your answers in your journal.

1. Are you concerned that someone might find your workbook or journal and read it?

2. What is your particular fantasy about what might happen?

3. Has this first chapter been more or less painful than you expected?

4. When you were exploring your hopes and dreams for this workbook (and for recovery in general), did you

really let yourself wish for the best? Or did you edit your dreams and wishes to keep them "realistic"? After you've given it deeper thought, what are your dreams (regardless of how unrealistic they may seem)?

5. As a result of reading the warning signs of denial about your own relationship to alcohol/drugs, do you find yourself wondering about your own use?

Dismantling denial includes looking at your own relationship to alcohol and drugs, not just to your parents'. Did you find yourself rationalizing your drinking by comparing it to your parents', thinking, "Well, I don't drink the way they did, so I don't have a problem" or minimizing your drug use by thinking, "I only smoke pot and everyone knows you don't get addicted to pot"?

If you are even slightly concerned by your responses, especially to those about your own drinking and drug use, we encourage you to check the Recommendations section below for suggested reading, to talk more directly to your therapist about this point, or to visit an AA meeting. People who grow up in alcoholic and drug-addicted families have a significantly higher incidence (approximately 25 percent) of addiction themselves. Gathering information about alcoholism and exploring your own relationship to alcohol and other drugs is a vital part of recovery, whether or not your use is like your parents'.

Many of the remaining 75 percent of ACoAs have emotionally charged, rigid views that cause them to be judgmental and hypervigilant about their relationship to alcohol and other drugs.

6. If you find yourself in this latter group, write your thoughts and feelings about a typical conversation that goes on in your head when you are offered a drink, etc. For example:

Bob: "Say, Marty, would you like a beer?"

Marty: "Uh . . ." (thinking: *Let's see. It's only four o'clock. I really shouldn't* [implication: only drunks like my parents drink in the daytime]. *But Bob isn't an alcoholic; he rarely drinks. It's Sunday, and we're not going to drive anywhere so we won't get arrested for drunk driving* [implication: as my parents did when I was ten]. *Well, maybe I could. It's hot out, and we've been working hard in the yard. A beer would feel good now. I could just have water.*)

Bob: "Marty, you awake? . . . Wanna beer?"

Marty: "No, I'll just have water."

What would the conversation in *your head* be?

7. If you were only able to pass by a Twelve-Step meeting while it was in progress but didn't go in, describe how you felt throughout the process of planning to go, walking or riding by, and leaving.

★ Recommendations

Two books* that provide further information about chemical dependence are

> *I'll Quit Tomorrow*, Vernon Johnson
>
> *Is Alcoholism Hereditary?* Donald Goodwin

The following books provide further information about the ACoA experience and alcoholic families in general. They may help you assess your family's relationship to alcohol and drugs, as well as your own.

> *It Will Never Happen to Me*, Claudia Black
>
> *A Time to Heal*, Timmen Cermak
>
> *The Secret Everyone Knows*, Cathleen Brooks

In addition, *Huckleberry Finn* (book by Mark Twain and film by Disney) is the insightful story of a young CoA's efforts to leave

---

*The complete reference for all books is provided in Appendix III: Bibliography.

home. In his adventures along the Mississippi River, a metaphor for the search for himself, Huck's survival skills are tested over and over again. Most ACoAs are heartened by Huck's resilience and humor.

If you are new to Al-Anon/ACoA meetings, and Twelve-Step Programs in general, we recommend two books:

> *Al-Anon Faces Alcoholism*
>
> *The 12 Steps for Adult Children*

Organizations to Contact for More Information:

The National Association for Children of Alcoholics (NACoA)—11426 Rockville Pike, Suite 100, Rockville, MD 20852, (301) 468-0985

Al-Anon (see your yellow pages for the local chapter)

Alcoholics Anonymous (AA) (see your yellow pages for the local chapter)

Children of Alcoholics Foundation—Box 4185, Grand Central Station, New York, NY 10163-4185 (212) 754-0656 or (800) 359-COAF

Johnson Institute—7205 Ohms Lane, Minneapolis, MN 55439 (800) 231-5165

The National Council on Alcoholism (see your yellow pages for the local chapter)

The National Council on Alcoholism and Other Drug Addictions—National Office (212) 206-6770, or (800) 622-2255

Suzanne Somers Institute for the Effects of Addictions on Families—340 Farrell Dr., Suite A203, Palm Springs, CA 92262 (619) 325-0110

Chapter Two

Our Common Ground

This chapter explores the different strands that spin together into the common thread running through ACoAs' lives. Just as you might walk through a messy attic to get an overview of what is there before beginning to clean up and organize things, so it is useful in the beginning of recovery to survey the range of characteristics that are often found in ACoAs.

Before exploring what ACoAs have in common, it is important to remind ourselves that, although there are many commonalities among us, there are also individual differences. With nearly thirty-five million Americans of all ages having a parent who is addicted to alcohol or other drugs, there are bound to be a lot of differences among ACoAs as well. We can never reduce ourselves to a single stereotype.

Some ACoAs come from families in which the chemical dependence remained largely hidden; others were raised by the town drunk. Some ACoAs were raised in poverty; others, in wealth. Some had broken homes; others lived in intact families. Some were physically and sexually abused; others were coddled and overprotected. Some ACoAs are white and male; others are members of minority groups or female. Some have become chemically dependent themselves; others have never used alcohol or other drugs.

These different experiences naturally lead to a range of ACoA characteristics. Although every characteristic may not apply to you, most ACoAs recognize several as being prominent aspects of their personalities. Much of this commonality comes from the fact that we all have lost a parent, physically or emotionally, to a mysterious disease. We all have had to deal with the disappointment of longing for our parents to be parents in the real sense. We have all had to come to terms with both loving and hating, needing and fearing a parent who was not fully present for us.

The characteristics shared by ACoAs are not wildly different from the normal problems of living experienced by everyone. In some cases, these problems *are* more intense for ACoAs; in other cases, ACoAs merely *see* themselves as having more frequent, and more intense, problems than "normal" people. Such negative self-perceptions take a toll and stem from a mixture of ACoAs' seeing themselves as coming from a defective family and having little sense of what "normal" families are like. They come about these feelings honestly because alcoholic families often have a pervasive sense that something is drastically wrong with the family, and that they do not fit into the surrounding community. In cases in which the alcoholic *is* actively rejected by the surrounding community, children are usually quite aware of this rejection and share in the embarrassment.

After looking at the characteristics most often found in ACoAs, we will then look at the roles ACoAs often took in their families. The following list* reviews many of the characteristics that ACoAs frequently identify within themselves and adds quotes from our groups that illustrate how these attributes pervasively affect people's lives.

Fear of Losing Control

Adult children of alcoholics maintain control of their feelings and behavior and try to control the feelings and behavior of others. They do not do this to hurt either themselves or others, but out of fear. They fear their lives will get worse if they let go of their control and get uncomfortably anxious when control is not possible. As a result, their emotional lives are often constrained, and their relationships lack the spontaneity needed for real intimacy.

A Primer on Adult Children of Alcoholics (Cermak, 1985, revised 1989).

> I don't like being in this group because there are so many
> eyes looking at me at the same time. I can't control what
> people are thinking of me if I can't concentrate one on
> one with them. This feels way too out of control.
>
> Bob

Adult children of alcoholics have often buried their feelings (especially anger and sadness) since childhood to accommodate to
their family's denial. Such restraint gradually erodes the ability to
experience or express any emotions freely. Eventually, all emotional intensity is feared, even that stemming from good feelings,
and is seen as loss of control. For some ACoAs, emotional intensity is equated with intoxication, because the only spontaneous
feelings they witnessed at home came from a bottle.

Fear of Feelings

> I know that I have to keep a lid on all of my feelings in
> this group. Even if I let myself start laughing too hard, it
> will begin feeling out of control, because I won't be able
> to watch how you are reacting to me when I'm feeling
> too much. . . . Besides, it feels like any strong feelings
> will let the barn doors swing wide open, and everything
> will be able to get out then.
>
> Sharon

Adult children of alcoholics who experienced verbal or physical
violence whenever conflict arose between their parents often remain frightened by people in authority, angry people, and personal criticism. Common assertiveness displayed by others is
often misinterpreted as anger. As a result of their fear of conflict,
ACoAs are constantly seeking approval, but they lose their identity in the process. They often end up in a self-imposed state of
isolation, always accommodating to others in order to keep from
"rocking the boat."

Fear of Conflict

> After the group had sat silent for a few moments, Brian
> and Bill began to speak at the same time. "You go
> ahead." "No, you go ahead." "You were first." "No, you
> were." The group fell into silence again, and no one took
> the risk of speaking lest they conflict with the other per-
> son's need to talk.

Overdeveloped Sense of Responsibility

Adult children of alcoholics are hypersensitive to the needs of others. They needed to develop this trait in order to react quickly to the self-centered personalities of their intoxicated parents. Their self-esteem often comes from making bad situations work, but this also contributes to compulsive needs to be perfect and continually keep other people happy.

> I didn't want to talk last week because it seemed that Estella and Denise had so much on their mind. I didn't want to take the focus off of them, since they obviously needed attention. I never, ever, want to look like I'm so needy that others have to put their own needs second in order to pay attention to me.
>
> Brian

Feelings of Guilt

ACoAs are strongly influenced by feelings of guilt. They feel guilty for "driving their parents away" and for not getting them to stop drinking. Whenever they stand up for their own needs instead of giving in to others, they feel guilty. ACoAs can develop lifelong habits of sacrificing their own needs in an effort to be "responsible" and to avoid guilt.

> When I was driving home from group last week, I had this intense shame attack. I suddenly realized that I had taken over twenty minutes talking about problems with my boss and everyone had listened politely. But I felt so guilty for taking all that time without even asking if it was okay.
>
> Marion

Inability to Relax, to Let Go, and Have Fun

Fun is stressful for ACoAs, especially when others are watching. The child inside remains terrified. In order to survive, it exercises all the control it can muster to look good, to monitor how others are feeling, and to be prepared to cope with the return of chaos at any moment. Family life taught it never to relax its guard. Under such rigid control, it is no wonder spontaneity suffers; for spontaneity and control are incompatible.

> During a group meeting devoted to play, Bill stood rigidly in the corner, trying to fade out of sight. Later he

said, "I was looking forward to today. But, when I came in the room and saw that all the chairs were gone, I suddenly felt terrified that I didn't have any idea what you were going to ask us to do. It felt safer to stand on the sidelines, but it was also lonely. I kept thinking that I stood out and was ruining everyone else's fun. I felt isolated, but just couldn't join in."

Adult children of alcoholics are often burdened by very low self-esteem, no matter how competent they may be in many areas. Some learned to criticize themselves at the hands of an abusive, rejecting parent. Others castigated themselves to keep their needs out of sight. In most cases, they are amazed when they discover that harsh self-criticism is not the norm for everyone—it just seems so natural to them.

Harsh, Even Fierce, Self-Criticism

I tried to do the Feelings exercise, but I can't even begin to find the words to describe what I feel. . . . You'd think someone my age would be less of a fool!

Susan

Whenever ACoAs feel threatened, their tendency toward denial intensifies. This is the reflex response they learned in their families, and they often continue to use denial to maintain a sense of being under control. As a result, their coping skills as adults are often brittle and ineffective.

Living in a World of Denial

Is this the last meeting for our group? I had no idea we had finished. I didn't give any thought to the fact that this is a time-limited group after it started. Do we really have to end the group?

Susan

Intimacy gives ACoAs a feeling of being out of control. It requires self-love and comfort with expressing one's own needs. And few ACoAs witnessed examples of intimacy in the relationship between their parents. As a result, ACoAs frequently have

Difficulties with Intimate Relationships

difficulty entering into, or sustaining, intimacy. For many, intimate settings feel unsafe. And sexuality is often affected by their distrust of being vulnerable.

> Every time I begin to let a relationship become sexual, I have this sinking feeling that it's all over. I start needing the other person too much. I start feeling that they are going to abandon me. The whole relationship seems to become too important and too scary. . . . And it doesn't even matter if the sex was good or not.
>
> Gail

Living from the Point of View of a Victim

Adult children of alcoholics grew up in environments over which they had little control. In a very real sense, they *were* victims of their parents' disease. As adults, they may continue to see themselves as victims, and they are often attracted to other "victims" in their love, friendship, and career relationships.

> "The one thing I didn't like about the group is how one member spoke too much nearly every week." When asked why he had not mentioned this earlier in the group, when it could have been changed, Bill replied, "No one said we could bring things like that up."

Compulsive Behavior

Adult children of alcoholics may work compulsively, eat compulsively, become "addicted" to a relationship, or behave in other compulsive ways. Most tragically, ACoAs all too often drink compulsively and become alcoholics themselves.

> Ever since this group started, I have been unable to control my eating. I even buy a bag of M&M's and pour them into my pocket before coming to meetings. I can't stand feeling so agitated, and now I see better how my compulsions push everything back down again.
>
> Estella

Tendency to Confuse Love and Pity

There are few examples of mature love in alcoholic families. In many cases, what passed for love was really one parent feeling sorry for the other. As a result of this confusion, ACoAs often "love" people they can pity and rescue.

When my wife heard what I was saying about her drinking, she broke down into tears. She looked so miserable that my heart started to melt, and I knew that I would not be able to leave her even if she did start to drink again.

Bob

Fear of Abandonment

Adult children of alcoholics often grew up feeling chronically abandoned by an alcoholic parent in favor of a bottle. At the same time, they were terrified that the abandonment could become permanent at any moment, by divorce or death. As a result, they may hold on to relationships far too long in order not to reawaken the painful experience of feeling abandoned.

After a group member arrived fifteen minutes late because of a traffic jam, another member said the following: "I was sure that you had decided to leave the group because I disagreed with you last week. The moment I saw you were not in the group, I felt afraid that I had come on too strong and you weren't going to come to the group anymore." The late member looked confused and asked, "What did you disagree with last week?"

Tendency to Assume a Black-and-White Perspective Under Pressure

Under stress, people develop all-or-nothing patterns of thinking, feeling, and behaving. The gray areas of life disappear. As a result, ACoAs often mistakenly see themselves as facing an endless series of either/or alternatives.

When my wife felt disappointed about my having to work on Saturday, I felt like I had devastated her. I felt so guilty the whole day that I hardly got anything done. Then, when I got home, she was off with some friends at the beach. I still have trouble believing that someone can be just a *little* disappointed in me.

Bill

Tendency toward Physical Complaints

Research has established that the close relatives of alcoholics seek twice the average amount of medical care. As adults, children from alcoholic homes continue to suffer higher rates of stress-related and psychosomatic illness.

> Every time tax season is over, I get sick. I know it is a stressful time for the other bookkeepers, but I don't seem to be able to handle the stress without getting a bad cold, or flu. And I don't seem to be able to slow down until I get sick.
>
> Susan

Suffering from a Backlog of Delayed Grief

Losses experienced during childhood were often not grieved because the alcoholic family does not tolerate such intensely uncomfortable feelings. Later on, the normal losses and disappointments of life cannot be felt without calling up these past feelings. As a result, ACoAs are frequently depressed or unable to enjoy the quality of life they have achieved.

> I'm afraid to let myself begin feeling sad about my father's alcoholism. It seems like, if I start feeling sad about it, I won't be able to stop. All the sadness will rise up, and I'll be lost in a dark cloud that's so thick I won't be able to see out of it. I can't risk that. Not now. Too many important things are going on to risk that.
>
> Mark

Tendency to React Rather than to Act

Another long-term effect of traumatic levels of stress is hypervigilance—automatically scanning the environment for potential catastrophes. Those individuals who are best at hypervigilance are most likely to survive. Adult children of alcoholics remain hypervigilant long after such continuous alert is necessary.

> Oh, I knew the first group meeting who I felt safe with and who I didn't (pointing to people). You looked full of anger. You had a plastic smile I knew was hiding something. And you two seemed as scared as I was. I couldn't get a read on the rest of you, so you couldn't be trusted yet. That's my usual way of entering into new situations. I sit back and get a feel for the lay of the land before I start taking any steps.
>
> Bob

Ability to Survive

Most important, children of alcoholics are survivors. Everyone reading this workbook survived. Some of us survived against the odds. Some of us survived primarily by our wits; some, by grit; and some, with stunning creativity. Once most ACoAs view their childhood realistically, they begin to understand that their survival was no small accomplishment. In fact, it is the legitimate source for some pride.

> When I read my first book on ACoAs, the only thing I felt was that "I survived. I *did* survive." I wasn't even sure yet of any of the details of what I survived, but the feeling of being a survivor seemed right.
>
> Estella

To reiterate, not everyone with a chemically dependent parent will identify with every one of the above characteristics. Some characteristics are more likely to be present if you experienced violence in your family, others if your parents' intoxication was hidden beneath a dense cloak of denial. Nevertheless, most ACoAs recognize large parts of themselves in descriptions of the common thread that binds us together; and this discovery further dissolves the sense of isolation that most carry from their childhood into adult life.

The second way to describe the commonalities among ACoAs is to look at the family roles that they typically fall into. In *Another Chance: Hope and Health for the Alcoholic Family,* Sharon Wegscheider-Cruse identified four primary family roles assumed by children in alcoholic families. In reading about these roles, pay special attention to the feelings associated with each. If these are the feelings that you tend to have, especially during the difficult moments inevitably experienced in most intimate relationships, then this may be the role that you play, or aspire to play. The significance of these roles is that they arose within your highly stressed alcoholic family, where they contributed to survival. Unfortunately, these roles stick with ACoAs later in life as habits. And, as habits, they prevent adult relationships from achieving the intimacy that we all seek.

1. *The Hero*

   Behavior—always rising to meet the challenge, pulling the family through problems, competent, reliable, self-effacing

   Feelings—inadequate and guilty

2. *The Scapegoat*

Behavior—often calls attention to the family's problems indirectly by getting into trouble, but ends up becoming the focus of attention instead of the chemical dependence

Feelings—anger and pain

3. *The Lost Child*

Behavior—avoids being the center of attention by fading into obscurity, rarely requires much of the family's energy, thereby not adding to the family's burden

Feelings—loneliness

4. *The Mascot*

Behavior—cute, makes people laugh, plays the buffoon/clown to take people's attention away from the chemical dependence and to break the tension

Feelings—fear

Most ACoAs recognize themselves as playing one of these roles (especially when under stress), but research has shown that kids develop roles in healthy families as well. So what is unique about ACoA family roles? Why does recognizing the role they played in their families so often empower ACoAs?

The answer is that family roles are *imposed* upon children in alcoholic families—imposed by the *family's* needs. This is very different from healthy families, where children develop roles according to their own individual needs and talents. In alcoholic families, children are pressed into roles with such force that they begin to lose a sense of who they really are; in healthy families, children are free to explore different roles as a way of finding out who they really are. When ACoAs learn of these roles later in life, they often experience a jolt of recognition that the image they have tried to portray to the world is not who they really are.

The exercises for this chapter help you identify the ACoA characteristics and roles that have wound their way through your own life. Later on we will be able to make more sense of the origin of these characteristics.

· · · · · · · · **EXERCISES** · · · · · · ·

> I go out of my way to please people. If someone's upset, I immediately think I've done something wrong and I've got to fix it. Once, when a waiter was rude to me and forgot to bring what I asked for, I ate what he brought anyway and gave him a big tip. I thought he was angry with me.
>
> Bob

Although many people who join our groups at Genesis are familiar with the ACoA characteristics and roles described in the first part of this chapter, this knowledge is often used more as a label, a rationalization, or even an indictment of themselves. Some people identify nearly everything about themselves as "dysfunctional," to the point where the term carries little meaning. Our goal is to help group members develop an awareness of ACoA characteristics on a *personal* level and to explore how each characteristic can be a strength as well as a burden. On this level, understanding ACoA characteristics can become a key to unlocking one's potential, rather than remaining prisoner to one's limitations.

The exercises below will help you identify and personalize the problems and strengths commonly found in ACoAs. In sharing this information with one another, group members slowly notice a shift from feeling predominantly *alone, separate,* and *different* toward feeling a part of the group, connected and similar to other group members.

Read carefully the list of characteristics below and put a checkmark by the statements that you identify with, however slightly.

Exercise 4: Characteristics of ACoAs

Fear of Losing Control

_____ I am careful not to be too emotional.

_____ I like things in order.

_____ I feel anxious when I'm not on top of things.

_____ I would feel much better if I had more power.

_____ In my family, someone was out of control.

_____ In my family, physical abuse occurred.

_____ In my family, chaos erupted at a moment's notice.

Fear of Feelings

_____ I have a hard time expressing my feelings.

_____ I often don't know what I'm feeling.

_____ I sometimes think feelings are just a burden.

_____ I'm scared of what I might find if I let myself feel.

_____ In my family it was not OK (safe) to express . . .

_____ Guilt	_____ Pain
_____ Remorse	_____ Love
_____ Shame	_____ Anger
_____ Fear	_____ Sadness
_____ Joy	

Fear of Conflict

_____ If there's a conflict, I try to diffuse it.

_____ I tend to think that conflict is bad and leads to violence.

_____ I try to run the other way when there is a conflict.

_____ In my family, conflict meant violence.

_____ In my family, conflict meant someone got yelled at.

_____ In my family, conflict meant someone would physically/emotionally leave me.

Overdeveloped Sense of Responsibility

_____ I tend to feel responsible for everything.

_____ If extra work needs doing, I volunteer.

_____ I find it hard to say no when asked for help.

_____ In my family, I helped out and took care of things.

_____ In my family, I was praised for acting like an adult.

_____ In my family, I physically/emotionally took care of my father/mother (after a drinking binge).

Feelings of Guilt

_____ I feel guilty for having needs.

_____ I often feel guilty for being a burden on others.

_____ I tend to say "I'm sorry" a lot.

_____ I apologize for things that don't need an apology.

_____ In my family, someone was always blamed.

_____ In my family, I was held responsible for things I shouldn't have been.

_____ In my family, I took the blame for things I didn't do, just to stop the arguing.

Inability to Relax, Let Go, and Have Fun

_____ Having fun is a chore for me.

_____ When people laugh "too" loudly I get anxious.

_____ I feel like a loner a lot.

_____ I tend not to laugh without checking out whether other people are laughing first.

_____ In my family, loud laughing meant things got out of control.

_____ In my family, if I relaxed something bad happened.

_____ In my family, fun meant drinking.

Harsh, Fierce Self-Criticism

_____ I tend to be my own worst critic.

_____ I am quick to judge myself.

_____ I am my own worst enemy.

_____ In my family, I could never do anything right.

_____ In my family, blame, silence, or ostracism was a usual response to problems.

_____ In my family, being wrong had terrible consequences.

Living in a World of Denial

_____ I'm not in denial.

_____ When I feel threatened, I tend to get defensive.

_____ Sometimes I lie rather than admit a mistake.

_____ In my family, people denied problems.

_____ In my family, I could never figure out what they wanted of me.

_____ In my family, we avoided dealing with problems.

Difficulty in Intimate Relationships

_____ The closer I get to someone, the more uncomfortable I feel.

_____ I tend to sabotage getting close.

_____ I've never really felt safe with anyone.

_____ When I feel vulnerable, I feel threatened.

_____ In my family, getting close meant getting hurt.

_____ In my family, no one got close.

_____ In my family, we only got touched when we got hit.

Living from the Point of View of a Victim

_____ I feel helpless a lot.

_____ I feel that no matter what I do, nothing changes.

_____ When I'm just about to get something I need, it usually gets taken away.

_____ In my family, physical abuse (hitting/pushing/punching) occurred.

_____ In my family, verbal abuse (yelling/blaming/ screaming) was common.

_____ In my family, sexual abuse (inappropriate touching/ fondling/incest) occurred.

Compulsive Behavior

I tend to be compulsive about:

_____ being on time   _____ work

_____ sex   _____ shopping

_____ neatness   _____ self-help books

_____ food   _____ possessions

_____ alcohol and/or   _____ gambling
        other drugs
                               _____ religion

Tendency to Confuse Love and Pity

_____ I'm attracted to people I feel I can help or heal.

_____ I tend to be in relationships with someone who is wounded or unavailable.

_____ I feel closest when I'm helping someone.

_____ In my family, someone was always in trouble.

_____ In my family, I was a special confidant.

_____ In my family, being close meant being a helper.

Fear of Abandonment

_____ Letting go is hard to do.

_____ I hate saying good-bye.

_____ I've been in relationships for years longer than I should have been.

_____ When someone close to me leaves, I'm afraid I'll never see him or her again.

_____ In my family, my (mother/father) left at a moment's notice.

_____ In my family, people came and went without much warning, and I just had to cope.

_____ In my family, I was left alone.

Black-and-White Thinking

_____ When faced with problems, I have a hard time thinking of more than one solution.

_____ I tend to think in terms of good or bad.

_____ I often think there is only one right answer.

_____ If you're right, then I'm wrong.

_____ In my family, life was either dead calm or all hell was breaking loose.

_____ In my family, we used terms like *always, never, absolutely, totally.*

Delayed Grief

_____ When I tell stories about my past, I tend to speak without much feeling.

_____ I generally avoid talking about my family.

_____ I often think "the past is the past."

_____ As much as I try, I still feel haunted by the past.

_____ I remember being told "Don't be upset."

_____ In my family, sadness was forbidden.

_____ In my family, being sad was a weakness.

Ability to Survive

_____ I often feel like a combat survivor.

_____ I often feel that I can handle anything after having grown up in my family.

_____ In my family, the enemy lived in my house.

_____ I learned how to survive by being independent.

_____ I learned you can't count on anybody.

_____ In my family, as much as I prayed no one came to help.

Sharon had the following reactions to this checklist:

> I was absolutely amazed at how you had me pegged on the control thing. I mean I knew I was into control, but whoa! I checked off *every* item under "Fear of Losing Control." I definitely regulate how I express myself. I'm always keeping a careful eye on just how I'm acting around other people. I like things in order. I not only organize my spices in the kitchen alphabetically, I have the labels printed up on my computer and I measure the same distance from the top for each one. I never really gave it much thought but when the next sentence was, "In my family someone was out of control," it really hit me how much I never knew what was going to happen in my house.
>
> Sharon

Exercise 5: Personalizing the Characteristics

1. Read over the list of characteristics again, paying special attention to the items you checked. On a sheet of paper in your journal, on the left side of the page make a list of the characteristics you have identified.

2. Now, on the right side of the page, write a phrase describing each characteristic as you experienced it in your family.

For example, if the characteristic is "I have a hard time expressing my feelings," your personalized experience may have been "*I could never get angry at my father. I could never feel sad because I was afraid I would disappear.*"

To illustrate Exercise 5, some of Sharon's responses are listed on the following page:

Sharon's List—Exercise 5

Step One	Step Two
1. I'm careful not to be too emotional.	I always have my feelings in check. A lot of the time I know I'm feeling something but I just push it down. I think feelings really get in the way of making sound decisions.
2. I like things in order.	I organize my spices, my clothes are arranged according to their color and the season of the year, I even keep each food in the fridge labeled with the date I purchased it and the kinds of dishes I intended to prepare so I won't forget.
3. In my family physical abuse occurred . . .	About once a week someone got hit, if that's what you mean by abuse. Nothing hard. He (my father) didn't hit us with anything like a board. He'd just use a belt. When he was really mad he'd use the buckle end.
4. I feel like a loner a lot.	"Loner" doesn't even begin to describe the way in which I feel apart from people. I don't even feel like I know myself. I come on real dynamic in relationships, but the only men who seem to be interested are the ones who need a mother to take care of them, solve their problems, or mooch off of me.
5. I'm my worst critic.	That doesn't even begin to touch the way I jump on myself. I should write a whole page just about this.

For many ACoAs, the above characteristics are often experienced as hindrances. However, when we begin to look at these characteristics as tools that we needed to survive in an alcoholic family, they start to look more like strengths and assets. Sharon's statement below demonstrates awareness of how her self-criticism is a painful burden in her present life, but in the same breath she acknowledges how important her hypervigilance was in the past to keep out of trouble.

> I've always wanted to exorcise my self-criticism. It's like there's someone standing over my shoulder just waiting to judge me, to yell at me, call me stupid, ignorant, worthless. This all began when I was in the third grade. I remember drawing class. We were told to draw our guardian angels. The teacher said they were spirits who were always looking down on us and watching. I drew a black robed figure with horns and a belt standing on top of me. When my teacher noticed my drawing and asked me what it was, I said that this was the angel who told me how to stay out of trouble.
>
> Sharon

For many group members, once these ACoA characteristics are recognized, they are only seen in a negative light. Then they become the object of scorn. There is an attempt to eradicate them. Unfortunately, this only reinforces a harsh, negative self-image—like Sharon's ominous shrouded demon. The following exercise will help you identify the hidden strengths of these hindrances and thus develop a more compassionate perspective on how you survived your alcoholic family.

1. Look over the personal inventory characteristic list you have created.

2. Choose one of the characteristics and write a paragraph describing the way in which this characteristic has been a hindrance in your life.

    Be descriptive, and include your feelings. Don't write in generalities or in "recovery-speak." (*Recovery-speak* occurs when people use all the catch phrases of the recovery movement without describing their actual feelings.)

Exercise 6: Hindrances and Strengths

For example, in describing her fear of abandonment, Marion began with the following:

> My Inner Child forces me to stay in a marriage that is uncomfortable when I should Let Go and Let God.

This description was eventually revised until it looked like this:

> Yesterday I was afraid my husband was going to leave me. I know it doesn't make sense, but I get this way a lot. When I think about him leaving me, I get flushed, I break out in a cold sweat, and I start to panic. I knew he was only going to work, but I got scared and had to call his office. His secretary said he was out and I was sure she was covering for him and he was getting ready to leave me. I know it doesn't make sense. My husband has been faithful and devoted for all six years we've been together. When he found out I called the office in a panic, he was upset that after six years I still couldn't trust him. We had a bad argument. It's hard to accept that I have so much fear.
>
> Marion

3. Write another paragraph describing a way in which this characteristic has been helpful, a developed skill, and beneficial in certain circumstances.

For example:

> Because I expect my husband to leave me, I have been saving money in a special account. He doesn't know about it. I don't feel good about not telling him, but I keep thinking that if I can get to the point of trusting him we can use the money for a down payment on a house. I'm not a hoarder. I do spend money on myself. But every week I put twenty-five dollars away, just in case. I am a good saver.
>
> Marion

4. If you find yourself feeling stuck at this point and not able to find anything positive and beneficial about the hindrance you've listed, set it down for now. Choose another hindrance that you can see something more positive in and repeat the exercise.

5. Now choose at least one more characteristic and do the same. If you want to, you can do more.

Sharon Wegscheider-Cruse described the roles that ACoAs adapt to in response to the chaos of an alcoholic family environment—the Hero, the Scapegoat, the Lost Child, and the Mascot. This exercise will help you explore the ways in which these roles may have become second nature in your family. By identifying them you can begin to explore the way they have affected you, both in the family of your childhood and in your current relationships.

**Exercise 7:
Family Roles**

1. On a page in your journal, list the names of people in your family of origin (mother, father, brothers, sisters, significant live-in relatives, and yourself).

2. Think about the roles each of you played in the family and write these next to the names of your family members, along with some of the characteristics of each role. You may find that some members took on more than one role, or changed roles when older siblings left home.

As an example, here is Susan's list:

Father	The Lost "Child"—emotionally unavailable, usually at work
Mother	The Alcoholic—unpredictable, emotionally hurtful
Me	Family Hero—always reliable, but feeling inadequate
Jim, brother	Scapegoat—always getting into trouble, angry
Dana, sister	Mascot—cute, but terrified and lonely

Grandma   Family Hero—tried to hold family to-
            gether by taking over mother's respon-
            sibilities, very guilty

3. In your journal, write a paragraph describing a time
   when each person acted in accordance with his or her
   specific role in the family.

Estella wrote the following:

I remember this like it was yesterday. It could've happened a hundred times. My father comes home from a
night of drinking. He bursts in the door screaming,
"Why are you good-for-nothing little brats still up?" He
was the Terror in our family. Then, if he didn't fall on his
face in the doorway, he'd come after one of us to give us
a beating. We called that person "the Chosen One."
Usually it was me.
     The Chosen One had the responsibility of distract-
ing the Terror so the rest could hide, either in the garage
or under our beds. Then the Chosen One had to keep
Dad occupied until he passed out. Mom would cry like a
wounded martyr, in the other room, about how much
she had to put up with "just for us kids." I was the family
hero when I withstood Dad's attacks, and even let him
molest me, so the others could stay safely hidden. Later
on, Mom would point out all of Dad's good points and
make us feel guilty that we wished he'd get hit by a car on
his way home from the bar.
                                              Estella

**Exercise 8:
At What Cost?**

Whenever we take on a role in our families, we often sacrifice our
true selves. Unfortunately, in alcoholic families, roles tend to become fixed and rigid in order to maintain the status quo. When we
sacrifice our individual needs for the tenuous and temporary
peace of the household, we all pay a price.

I've always been the family Hero. As the oldest I was responsible for taking care of my three brothers and sister.
When I was fourteen, my alcoholic aunt got divorced

and came to stay with us. At the same time, my grand-mother had been living with us for about five years. She was an invalid, and as the oldest I had the responsibility of taking care of her a lot. One time, my mother just couldn't stand taking care of Grandma and us, with her sister being drunk all the time. She and Dad took off for the weekend and left me with the job of taking care of Grandma, Aunt Mary and the kids. I remember that whole summer all I did was take care of Grandma, Aunt Mary (I hated it when she got drunk), and the kids. I can't remember a single time I went out to play with my friends.

Sharon

This exercise will help you explore the cost of taking on the role of the Hero, Scapegoat, Lost Child, or Mascot. In your journal, answer the following questions:

1. What was it like to take on the role you played in your family?

I loved it and I hated it. I loved it because I got to do all sorts of grown-up things. I drove when I was fourteen because some-one had to get the groceries and drive Dad home when he was drunk. And I hated it because I never got a chance to play with friends. At twelve, I was doing the laundry. At thirteen, I was cooking three nights a week because my mother was working late, and at fourteen I had to drive the car down to the bar to pick up Dad whenever he got drunk.

Bob

2. How did it *feel* to be the family Hero, Scapegoat, Lost Child, or Mascot?

Being the hero made me *tired.* I can't tell you how many times I fell asleep in school or missed the bus in the morning because I was dead asleep and got up late. Or the times my father would keep us up all night with his screaming. Then he'd sleep all day and we'd have to go to school at 7:30 in the morning.

Estella

3. How do you feel about the roles taken by other family members? In other words, if you're the family Hero,

how do you feel toward the family Scapegoat, the Lost Child, the Mascot? If you are the family Scapegoat, how do you feel toward the family Hero, the Mascot, and the Lost Child, etc?

4. Can you identify specific problems in your relationships and feelings toward your siblings today that might be directly connected to the roles each of you played in the family?

5. Are you aware of any resentments that you still harbor toward your siblings that stem from the role they played in the family? Take the time to make a note of these.

Feeling Exercise

Take time to do the Feeling Exercise as described in chapter one (page 15).

Journal

Respond to the following questions by writing in your journal:

1. What is it like to realize you have a lot in common with thirty-five million other Americans with a chemically dependent parent?

2. When you took the time to look closely at the role(s) you played in your family, what was the *payoff* for the role you played?

For example, the Hero may take on a great deal of work and responsibility but also may receive the family's praise, may feel elevated to the level of adult, and may experience a sense of righteous power over others in the family. The Scapegoat may get a lot of blame from everyone, but he also has the opportunity to do all the forbidden, taboo things that the family defends against, like being promiscuous, wild, different. The Lost Child may be isolated and forgotten, but she also enjoys peace and solitude away from the fracas and chaos that envelop the rest of the family. The Mascot may be responsible for releasing all the tension in the family by distracting everyone with jokes and antics, but he also is the beneficiary of the laughter and is the life of the party. How was it in your family?

3. What do you feel was the cost of playing out your specific role in the family?

For example, frequently in alcoholic families, the family Hero is the responsible one who gets good grades, takes out the garbage, and helps Mom with Dad when he's drunk and needs to be picked up off the floor, driven home from the bar, etc. The price may be a lost childhood sacrificed to a pseudo-adulthood, the need always to be responsible for helping others and never just to play around. The Scapegoat may get to do all the forbidden things in the family or culture but may also be beaten, ostracized, and kicked out of the family. The Lost Child may have the solitude of being left alone but also may feel an intense sense of loneliness and depression and experience profound difficulty feeling close to people. And although the Mascot may be the class clown and the family jokester getting all the laughs, the ability to be warm, sincere, and genuine may become elusive and end up as a powerful barrier for the Mascot in intimate relationships.

4. Now that you've looked at how you and your brothers and sisters have taken on these roles, there is another, potentially more difficult and painful task at hand: considering the way in which you resemble one or both of your parents.

Most of the group members can explicitly recall, usually after some very traumatic family event, saying to themselves, "I will never be like them! Never!" And yet we all have some characteristics of our parents. It is inevitable.

5. Although you may feel some resistance, describe some of the characteristics you find in yourself that seem similar to those of your alcoholic and nonalcoholic parent.

Keep in mind that within each characteristic lie both a hindrance and a strength. For example, in Estella's family, although her father suffered from a profound mental illness as well as being an alcoholic, he was creative, artistic, and at times full of vitality.

> My father was a musician, an alcoholic, and he was a manic-depressive. He was extremely creative. There would be times when we'd draw together and make up stories for hours. There were days he'd play his saxophone for us and we'd sing together. We made our own instruments and had a little band together. I would be the conductor, and he would play along with the rest of us kids. I got my artistic temperament from him.
> Estella

★ Recommendations

The following books provide more detail about ACoA characteristics:

A Primer for Adult Children of Alcoholics, Timmen Cermak

Adult Children of Alcoholics, Janet Woititz

A Guide to Recovery for Adult Children of Alcoholics, Julie Bowden and Herb Gravitz

Safe Passage: Recovery for Adult Children of Alcoholics, Stephanie Brown

Another Chance: Hope and Health for the Alcoholic Family, Sharon Wegscheider-Cruse

The film *The Great Santini* tells a powerful story of a military family struggling to cope with an uncompromising, rigid, alcoholic father. Robert Duvall plays an authoritarian fighter pilot who, in between binges, treats his family like a bunch of raw GIs. His struggle for control of everything but his drinking makes him monumentally self-centered and lonely. As you watch, notice the roles that each of the children plays in the family, and then look back over the information and exercises about alcoholic family roles in this chapter.

Chapter Three

Remembering the Past

It is now time to begin looking at your own unique history. In the Twelve-Step Programs, this is called "telling your story." And you *do* have a story to tell: In the receding horizon of time, four people were born. Each grew up in a different family, until they eventually formed two couples and gave birth to your parents. Your mother and father learned about the world from their own families of origin. Although the world your grandparents lived in no longer existed at the time you were born, what your parents learned from them became the furniture of your own childhood. At some point, the use of alcohol or other drugs began to take over your family's life. Perhaps one of your parents grew up with an alcoholic; perhaps not. But when your own parent's personality began spiraling into compulsion, pain, and denial, the rest of the family had their lives turned upside down as well.

Yes, you *do* have a story, and there are highly productive ways of relating to it. They begin by allowing yourself to remember the past as clearly as possible. They end by permitting you to stop repeating it.

It is very helpful to look carefully and honestly at the past if you want to make changes in your current life. Remembering the past—both the factual details and the emotions that colored each moment—usually gives us a more sympathetic perspective on our problems. We see that they arose for good reasons. They arose out of our experience, not as manifestations of flaws in our inner character. Accurately remembering the past also helps us make more effective changes designed to address the actual problems underlying the pain in our current lives.

If you have no desire to change your life, however, there is little reason to plunge back into painful memories. In some cases, I have agreed with ACoAs who are comfortable with their present lives that it makes little sense to revisit their past. My advice was that, if they ever *do* encounter problems that resist resolution, then it might be useful to explore where their coping strategies came from.

The past affects us for one understandable reason: *PEOPLE LEARN BY THEIR EXPERIENCE*. It is this fact, in combination with our insatiable curiosity, that makes human beings so successful on this earth. But, our experience can work against us as well. If what we learn from our families does not give us accurate information about the world at large, we may enter adulthood with a confusing mixture of strengths and disadvantages. Although everyone embarks upon adult life with both strengths and weaknesses, the particular legacy bequeathed to ACoAs can be immensely destructive.

The following, particularly tragic example illustrates how the past haunted one ACoA. Roger was arrested for murder only a few months after his eighteenth birthday. Throughout his *entire* life, from conception on, he had been the victim of profound neglect, abandonment, and terrifying physical and emotional abuse, largely stemming from his father's behavior when intoxicated. Not more than six months before the murder, he was finally big enough to stand up to his father—an act that required monumental bravery and tremendous physical risk. The shift of power between the two was almost dizzying for Roger, while it left his father reduced to a shadow of himself. In his victory, Roger was suddenly truly alone. His anger no longer was constrained by fear of his father, and it exploded in seemingly arbitrary directions.

When I was asked to consult in Roger's trial, I was struck by the depth to which the past had narrowed his options. Tried as an adult, he was clearly still an adolescent emotionally. Because his body had grown tall and muscular and his passions had been intensified by puberty, he looked to the outside world like an adult. But appearances can be deceiving. On the inside, he was still huddled down to protect himself against a hostile world, locked

into the experience he repeatedly had had as a child when his father tied him up and kicked him without mercy. We learn by our
experience. And, when this experience is distorted, it may take
many years and lots of help to sort it out. Roger never had the
time and help he needed.

Although it may be obvious that Roger's childhood experience affected how he perceived the world and limited the ways he
had for coping with events, the same kinds of effects are present
in more subtle ways in the case of most people who grow up with
a substance-abusing parent. Even when past experiences of having to rely only on ourselves do lead to mature and effective independence, the past has still affected who we are today.

Recovery requires that each of us put a good deal of energy
into recalling the specific, detailed events that make up our past.
In Twelve-Step Programs, this is called taking a "searching and
fearless moral inventory of ourselves." In order for this review to
be as accurate as possible, we must approach it with as little judgment as possible. Remembering the past begins with looking at
"what was" and "what we felt," not with evaluating, analyzing,
understanding, and judging.

We must deal with the realities of our past if we are to have
any hope of grieving for them, healing them, and freeing ourselves from them. Unfortunately, as children we often tried to
deal with our experience by avoiding it, ignoring it, disconnecting
from it, rising above it, denying it, not paying attention to it, or in
some other way trying to keep it from having power over us. Many
alcoholic families hold together only because every member is
contributing to a group denial of the family's experience, working
desperately to make it less real, less powerful, and less obvious to
the outside world. As a result, you may have been supported by
other family members whenever you ignored or forgot the painful events that kept your family in turmoil.

Although this strategy did help you tolerate the pain and did
contribute to your surviving high levels of stress, it has also kept
you isolated and out of touch with your experience. This isolation
is a burden that leaves people unaware that others have had very
similar experiences. Isolation causes people quietly to "accept
their fate," because they have no hope that others can understand
them. And isolation contributes to people's disconnecting from
their experience in order to diminish their pain.

In her important early book, *It Will Never Happen to Me,* Claudia Black described the psychological straitjacket that alcoholic families often impose on every member when she formulated her three rules: "Don't talk. Don't trust. Don't feel." When these rules are imposed on children and when children "mature" and learn to impose these prohibitions on themselves, reality is hidden from view. Remembering the past usually means violating these rules. Remembering means throwing off the yoke of admonitions and punishments that greeted anyone who talked about the drinking or who had angry, sad, or fearful feelings about it.

Remembering the past is a conscious act of reconnecting with your experience—of bridging the gulf that developed between yourself and your feelings. When you work to make the past real again, you are working to make *yourself* real again. Just as people work to remember the Holocaust or the trauma of Vietnam in order to heal themselves, ACoAs find more freedom through remembering than through forgetting. This wisdom is reflected in the book *Alcoholics Anonymous* (often called the Big Book) when it says that "the family may be possessed by the idea that future happiness can be based only upon forgetfulness of the past. . . . Cling to the thought that, in God's hands, the dark past is the greatest possession you have . . ." (chapter 9, "The Family Afterward").

At the same time, AA cautions that "it is possible to dig up past misdeeds so they become a blight, a veritable plague." We can get lost in the past. We do not heal ourselves when the past is used to justify our current misery, to relieve ourselves of the responsibility to make necessary changes, or to wreak revenge on others. Healing occurs when remembering the past serves the same purpose as referring to a map when you are lost. The past can orient us. It can help us know where we are today and where we can go tomorrow, by telling us precisely where we have been. And it can help us not to repeat the wrong turns that have kept us lost.

Recognizing the past for precisely what it is, no more and no less, frees up a lot of energy that has been expended to keep the truth at bay. Whether we are aware of expending this energy or not, it saps the vitality from our lives. It weakens the healing processes within each of us. It diminishes our resilience. Remembering the past is valuable simply because it is *truth* that sets us free. The truth has healing power, much as clear water washes out germs that infect a wound. Unfortunately, the habit of keeping the truth at bay may not be easy to stop all at once. Once memories have been buried alive, without a headstone, we can lose track of where they lie.

As long as you remain isolated in the straitjacket of not talking to others about your experience and disowning your feelings about the past, memories may remain few and far between. But, do not fall into the trap of believing that just because it *feels* as if your past is irretrievable that this is indeed fact. When ACoAs tell what they do remember of their own story and listen to others tell theirs, they begin breaking the isolation that contributes to forgetting. There are things that can be done together that cannot be done alone. Together, people can help one another slip out of their self-imposed straitjackets.

Many ACoAs avoid remembering the past because of fear. They fear what they will find, or they fear the intense feelings that will be released. If you share this fear, do not try to jump over it. Do not try to dismiss it. Do not try to banish it. Do not judge yourself harshly for it. Begin remembering the past by acknowledging your fear of it. And allow yourself to entertain the possibility that the fears are there for good reasons. Most people find that, when they discover these reasons and explore them in detail, the fear begins to lose its power.

The primary goal of the following exercises is to develop a greater *willingness* to know the past. Whether many memories come back, or not, is less important than whether you develop a new relationship to the past. Are you *open* to knowing more of the truth? Openness paves the way toward healing.

· · · · · · ·   **EXERCISES**   · · · · · · ·

You know, I really don't want to remember what happened in the past. I still have terrifying nightmares about childhood. For the most part, I feel numb when I talk about my family. I'm real good at telling my story at meetings but people say it sounds flat. I can't get to the feeling. I'm afraid I wouldn't be able to handle it. I actu-

ally think that I'd explode if I started to remember
any more.

Gail

In this chapter, we stressed the importance of remembering
the past. Telling your story breaks the silence created by the alcoholic family rule of "Don't talk." Reaching out of your isolation
toward others breaks the rule of "Don't trust." And sharing the
emotional truth of your life breaks the rule of "Don't feel."

The following exercises will help you tell your story in three
steps.

- *Step 1—Prepare a family genogram.*
  This will give you a picture of your family in graphic form
  and help you identify patterns that have affected individuals and relationships throughout the family as a whole.

- *Step 2—Write a family history.*
  This will create the historical context within which your
  own life experience has unfolded.

- *Step 3—Add the emotional dimension.*
  This will draw a more accurate picture of what it was like
  to be a small child in your family.

It is important to keep an open mind in performing this exercise. Some group members assume that they can skip this exercise by rationalizing, "Well, I've told my story hundreds of
times in meetings; I don't need to write it here." It may be true
that you've told your story to friends, to a therapist, or in Twelve-
Step meetings, but this exercise is different. We have found that
committing your life story to paper has a powerful significance
beyond merely thinking it through or telling the story verbally to
others. *Writing* your story is committing it to a concrete form that
you can read over, elaborate on, and examine again and again.

Another rationalization we hear for avoiding this exercise is
"I already know my story." This may be true, but we've found that
many personal histories have become condensed into concise,
stereotyped vignettes. These canned stories may make "good
sharing," but often at the cost of genuine aliveness. In order for

our own histories to remain alive, we must continually find ways to keep them growing, in depth and in detail.

> I thought you were just giving us a line when you told us to write our story down on paper. I'm one of those people who's told my story over and over again in meetings to the point where I even put myself to sleep when I tell it. Well, I spent all weekend working on it and I'm still not finished.
>
> I got this huge roll of white butcher paper and started to write down all my memories of my family. I just sat down and started writing. It was amazing! It just poured out of me. There are still blank spaces. For some reason, I don't have any photographs of me from nine to eleven; and I don't seem to remember much about that time. I got out all my family photographs and I've made this collage. Its amazing. I've always felt so insubstantial. Like I didn't have any weight. This is like my saying, "I do exist."
>
> Susan

We encourage you to approach the following exercises with both a willingness to record what you already remember and an openness to discover what may lie deeper in the heart of your past.

**Exercise 9:
The Family Genogram**

The genogram will be an essential reference for later discussions and questions about your family.

What Is a Genogram? Basically, a genogram is an elaborate family tree. It uses circles and squares to represent family members, lines for relationships, and other symbols to stand for specific characteristics such as divorce, violence, alcoholism, mental illness, codependence, etc. Genograms are particularly useful for unveiling historical family *patterns.* For the purpose of this exercise, we will look at relationships over at least three generations.

In drawing up your family genogram, you may initially discover how little information you know. This is especially common in alcoholic families where denial is rampant, secrets guarded, and family shame is passed down from generation to generation. To gather more information, you may want to consider talking or writing to your parents, grandparents, siblings, aunts, uncles, cousins, etc. *As before, we offer a note of caution: we encourage you to choose your confidants carefully.*

Creating a Genogram. A genogram can be relatively simple or detailed and complex. In this exercise, we will draw a basic one that provides the following information: family members, gender, age, death, marriage, divorce, miscarriages/abortions, names, chemical dependency, and codependency. To help you create your genogram, we've included a legend (below) for reference.

GENOGRAM LEGEND

□	–	Men	○	–	Women
Dan	–	Name	38	–	Age
b. (date)	–	Born	d. (date)	–	Death
m. (date)	–	Marriage	/	–	Divorce
M	–	Miscarriage	A	–	Abortion
ꝑ	–	Alcoholism/ addiction	*	–	Sober
ꟼ	–	Codependence	MI	–	Mental Illness

If you want to include more detail in your genogram, you can create your own symbols or note additional information that you feel is significant for your family. If you need more space than a single journal page, start with a large sheet of paper. You can always reduce the information and put it in your journal later.

Let's begin by drawing your immediate family, including you, your brothers and sisters, and your parents.

1. Place a symbol for yourself (squares indicate men, circles, women) in the middle of the page. Put your name and age immediately below the symbol.

2. On either side of your symbol and a few inches apart, place squares or circles for your brothers or sisters, respectively. Write their names and ages below as you did for yourself.

Note Marion's family in figure 1. She has two younger brothers and an older sister. She put herself second from the left in descending order of age.

figure 1

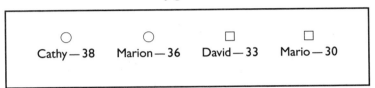

3. Now we'll put your parents in the picture. Place a square for your father and a circle for your mother above you. Put their names and ages in as you have done with your siblings.

4. Next, draw a horizontal line between your parents, to indicate their relationship. If they are divorced now, place a slash ("/") along the line between your mother and your father, along with the date of their separation. Draw vertical lines connecting you and your siblings to the horizontal line between each person's biological parents (see figure 2).

figure 2

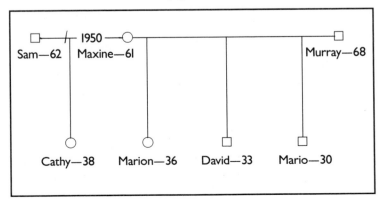

In Marion's family, her two brothers are full siblings, and her sister is a half sibling from her mother's previous marriage. To include her half sister, Cathy, and her relationship to the family, Marion drew Cathy's father, Sam, on the same generational level as her own parents, with a symbol and the date for her mother's divorce from her first marriage.

5. Now let's return to you and your siblings. If you are married or want to include significant-other relationships (SO), put a symbol for your spouse or your current SO next to you with a name and age. If this is your second marriage, include your first spouse as Marion did. Do the same for your siblings and their husbands, wives, or SOs. (See figure 3)

figure 3

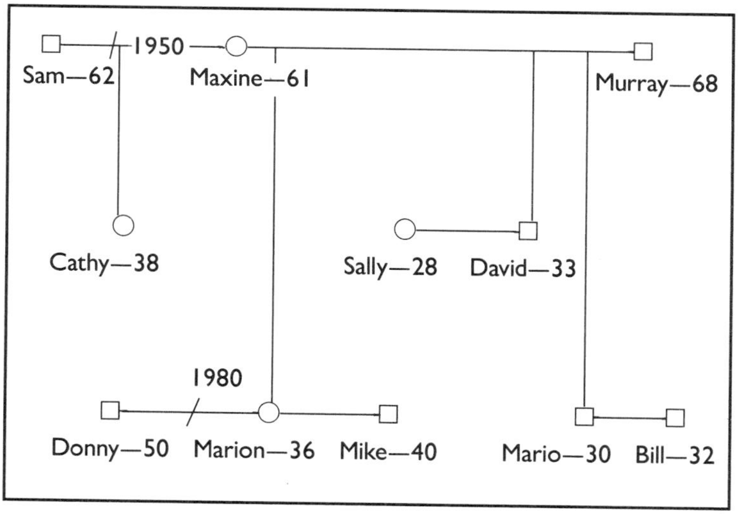

Marion's genogram shows that she was first married to Donny and is currently married to Mike. Her half sister, Cathy, remains single. Her brother David is married to Sally. Her brother Mario, who is gay, has had a long-term relationship with one man.

As you can see, the more people and relationships Marion included, the more space she needed. In our Tuesday group, only

Bob, Bill, and Susan brought the final draft of their genograms the first week of this exercise. The rest of the group took over a month to finish. As they added more and more information, they needed more and more space and redrew their genograms several times.

6. Now let's add your children and your siblings' children, if there are any. Draw solid lines down to these children. At this point you can also include miscarriages (M), abortions (A), and deaths (d.), as in figure 4.

figure 4

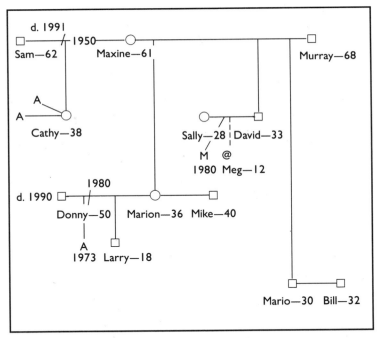

Marion's genogram now shows that she has an eighteen-year-old son, Larry, from her first marriage to Donny. She also had an abortion when she was with Donny, before Larry was born, which she represented with an "A." Cathy, Marion's older half sister, has had two abortions. Her brother David and his wife, Sally, have had one miscarriage.

We can also see that David has an adopted daughter named

Meg. If children are adopted, you might create another symbol for adoption as Marion did by putting a small "a" in Meg's circle. Marion decided to use a dotted vertical line between Meg and her parents, in addition to the little "a," to indicate the adoption.

There were also two recent deaths in Marion's immediate family. Her mother's first husband, Sam, and her own first husband, Donny, both died in alcohol-related accidents the year before. You may want to note briefly the cause of an individual's death in order to recognize patterns that run through your family.

7. Now let's indicate which family members are chemically dependent and codependent. (If you are not clear about what codependence means, come back to finish this part of your genogram after reading chapter 7.) We use square flags for alcoholics or drug addicts and triangular ones for codependents.

figure 5

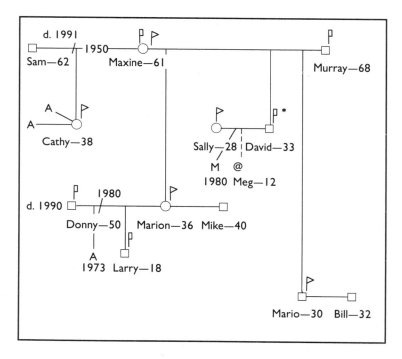

In Marion's genogram, both her parents are alcoholic. Her first husband, Donny, was addicted to cocaine, her brother David is recovering from alcoholism, and Marion has serious concerns about her son's marijuana use. In addition to her own codependence, Marion identifies her mother, Cathy, Mario, and her brother David's wife as being codependent.

Your genogram now presents the men and women, marriages, divorces, abortions, miscarriages, births, deaths, and relationships to alcohol, drugs, and codependency that exist in your immediate family. If you want to, you can continue to add more detail or stop at this point. What you've done so far will be sufficient to answer the questions at the end of this chapter.

You will use this genogram as a reference in later chapters, as it continues to grow into a valuable document that chronicles your family's history.

**Exercise 10:
Writing Your Story**

Your family genogram is like the outline of a novel. It gives you a historical map to use in writing your story.

Begin writing your life story in your journal by fleshing out the genogram from Exercise 9. Your initial job is to be the witness who chronicles your family's history. Like a reporter, you are passing on to others all the events you remember—pleasant and happy events as well as the uncomfortable and painful ones.

Many group members have found it best to begin this exercise by telling the background history and myths of their family's origins: What are the oldest ethnic, cultural, and religious traditions influencing your ancestors? Who emigrated (how and why?) to this country and eventually to the state and city in which you were born? As you write, include as much detail as you want to. Include major life events as well as small details that breathe life into the story.

If you find this task daunting, consider this a *work in progress* that you will add to over the following weeks, months, or years. Your story may grow as each chapter of this workbook reminds you of more events in your family's history.

Most group members at Genesis find that writing their story for the first time produces tremendous anxiety. The most important tool for dealing with this anxiety is the support that group members provide, both through understanding one another's nervousness and struggling openly with telling their own stories. Therefore, if you are working through this book on your own, this is a particularly important time to get to your first Twelve-Step meeting (if you haven't yet) or to increase the number of meetings for a while.

Finally, we encourage you to avoid using this exercise to reinforce a sense of being victimized. For the moment, try to be the witness, whose role is simply to record, openly and honestly, exactly what happened in your family.*

> This exercise is very painful for me, but I feel it's been helpful to see how distorted a picture of my life I have carried around with me for so long. When I sat down to write out my family history (after procrastinating for a couple of weeks) the first thing that came into my mind was the story my father told me about Aunt Gail, whom I was named after. Even to this day I can remember him saying what a nice woman she was. But then he'd say, ". . . even if she was from your mother's family." My aunt Gail died in her twenties when she and her husband, my uncle Marco, were drunk and were in a car accident together. My father to this day hasn't forgiven my aunt for being the one who was driving. My father looked up to Marco. So—I was named after my aunt Gail, my mother's sister, another alcoholic. This is about all I can handle now. I'll come back to it later.
>
> Gail

In the previous two exercises, we have moved from the outline to the narrative of your life story. The final step in recording your family's biography is to add the emotional dimension by recalling how it felt for *you* to experience each of the events in your story.

Exercise 11: The Emotional Dimension

---

* See *A Time to Heal*, pp. 49–75.

In this exercise we would like you to add the feelings, both good and bad, that you remember during the different events recorded in the above narrative. For things that occurred before you were born, make note of the feelings you have as you tell the story now. If you can't remember having feelings during some significant events, record that you have come up blank and guess briefly what you imagine someone in each situation might *have felt.*

Sharon found that she could easily acknowledge the traumatic and painful effects of her father's alcoholism on her and the rest of her family, but it was extremely difficult to admit to the fun that she had had with him when they would go to the park for walks and sing folk songs together. She only wanted to remember the bad times because evoking the good ones opened up such a well of sadness that she was afraid she'd never stop crying.

One story Bob told was how his father would "discipline" him when he was drunk. Bob was convinced, and he tried to convince the group, that being whipped to the point of bruising and bleeding was not abusive because his father said it was his right to "teach him a lesson," and lessons weren't abuse. His father would justify the beatings by listing all Bob's faults while preparing the strap.

When Bob used the word *strap,* a hush came over the group. In the silence that followed, the entire group lowered their heads. One by one, everyone told how they felt when they heard Bob talk about the "strap." Sharon said she felt helpless. Denise felt sadness and hurt. Then Bob interrupted and said that if he allowed himself to have feelings, he would be in a complete and total rage.

Feeling Exercise

Take time to do the Feeling Exercise as described in chapter one (page 15).

Journal

Take some time to think about the process you went through in creating the genogram and writing your family's story. In your journal, write your responses to these questions:

1. What did it feel like to think about asking family members for information to help complete this exercise?

2. Did you tell your family why you wanted the information? If not, why not?

3. If you did ask relatives for information, was it useful, or was it further confirmation that your family continues to be locked in denial?

4. What was it like to see your story written down in front of you?

5. Do you notice any subtle ways that you edited out certain events and left them untold?

6. What was it like to add the emotional coloring to events in your story?

7. Did you find yourself avoiding or minimizing your feelings by telling yourself not to "complain"?

You are *not* complaining when you are struggling to give witness to pain that came at the hands of people whose role in life was to raise you, protect you, and teach you. Breaking the silence means that you have a right to chronicle the events in your life—to acknowledge the truth of what happened and its effects on you. You are banishing the process of denial and clearing the way for the healing to begin.

> I was surprised to realize how little information I have about my parents and what my early childhood was like. I just don't seem to have the memories. So I called my mother, because my father died six years ago, and figured I'd ask her about it. Maybe it's still too soon after his dying; I don't know. She wouldn't talk about our family. She gave one or two word answers confirming the old stories, but she just wouldn't talk about the family when I was growing up. I have no idea what that's about. Next week I think I'll call my aunt, my father's sister.
> Mark

★ Recommendations

Further information on constructing genograms can be found in McGoldrick and Gerson's *Genograms in Family Assessment.*

If you have a difficult time remembering your early years, we recommend several movies. *Shattered Spirits,* a made-for-TV movie with Martin Sheen and Melinda Dillon, is a dramatic illustration of how parental alcoholism can terrify a family. *Desert Bloom,* with Jon Voight, portrays the ambivalence children can have toward an alcoholic parent. *Soft Is the Heart of a Child* (Operation Cork) and *The Mirror of a Child* (Johnson Institute) are two effective movies that you might be able to borrow from a local chemical-dependence treatment center. While watching these movies, pay attention not just to the drama revolving around the alcohol but also to the tension, the silences, the empty spaces, and the deceit that permeate day-to-day life in alcoholic families. Although no children are portrayed in *Who's Afraid of Virginia Woolf,* with Elizabeth Taylor and Richard Burton, this film is so intensely evocative for people who grew up in alcoholic families that it may help you recall memories of your alcoholic family.

The following books can also stimulate memories of your own childhood:

> *This Boy's Life, A Memoir,* Tobias Wolf
>
> *Keeping Secrets,* Suzanne Somers
>
> *Potato Chips for Breakfast,* Cynthia Scales

As an antidote to the tendency of ACoAs to take responsibility for their misfortunes, we also recommend the book *When Bad Things Happen to Good People,* by Harold Kushner. His message is good preparation for the exercises in chapter 8, when we explore the guilt and shame associated with familial alcoholism.

Chapter Four

Welcoming Feelings

Exercises in the last chapter placed great importance on the feelings that ACoAs had during childhood. In this chapter we explore more deeply the *relationship* that you currently have with that ebbing, flowing, changing river of feelings that flows through each of us. Feelings themselves are rarely the source of problems. It is a *dysfunctional relationship* to feelings that causes traumatic experiences to continue to bedevil people.

Let's dispel a few myths that our culture—and many therapists—promote about feelings:

Myth #1: Feelings are accurate guides to the truth.

Wrong. Feelings give us information about our *inner* world. But it is quite possible to *feel* mistreated when we are actually being treated fairly. It is important both to identify accurately the feelings you have and also to explore their meaning rather than assume they tell you the truth about the outside world.

Myth #2: Feelings can be controlled by keeping them out of awareness.

Wrong. Feelings live on and affect us even when they are kept out of consciousness. They are as inevitable and continuous as breathing. Whether you are aware of their presence or not, they have an impact on your life. When they are kept out of awareness, feelings find ways to disguise themselves or gather enough strength to emerge in unexpected ways, and at unexpected times.

Myth #3: Feelings are more important than ideas.

Wrong. Feelings and ideas are of equal importance. You need both your heart and your head to navigate successfully through life, just as you need both a right leg and a left to walk in a straight line.

Myth #4: Feelings are a burden that must be managed.

Wrong. Feelings give us vitally important information. Although they may rumble through your chest, twist your bowels, and heat up your groin, they have no stake in bringing you to your knees and destroying you. Feelings can generally be trusted to have a natural course, during which time they wax, then wane. The information they give you about yourself is invaluable. The greater burden is being without this information.

What constitutes a healthy relationship to this continuous river of feelings? As with so many things in life, having the "right relationship" to feelings requires finding a middle ground—a golden mean. In the case of feelings, this golden mean exists in a balance between giving feelings enough freedom to be exactly what they are and maintaining some control over the impact they have on how we live our lives. We must learn not to control our feelings while simultaneously not allowing them to control us. Such a balance comes through the art and discipline of *welcoming feelings.*

When feelings are welcomed, they are treated like an honored guest who unexpectedly knocks at our door. If Mother Teresa showed up at my house, I hope I would invite her in *unconditionally* and say that my home is hers. I hope that I would not first extract a promise that she would stay for only three nights, as I might with an unwanted relative. Exercising such control up front comes from fear that a guest cannot be trusted. With Mother Teresa, however, if the house arrangements were not working, I *could* tell her. She *would* listen. She'd have my best interests at heart, and that premise would not have to be established before extending her an invitation.

Children of alcoholics often develop a dysfunctional relationship to their feelings, believing both that they *can*, and *have* to be, controlled. ACoAs develop unrealistic ideas about the natural limitations of human willpower and control because their alcoholic parents (and often the nonalcoholic parent as well) are deeply confused about the same issue. Just as the alcoholism is blamed on a lack of willpower, the anger and fear that family members are feeling is blamed on a lack of self-control. ACoAs are unwittingly encouraged to strive for unrealistic levels of self-control in order to feel good about themselves. The underlying message is that greater control is always possible, through greater exertion of willpower.

There is nothing wrong, in and of itself, with defending ourselves against feelings. We all do it; resistance to being overwhelmed by feelings is part of being healthy. When traumatic events occur, for example, the ability to defend ourselves against being overwhelmed permits us to take action—to get out of danger. But people frequently make the mistake of believing that just because they have restricted their *awareness* of feelings, the feelings themselves do not exist.

Controlling feelings is an illusion. We only control our awareness and expression of feelings, not the feelings themselves. This illusion, however, is the fulcrum around which alcoholics manipulate other people, and around which they inadvertently manipulate themselves as well. This manipulation is in force when an alcoholic family falls into the illusion of seeing the denial of feelings as a sign of caring and maturity.

The dismantling of this illusion is also the pivotal point around which many peoples' lives turn when they enter recovery. For many alcoholics, and for their children as well, developing a healthy relationship to feelings is the eye of the needle through which they must pass in order to enter recovery. Passage through this eye is impossible if you are still carrying an overblown idea of what your willpower can accomplish. Only someone with a right relationship to willpower can find a right relationship to feelings. The art and discipline of *welcoming* feelings requires that people become willing to rethink everything they "know" about their relationship to emotion, most especially the degree to which emotions can be controlled.

As we described in the last chapter, when group members

begin exploring old memories, many of them find that few feelings arise with the memories. Others find that powerful feelings begin to emerge, but that they are automatically fought back down. Most people discover that they are so practiced at controlling feelings that the process occurs offstage, out of everyone's view—even their own. Before the feelings become strong enough to emerge into awareness, their ever-vigilant unconscious notices the emotion and manages to keep them from gaining any attention. Something is amiss. Why would people lose access to what is so human about themselves?

The most common emotions to well up as ACoAs begin reviewing their past are guilt, shame, sadness, anger, and fear. Let's look briefly at each of these powerful feelings.

Guilt arises because people from alcoholic homes are so often held responsible for the alcoholic's drinking and become so practiced at keeping the family's dirty linen out of public view. The appearance of propriety is so vitally important to most alcoholics that their children feel guilty for betraying their parent if they talk about the truth. Breaking the silence, for many children of alcoholics, automatically leads to guilty feelings, as though their truthfulness were motivated by disloyalty.

Shame is often the feeling that comes up for ACoAs raised in families that were so publically dysfunctional that little sense of propriety remained. The embarrassment of being the son or daughter of a public drunk goes to the core of many children. Group members talk of feeling that, underneath all the layers of maturity and competence they have established, there is a basic sense of being somehow contaminated, even evil, by association. Something is wrong deep inside, so wrong that it is intensely shameful to allow anyone else to see it.

Sadness is present because the losses are real. Perhaps a parent died because of his addiction. Perhaps the family fell apart—or blew apart. Perhaps the emotional distance simply grew until it became a chasm so wide that the other side moved beyond sight. When a parent is still drinking, the loss may still be growing. Each year that is lost to intoxication is one more that has to be grieved for.

Anger consumes some ACoAs; it runs so deeply and is so impotent at changing the past. For other ACoAs, anger is inconceivable; it threatens to explode if it finds the light of day. And for others, anger simply does not seem to exist; it has been locked away so completely that it has been forgotten.

Fear comes out of the darker corners of our minds and is often one of the most difficult feelings to tolerate. Frequently ACoAs have grown up in an atmosphere of such fear (of physical danger, of loss, of humiliation, etc.) that it has become part of their daily lives. Allowing others to see our fear makes most people feel very small and far too vulnerable. Both of these reactions only increase the fear. A spiraling panic can threaten to overwhelm us very quickly. Tolerating our experience of fear is very difficult.

Not all feelings are kept out of awareness by an unwillingness to experience them. The most traumatic experiences can generate a numbness that overtakes people like a knee-jerk reflex. If you find that exploring the past has left you with very little feeling, the very depth of disconnection from your experience may be the "smoking gun" that establishes how frightful things were. More specifically, such numbness is often evidence of how pervasively ACoAs experienced the threat of being overwhelmed by their feelings. The intensity of confusion, fear, anger, sadness, and shame was so great, perhaps on a daily basis, that a rupture began to occur between themselves and their experience. Many ACoAs enter our groups only partially connected with their immediate experience; they have chronically dissociated from themselves.

However, once feelings get slotted away into the unconscious, they remain there in exactly the same form as when they were first stowed away out of sight. To the unconscious, time is irrelevant. Feelings that we bury alive remain alive. They never really fall into the past. When ACoAs begin to scratch the surface above the graveyard of their old feelings by looking at what really happened during their childhood, ghosts can unexpectedly spring out of the ground and begin to bedevil them. This may initially feel overwhelming. However, when group members *feel* as if they are going to be overwhelmed by emotions, we remind them that this feeling does not mean that you *are* going to be overwhelmed.

The goal of recovery is to develop a new relationship to your feelings.

This new relationship recognizes that your feelings need your attention to be free; and your health depends on their freedom. Think of your feelings as being like your children. When you do this, you no longer listen to them only to shut them up. You listen to them because it enriches you and because they deserve to be heard. When listening closely to them is your sincere goal, then the relationship deepens, and they find it easier to grow and become who they really are.

Welcoming your feelings, whatever they may be, is a step toward greater health.

• • • • • • • **EXERCISES** • • • • • • •

Almost unanimously, our ACoA group members talk about having problems experiencing, identifying, and validating their feelings. Many, like Brian, deny the importance of feelings outright with an arrogant defiance and minimize their importance:

> You know, I'm having a hard time with all this focus on feelings. What's the big deal about feelings? I get by just fine without all this touchy feely stuff. They just make life more difficult.
>
> Brian

Others have a hard time recognizing feelings at the moment when they arise.

> Sometimes I know I'm feeling something, but I just can't get at it. I know something's going on 'cause I feel fidgety and in a fog. I can go for days like this, and then suddenly it will hit me—I'm really angry!
>
> Sharon

And still others confuse thinking with feeling.

> I feel that you're treating me like the brother you don't like. I feel that your anger at me doesn't have anything to do with me. I feel you should just let go of your anger.
>
> Denise

An important step in recovery is the exploration and integration of your capacity to feel. This may involve developing an awareness of your feelings in the present just as much as discovering your feelings about the past. It may include pleasant feelings like joy, happiness, and love as well as unpleasant ones like irritation, anger, and loneliness.

It's important to emphasize that we are not valuing feeling *more* than thinking. The capacity to think is essential to our ability to function in the world. For many ACoAs, however, thinking was used during childhood as such an effective shield against being overwhelmed by powerful emotions such as fear, anger, and shame that this shield became permanent—and so thick that less intense feelings, like irritation and pleasurable feelings, were also excluded.

The following exercises explore:

- your range of emotions
- your emotions and their impact on your body
- your family's emotional range

Later in the workbook we will explore the specific feelings of anger, guilt, shame, and sadness.

The following exercise will help you become more aware of the range of your feelings and the extent to which your emotional life may have been constricted as a result of having grown up in an alcoholic family. The exercise will use the feeling lists that you have compiled over the last few weeks.

Exercise 12:
Your Emotional Range

Emotional constriction tends to show up in group members who find themselves using a very limited vocabulary for most of their feelings. For example, after several weeks in the group, Sharon gave Brian some feedback about their interactions.

Brian, I want you to take this the right way. I don't mean this as criticism. You come across as very bright and articulate, but I just can't get a sense about what's going on inside you. I know you're upset; but other than that, I

honestly can't tell. The only words you use to describe
what's going on are "okay" and "not too bad."

Sharon

In her own way, Sharon was trying to help Brian become
aware of how his limited range of feelings and his constricted vocabulary of feeling words made it difficult for her to understand
what was going on with him below a surface level.

Let's explore the range of your feelings.

1. Look back over your Feeling Exercises for the last three
   chapters. Make a master list of all the feeling words you
   have written down so far and look at the words you have
   circled in the Feelings List.

2. Is there much range in intensity among your feelings?
   For example, in the last three weeks have you gotten *irritated* or *peeved* but not *angry* or *mad*? Have you gotten *slightly blue* but not *depressed* or *anguished*?

3. Do you sense a way in which you actively or unknowingly
   stifle, block, withhold, disguise, or dampen the intensity
   of your feelings? How do you do this?

4. If you sense that you are dampening the intensity of
   your feelings, what do you think you might be protecting
   yourself from?

5. Looking at the list again, where do the holes appear
   (places where you didn't seem to have had much feeling
   in the last three weeks)?

6. Do you notice that other people have emotions that
   seem foreign and out of your range? If so, list these
   emotions in your journal.

At first I thought this exercise was going to be easy because I'm so verbal. I'm a writer, and I use words all the
time; it's my living. But, you know, I was amazed. Every
night before I went to bed I would turn off my computer, go to the workbook, and sit and think. All the feel-

ing words I came up with were the feelings of people in the stories I was writing about. Then I realized what I was doing and tried to focus in on what *I* felt throughout the day . . . I found a blank. I wonder why I write about other people's lives so easily when I can't figure out what I'm feeling?

I started to see how unconnected I feel with the people in my life, as well as with my own feelings.

Brian

Initially, Brian had a hard time with this exercise because he tended to intellectualize his feelings. As he was able to describe the way in which he distances himself from his feelings, he became aware of how he also feels separate from the people in his life. At first he chalked this up to being the only African-American in the group, but he soon realized that his feelings of separateness occur in all settings. Slowly he discovered the sadness and depression that lay beneath his intellectual exterior. Although this was hard for him to acknowledge openly, he got some positive feedback from Sharon that helped him persevere:

When you talk about how lonely you are, I feel closer to you, Brian, because I know what it feels like to be lonely. When you talk from your head, you feel very distant. Until now, I didn't want to get close to you.

Sharon

Sharon then described her experience with the exercise:

This wasn't as hard as I thought. So much of my life I feel as if I'm in a fog, just wandering. I thought for sure this was going to be the same. I couldn't believe how much I got into this exercise. I tore out the Feelings List and kept it in my purse. Whenever I thought I was feeling something I'd pull it out, search through the list till I came to the word that fit and check it off. It's the strangest thing, but the more I seemed to be able to label my feelings, the more solid I felt.

Sharon

Here's a portion of Sharon's list:

Monday	*Tuesday*	*Wednesday*	*Thursday*
tired	exhausted	irritable	embarrassed
groggy	irritated	worthless	ashamed
expansive	wounded	inferior	worthless
energized	depressed	fraudulent	tired
alive	hurt	cold	condemned
excited	furious	defeated	unsupported
motivated	angry	deflated	understood
	pissed off	discouraged	valued
	anxious	unworthy	savored
	tired		respected
			needed

Take a break before going on to the next exercise.

Exercise 13:
Emotions and the Body

The charge and power of emotions, communicated throughout the body by our nervous system, are often felt as internal sensations (e.g., tingling, heat, cold, churning, tightness), movements (e.g., twisting, fidgeting, trembling), or the physical equivalent of mood states (e.g., expansiveness, emptiness). To help identify your feelings more readily, this exercise will focus on body sensations that accompany feelings. By becoming aware of your body's responses to feelings, you can learn to identify your feelings more quickly and precisely. For example: If I notice the hairs standing up on my neck, I can ask myself, "Hmmm, this tends to happen when I'm scared. Am I scared at this moment?"

If you have a difficult time with this exercise, don't give up. Take a break for a day and let it sit. Then try again.

1. For the next week, pay attention each day to the sensations in your body that are present when you are experiencing feelings, from the slightest irritation or pleasure

to the strongest rage or ecstasy—and, of course, everything in between.

2. Notice *where* in your body you tend to feel sensations: in your heart, your head, your stomach, your knees . . . Some of you may actually notice the sensation first and then the emotion.

3. Pay attention to whether you sense *movement* associated with emotions in the body. Do you get a *sinking* feeling in your heart when you feel sad, a *churning* in your stomach when angry, a *surging* in your temples when frustrated, or a sense of feeling *bubbly* when excited?

Today a nurse on my floor was fired. When my supervisor gave me the news, I felt cold. Literally, my hands felt cold. I noticed I had trouble breathing. I was breathing very deeply, but still could not catch my breath. My mind went blank for a few minutes, and I don't think I heard the rest of what my supervisor was saying. I think I was scared. There I go thinking my feelings again. Let me try that again. I was . . . I *am* afraid. My stomach feels queasy, not quite nauseous. I am definitely afraid.

Sharon

4. When you've done this for a few days, look over your Feeling Exercises for the last three weeks again. Do you remember any physical sensations associated with these particular feelings? In other words, when you feel sad, do you get nauseated and have a low energy level? Do you experience your sadness in your chest or stomach? Are you weak in the knees? When you are upset and angry, do you get hot and tense or energetic and filled with vitality?

I'm still having a hard time with this. I'm getting better at noticing my feelings, but I don't seem to have much physical reaction to feeling things. Maybe I'm doing this wrong. But come to think of it, I do notice a kind of empty feeling in my gut a lot of the time—especially

> when here with the group. It's as if there's an iron band around my chest and stomach keeping everything in.
>
> Brian

> As I said, this was easy. I always notice my body when I'm feeling something. When I'm sad, I feel this pressure on my chest. When I feel happy, I feel somewhat light-headed; I feel like jumping. I hate feeling down, and I especially hate feeling angry. When I feel angry, I feel like my head is going to burst.
>
> Sharon

Brian was still struggling with identifying his feelings and how his body responds to emotions, but he was able to identify the bodily sensation of constrictedness ("It's as if there's an iron band around my chest and stomach keeping everything in"). For Brian, this is an important step toward identifying the presence of feelings.

Sharon had an easier time identifying both her feelings and her physical responses. What she began to learn was the way in which she had some feelings that were more acceptable to have—i.e., happiness—and others that were not acceptable—i.e., anger. When she was able to talk about her "unacceptable emotions" in the group, Brian said,

> Sharon—remember when you said you felt closer to me when I talked about feeling lonely? I think I'm feeling closer to you now that I know you have unacceptable emotions, too.
>
> Brian

Exercise 14: Your *Family's* Emotional Range

Remembering the past is healing when ACoAs recover the lost and suppressed emotions that they had as children. By recovering the past, ACoAs gain not only a deeper sense of who they were as children, but they also open the doors to feeling more deeply who they are as adults. They increase their capacity to experience their feelings *in the present moment*.

This exercise will help you explore the emotional landscape of your family as a whole. Understanding the range of emotions expressed in your family often sheds light on your own experience, or *lack of experience*, with feelings.

1. Refer back to your genogram. On the genogram, or on a separate page in your journal, record the emotions you most associate with each person. If you need to, refer to the Feelings List.

2. When ascribing feeling words to people in your family, do you notice any similarities with your own lists?

3. Is there a consistent pattern of who expressed most of the family's rage? Who felt the fear? The anxiety? The sense of responsibility?

4. Do you remember any family myths about the emotional states of certain individuals? For example, "She was angry from the moment she came out of the womb" or "You were so easygoing, you never gave us any trouble. You were such a good, happy girl."

I knew that I was one of the people in my family who didn't express much emotion, but I couldn't believe how similar I am to my father. When he got home and saw that my mother was drinking, he never said a word. He'd just hang up his coat—I can see it as if it were happening now. He'd hang up his coat . . . we had a rack in the corner near the door . . . put his hat on the table just beside the hallway, kiss my mother, and sit down in his chair in the corner and read the paper. That was it until dinner. If she'd been drinking a lot during the day and dinner was late, we just waited. If Mom couldn't get it together for dinner soon enough, without skipping a beat he'd just say, "Looks like a good day to eat out. How about pizza?" And we'd all pile into the station wagon and head for Pizza Hut. Mom, too. Even if she almost had dinner ready, we'd just go out. I never found out what happened to the near-dinners, and we never talked about it.

Brian

Feeling Exercise

Take time to do the Feeling Exercise as described in chapter one (page 15).

Journal 📖

In the group session on feelings, people quickly learn to deepen awareness of their emotions and body sensations. Being aware of distinctions among physical sensations can help you discover subtleties in your emotional life as well as give you more information about how you *feel*, as compared to how you *think* you feel.

Estella initially identified herself as feeling angry at her roommate for leaving the sink piled high with dishes over the weekend. In doing the exercise, she realized that her angry feeling was also accompanied by an intense knot in her stomach, flushing on her face, and a sense of feeling caged. Only then did she understand that she had mislabeled her feeling; she was *furious*, not just angry! Once she had this information, she knew she couldn't let the incident pass without talking to her roommate.

1. Reflecting back on the chapter exercises, what did you learn about yourself?

2. How have you become more sensitive to the full range of your feelings?

3. Did you find that it is easier to have feelings about some members of your family than others? For example: Was it easier to be angry at the alcoholic but not the non-alcoholic parent?

4. When you began paying closer attention to your bodily sensations and the relationship to your feelings, what did you discover about yourself?

5. What things distract you when you *begin* feeling strong emotions? Television, magazines, the radio, food, sex, sports, alcohol, drugs?

6. What did you learn when making a chart of your family's emotional range?

7. Did the exercises confirm any of the impressions, feelings, or thoughts you had about your family?

One of the big eye-openers for Brian in this week's exercise was just how much he was like his father. He had always thought of his father as capable, strong, in control. He never realized how closed off his father had been in order to be able to deal with his mother all the time and how little his father actually protected him from his mother's alcoholism. Eventually Brian discovered that his feelings about his father were not absent—he was filled with anger.

> I really focused all my anger, when I was in touch with it, at my mother for her drinking. I felt that she was always the bad one—not so much because of her drinking, but she just couldn't seem to get it together. But now that I think about it, while my father *did* take us out for dinner, he never tried to do anything about her drinking. I remember his saying, "It's just her way." *What the hell does that mean! What was I supposed to do when she was drunk in the kitchen before he came home?* What was I supposed to say when my teacher asked me what I did on the weekend? "Well, Mrs. McCleary, I took my mother to the hospital again, but she's okay; it was just her drinking again." Why didn't he ever do something more than take us out to dinner!
>
> Brian

★ Recommendations

The search for buried feelings is often described within the recovering community as the search for the child within. *Healing the Child Within,* by Charles Whitfield, helps explore the concept of the "child within." In addition, two children's books are nice introductions to talking about feelings: *Feelings,* by Aliki, and *C is for Curious: An ABC of Feelings,* by Woodleigh Hubbard.

In the spirit of struggling to recover your aliveness, we recommend several films that tell moving stories about the potential gains, and possible limitations, in awakening our emotional lives. Although they do not chronicle the effects of parental alcoholism, notice whether you find yourself identifying with the emotional struggles portrayed in the films.

Pump up the Volume, with Christian Slater

Awakenings, with Robert De Niro

Edward Scissorhands, with Johnny Depp

Dead Poets Society, with Robin Williams

Stanley and Iris, with Jane Fonda and Robert De Niro

Chapter Five

Survival

Many CoAs die during childhood, but the vast majority survive *physically* despite the increased risks to their health and safety. Living with someone who is frequently intoxicated forces a child close to the precipice of a wide variety of dangers: "Who will take care of me if the house catches fire? What will happen if Mom falls asleep when she's smoking? Who will protect me when Dad throws a chair down the stairs? Who will take me to the doctor when I'm sick?" Children naturally move into a survival mode when their parents are *incapable* of protecting them from these, and countless other, day-to-day dangers. As a result, most children of alcoholics begin to take responsibility for their own survival, to the exclusion of all the other things that kids normally do, like playing, learning, and growing. They age too fast, in a world they cannot trust.

Emotional survival is at stake for those CoAs who survive physically. Their growth into unique individuals, their ability to discover who they are, their own likes and dislikes, their own talents and needs, are all in jeopardy. Even though their physical health may not be threatened, protecting their emotional health becomes a full-time task. Again, the result is that many CoAs age too fast, in a world they cannot trust.

Not all children of alcoholics do survive emotionally. As a group, CoAs are at higher risk than the general population for a wide variety of problems and pains, including hyperactivity, learning disabilities, stuttering, behavior problems at school, becoming runaways, teen pregnancy, dropping out of school, and coming into contact with the juvenile-justice and foster-care systems, to name a few. In fact, you encounter most of the normal problems of living and growing up in modern America more frequently, and more intensely, if your parent was addicted to alcohol or other drugs.

One cornerstone of the ACoA movement has been the lifting of denial about the past and the willingness to move beyond simply considering that the past was a hard time, a stressful period of your life, and to begin acknowledging that these stresses crossed an invisible line into the realm of being truly *traumatic*.

Trauma, by its very definition, means that circumstances temporarily overwhelmed you. It was not possible to find meaning in events as they were occurring. It was not possible to pay attention to all your feelings at a given moment because they were too intense to tolerate. Trauma means that your defenses were breached, your feeling of security threatened, and your very sense of identity thrown into turmoil. In other words, your natural "fight or flight" responses were activated. Evolution, and its rule that the fittest survive, has given us a brain that responds to overwhelming danger by preparing our entire body for defense: our heart rate increases, the blood begins to flow to our muscles rather than to our intestines, adrenaline floods our body, and we are prepared to make maximum efforts to survive—whether that means fleeing or fighting for our lives. Of course, it rarely comes to either of these choices, but we are ready. We have reflexively clicked into the survival mode.

What happens when people enter the survival mode too frequently and stay there much of the time? Often the consequences of being traumatized take years to appear, as the cumulative strain of remaining on "red alert" begins to take its toll. For this reason, the concept of *Post*-Traumatic Stress Disorder is quite relevant to children of alcoholics. PTSD affects people who have experienced high levels of stress that lie outside the range of normal human experience. They often suffer a confusing mixture of paradoxical feelings, at times flooded by old fears that activate them into a fight-or-flight mode, even when current events clearly don't seem to to warrant such an intense response. They are at the mercy of *reexperiencing the trauma* whenever anything resembling the original stresses reappears and triggers their survival reflexes. Then, a maelstrom of emotions wells up and takes over. They are powerless against this reflex. The emotions seem raw, as though earlier feelings have reappeared in their original form. In this way, children of alcoholics may "overreact" whenever a boss treats them arbitrarily; or they may regard legitimate criticism by their mate as unjust and threatening. Among people who have suffered the worst trauma (e.g., combat veterans or victims of physical and sexual abuse), reexperiencing the trauma may be so severe that they lose contact, momentarily, with their immediate experience and begin having a flashback.

Paradoxically, trauma also leads people to develop *psychic numbing*, which is essentially the opposite of what has been described above. Psychic numbing describes a survival reflex in which we disconnect from ourselves. A gulf opens between ourselves and our experience. We stop reacting to our fate. We dissociate from our feelings. When this occurs, it leaves us freer to "take care of business." Doctors and nurses in emergency rooms are able to respond to the most horrible and disfiguring injuries without responding at the moment to the human tragedy before them. In the same way, children of alcoholics are able to pull their unconscious father into bed, clean up his vomit, and comfort their bleeding mother, without pausing to feel the grief and horror that would be a normal response to such a family tragedy.

Psychic numbing creates a synthetic peace—a floating calm that comes from being disconnected from the crumbling world that surrounds you. Unfortunately, once this disconnection from the world occurs, it takes on a life of its own. Like a new reflex, it can arise whenever you begin to feel vulnerable. As a result, psychic numbing often prevents relationships from achieving much intimacy, which requires a degree of vulnerability. Psychic numbing paradoxically intensifies the isolation that children of alcoholics feel, even as it seems to make that isolation more tolerable.

Trauma intensifies all feelings and creates all-or-nothing, black-and-white thinking, feeling, and behavior. As a result, feelings either come into awareness full blast (reexperiencing the trauma) or remain out of awareness (psychic numbing). This increased intensity and either/or experience causes CoAs to become quite *hypervigilant*. They learn to scan the environment, constantly looking for the earliest signs of impending disaster. Chronic anxiety becomes a way of life. Although such vigilance may be an asset in some professions (air-traffic controllers and intensive-care nurses, for example), it rarely benefits relationships, which require trust for intimacy to emerge.

And finally, there is another heavy, and unexpected, price that people often pay for surviving guilt. *Survivor guilt,* and the chronic depression that accompanies it, plagues many veterans of military combat and many members of alcoholic families. Children of alcoholics are battle-tested veterans, old beyond their years. They often not only bear the scars and cynicism of battle but also are left with the dilemma of understanding how such great pain can come from the family that was supposed to protect them from the world's problems. They question why they were able to survive when others (perhaps the alcoholic or younger siblings) may not have been so fortunate. This dilemma is especially strong with those ACoAs who must separate themselves from their still-drinking parents in order to protect their own health.

At the same time that children may be traumatized by alcoholic families, they also may be challenged by them. Even as children are scarred by living in chemically dependent families, such families can also become the crucible in which a child's mettle is tested, purified, and strengthened. With enough support, many children of alcoholics meet the challenge of their family successfully. These CoAs have been called "invulnerable children," but this is clearly a misnomer. Many kids appear invulnerable by separating from their experience, numbing their feelings, and resigning themselves to living in the isolation that comes from depending only upon themselves. They survive their family of origin, they become successful during early adult life (especially at work), but they frequently end up being drained and emptied by such "invulnerability" during their middle years. Such invulnerability may seem mature, but it prevents life from developing deeper meaning and richness. People often experience difficulty during later portions of their lives, when maintaining such invulnerability becomes too hard, and too senseless.

A crucible is used to melt metals and gather whatever gold is present. Alcoholic families become a crucible for children by putting them into a high-risk/high-gain fire that will destroy some, but strengthen others. Those who emerge still intact have often

had the benefit of enough support, and the God-given tempera-
ment, to be resilient, to survive, and even to thrive. But this does
not mean that there has not been an impact on them. And it does
not mean that they have become invulnerable.

In fact, successfully surviving the crucible often means that
ACoAs have maintained the ability to be vulnerable. They have
not closed off to the world. They have not developed a hardened
shell to hide within. It simply means that they have been challenged, they have developed many skills needed to cope with the
stresses of their family (often at a younger age than is normally
necessary), and their identity and self-esteem have not been
crushed in the process. We call the gold that has been purified
within surviving ACoAs *resilience.*

A leading family therapist who has carefully studied alcoholic
families, Steven Wolin,* has identified seven attributes that give
children the resilience needed to survive painful experiences.
These are the qualities that are called upon, and strengthened, in
many children of alcoholics by the crucible of their dysfunctional
families:

- *Insight* is the mental habit of asking oneself penetrating
  questions and giving honest answers. Insight is a process
  that starts with sensing something is wrong and gradually
  grows into knowing, then to understanding. With insight,
  CoAs become aware that their family's problems stem
  from a parent's behavior and not their own inadequacies.

- *Independence* is the best possible bargain a survivor can
  drive between the competing needs for safe boundaries
  between children and their troubled parents and the
  longing for family ties. With independence, CoAs are
  able to withdraw enough from their families to feel safe
  again.

- *Relationships* require the give-and-take work necessary
  to derive love, acceptance, and emotional gratification

---

* Steven and Sybil Wolin, *The Resilient Self: How Survivors of Troubled Families Rise Above Ad-
versity* (New York: Villard Books, 1992).

from other people. CoAs with a natural tendency to seek relationships often find neighbors and teachers who can give them some of the validation that is lacking at home.

- *Initiative* creates the buoyancy, capacity for problem solving, and belief in personal control found in children who do not buckle or accept a view of themselves as either worthless or helpless. CoAs with initiative are less likely to sink back into the morass of their family and more likely to keep trying to find solutions and relationships that bring comfort.

- *Morality* is the foundation of ethical conduct which gives resilient survivors the basic necessities of purpose, self-respect, and dignity. CoAs who can find purpose and meaning in sources outside their family (e.g., religion, patriotism, etc.) have an internal rudder to steer their lives.

- *Creativity* means expressing and resolving inner conflicts in symbolic forms that have aesthetic value. CoAs with an artistic or athletic inclination find avenues for expressing emotions and wrestling with conflict that is generated within their family.

- *Humor* finds the comic in the tragic. CoAs with a sense of humor have a sense of perspective. Their appreciation of the absurd in life, and in their family, is a form of insight.

Most ACoAs emerged from their families with a mixed bag of resilient qualities and psychological bruises. Some emotional damage has been sustained: you may quickly jump back into the survival mode, even when it is no longer necessary, and this keeps you more distant than is truly necessary from potentially good relationships. But you have also developed some pride and competence in dealing with the adversities of the world, and often at a very young age. Carrying this mixed bag, you enter adult life, you form friendships, you strive for intimacy, and you conduct your professional lives—all with confusingly mixed results. And, with this mixed bag, you pick up a workbook like this and hope to make some sense of yourself.

How did you survive? In the previous chapters, you looked at *what* you had to do to survive. But *how* did you survive the events and feelings that you experienced? Did you numb out? Do you continue to reexperience the sense of trauma? Are you hyper-vigilant? Do you continually feel responsible and guilty? In understanding these costs, you will begin to make better sense of these facets of your personality. And you will be better prepared to make different choices about when to protect yourself, and how.

The ACoA recovery movement involves moving beyond only counting the costs of having an alcoholic parent and focusing on the resilient qualities that you possess as well. Being a true survivor requires more than holding your breath long enough to reach the surface. Survival often takes amazing creativity, courage, perseverance, and luck. What kinds of resilience did you find within yourself to help you meet the challenge of your family? How were they strengthened by your experiences during childhood? How do they benefit you during your adult years? And how can they be put to work in the service of your recovery? The following exercises will help you answer these questions.

· · · · · · · · **EXERCISES** · · · · · · · ·

> I really can't relate to all these stories about how difficult childhood was, even though my story is pretty much the same as most of yours. My father was a drinker, he hit me and my sisters, and he molested us. My mother was useless. She always tried to make things right, but she just didn't have what it took. I just realized how crazy things were and did what I could. I toughened up. No one is going to do it for you. Life is not a party.
>
>   Estella
>   (speaking with little
>   emotion)

One of the most difficult aspects of recovery is facing the truth about your past. In virtually every group at Genesis, at least one person asks, "Why do we have to go back? Can't we just let sleeping dogs lie?" The question is telling. Such protests convey a profound fear of the unknown—of the sadness, of the hurt, and of the anger—that lies just below the surface. Facing that unknown together is often the best way to keep the fear from becoming overwhelming.

Exercise 15: Home

This exercise uses the maze of rooms that made up the apartment(s) or house(s) that was home to your childhood. As you explore these rooms, you will find places where important childhood events took place. Strong emotions will be associated with these places, from terror and pain to tenderness and joy. We encourage you to take time with this exercise. Many group members take several weeks to complete the following questions.

1. On a page in the journal (or a larger piece of paper) draw a basic floorplan of the main house (or apartment) you grew up in. You might consider consulting family pictures or contacting family members to help refresh your memory. Some people have pasted pictures from each room to the floor plan as a reminder.

Here's Bill's floor plan as an example:

Diagram A

Backyard

Shed	Stairway to upstairs
Family room	Kitchen
Living room	Dining room

Porch

1st Floor

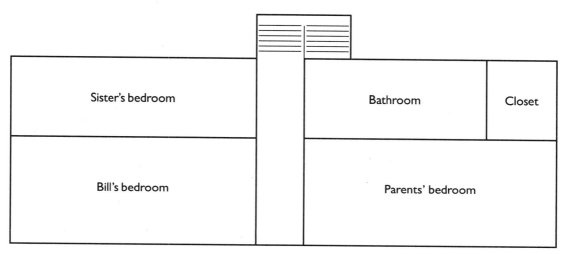

2nd Floor

2. With the floor plan and some pictures of the house (if available) in front of you, imagine you are standing outside, in front of the house. Take a mental walk from the street up to the front door. Specifically notice each of the following:

   • sights, sounds, smells

   • images and memories of events

   • feelings

3. In your mind's eye, open the door and step inside. Notice how you feel. Do any memories arise as you cross the threshold into the house? Write these down in your journal.

4. Writing in the journal as you mentally move throughout your house, go into each room, each closet, every corner, toward every window, door, into the basement, the bathrooms, the bedrooms, the laundry room, the backyard, the garage. (*Note:* Some group members have been helped in this exercise by dictating their thoughts into a tape recorder and transcribing them into the journal later.)

I don't know why this is the first memory that comes up, but I'm standing on the sidewalk, looking at the porch. My father is standing in the doorway with a beer in his hand. I can't be more than five or six. He's drunk. It's eleven o'clock on a Saturday morning. He's yelling at me, but I don't hear anything. I can just see his lips moving. He slips on the steps and falls. I don't hear him fall. I just see it.

Bill

Remember what the textures of the floor felt like in your bare feet, the carpeting, the stairs, the grass in the backyard, the cement in the walkway.

I walk toward my father. I feel the roughness of the cement of the walkway. My mother comes out of the house in her robe. She's drunk. Her hair is a mess. She seems to be yelling at me to help my father. I see her mouthing the words, "Give me a hand with your father," but I can't hear her voice. We struggle with him. He's fighting us. We get him into the hallway. The floors are wood. There are broken dishes in the hallway. I don't feel a thing.

Bill

Remember what each room smelled like, especially the kitchen.

Remember the sounds of each room. With each step, focus attention on your feelings and let memories of what happened emerge if they want to.

Record this information in your journal.

We get my father into the living room and put him on the couch. My mother collapses next to him. I hear her say, "Go out and play." I smell her breath. It stinks from cigarettes and alcohol. I feel like throwing up. I walk outside and sit on the porch in the sun. The porch feels warm and soft. I look at the beetles crawling in the dirt next to the steps. I don't know why I did this. . . . I dragged one of the beetles onto the cement and squashed it with a stick. The sun feels warm. It feels good.

Bill

Take a break for a few days at this point before going on to the next exercise. The time will let memories evoked by this exercise percolate slowly through your mind without your being distracted by material from the next exercise.

This exercise explores specific ways in which surviving your alcoholic family changed you. The first part uses the previous exercise to identify any effects of trauma (hypervigilance, psychic numbing, reexperiencing the trauma, and survivor guilt) that may still endure. Then the second part focuses on the resilient parts of your personality. As you examine the effects of the past, you may come to understand better who you are today—and what new choices are available to you regarding when, where, and from whom you protect yourself.

**Exercise 16:
The Seasoned Warrior**

The Effects of Trauma

Looking back over what you wrote as you walked through each part of your childhood house, do you find any effects of living on a battlefield: reexperiencing the trauma, psychic numbing, hypervigilance, and survivor guilt? Write in your journal any things from your own life that resemble the following examples:

- Reexperiencing the Trauma

    Are any places associated with a feeling of being overwhelmed?

    Did any feelings come back with their original intensity?

    Was there any sense that the intensity of feeling connected to certain places was more than you can bear right now?

    Did you ever have more of a sense of "reliving" events, as opposed to simply remembering them?

    Did the exercise stimulate any memories that have continued to intrude into your awareness, or that have reappeared as distressing dreams?

I went through the whole Home Exercise without much feeling—until I got to the closet in my bedroom. I still haven't opened that closet again, even mentally. When I approach it, I get this horrible feeling of stark terror. The fear starts in my chest, then grabs up at my throat. I cannot scream. . . . I know that that closet is where I used to hide from my drunken father when he tried to molest me. Sometimes he wouldn't find me. But sometimes the door would open, and his big hand would reach in and grab my arm. [Estella stopped and waved for us not to talk as she regained her composure.] I'm not ready to think about being back in the closet. Not yet.

Estella

- Psychic Numbing

    Were areas of your house blank, without memories?

    Did you remember any painful or scary events but found no access to any feelings about them?

    Did you feel more detached from yourself as you walked through certain parts of your home?

    Did you become "matter-of-fact" or bored during parts of this exercise?

In the examples given from Bill's journal during the Home Exercise, it was clear that he protected against being overwhelmed by the experience with his drunken mother and father by dissociating from the sound of their yelling and screaming. He blocked out the most unpleasant and disturbing aspect of the experience in order to survive and do what he needed to do. Unfortunately for Bill, there wasn't someone readily nearby to help him. As an only child, Bill took comfort in the only way he could: he found warmth in the sun where there was no warmth at home. He also took out his rage, as many children do, on those around him who were smaller and vulnerable to his anger . . . he killed bugs.

- Hypervigilance

    As you moved through the house, did you find yourself scanning the environment, reflexively looking for signs of danger?

Did you find your heart racing or your skin perspiring?

Did you get irritable during the exercise?

Did you have difficulty concentrating during the exercise?

There was no fighting in my family—not even any raised voices. But the tension that we all felt was beyond description. When I imagined walking up to the front door of my house, I began to feel all the old tension. I felt nervous as I thought of opening the door. It was like going into an oven. I had to take a few deep breaths before going in. It wasn't anger or fear that lay in wait for me just around the next corner. It was shame. I always had to be on the alert, ready to dodge a dart of shame one of my parents threw at me. . . . This exercise was exhausting for me.

Marion

• Survivor Guilt

Did you feel depression in your house (not just sadness at what was lost, but a sense of demoralization as well)?

Was there a feeling of being responsible for the events you remembered?

Was there any embarassment or guilt for having left the house, and those in it?

Was there a sense of never having really left emotionally?

When I imagined walking through the house, I felt that this is still my real home. I have never found a place that I can attach to as much as that house. Even though my father was alcoholic, and I had to watch him beat my mother up on the weekends, I still wonder what I could have done to make things be different. I was too passive back then. I wish I could really go back and have another chance to help my parents with what I know now.

Denise

Discovering Your Resilience

1. Looking back again at what you wrote as you walked through each part of your childhood house, do you find any examples of what we have described as the qualities of resilience: insight, independence, relationships, initiative, morality, creativity, and humor? Write in your journal any evidence you found of having had the following qualities:

   - Insight

     Did you sense that your family was different from your friends' families?

     Were you aware that your parent was drinking too much or using other drugs? At what age did you become aware of this?

     Did you understand that your parents' personal problems were causing the family problems?

   I remember the day I was playing "drunk" with my next-door neighbor. We were staggering around, talking dumb, and falling on the ground. All of a sudden I stopped laughing. I had to quit the game, because it wasn't funny for me anymore. I understood that getting drunk, the way my father did every night, was not a joke. I was eight years old.

   Denise

   - Independence

     Did you remember how often you left the house, wandering around the neighborhood rather than spending time at home?

     Did you remember any events in which you refused to participate, watching as others spun out of control?

     Did you vow that this was not your home for long, that you were getting out as soon as possible, or that you did not belong to this family?

Did you tolerate being in your home by reminding yourself that it was only a temporary situation?

Both of my parents are alcoholic, and I'm an only child. The first thing I thought of when I imagined walking through our trailer house is that I left when I was sixteen and have not been back now for two years. When I walked into my old bedroom, I imagined that it had already become a den. All my stuff had been stored somewhere, and I was glad to see that any evidence that I had come from the family was gone.

                    Gail

• Relationships

Did the mental return to your childhood house bring up any fond memories of being with either of your parents, a brother or sister, a neighbor, relative, or pet?

Did you recall trying to serve as the bridge between people in your family?

Did you persist in trying to be in a relationship with family members, rather than withdrawing?

Were most of your memories of other people and your connections to them?

Were you a social person with memories of having friends in your house?

Do you remember having behaved in ways that brought help to your family?

Lots of my memories from childhood involve my three brothers and my sister. It's amazing how little I remember of my parents. The most common memory is sitting in my big brother's room, playing cards with everyone, while my parents' angry voices could be heard downstairs. It seems as though we kids were always together, especially when things got bad. I remember one time that I called my sister when she was spending the night at a neighbor's house. My father had just knocked my mother out, and my sister immediately made an excuse for coming home to be with me. The greatest part of that memory is that I *knew* she would come home for me.

Sharon

- Initiative

    Did you encounter feelings of helplessness and apathy when you walked through your house, or did you remember continually trying new things to help the situation?

    Did you remember ways that you found to take care of yourself?

    Were you always suggesting possible solutions to the family's problems?

    Did people look to you to help clean up messes (literally or figuratively)?

    Did you help lead the campaign to get your alcoholic parent to stop drinking?

    Did you find ways to use school, friends, athletics, art, church, etc., as a refuge?

When I walked through the garage, I had the most vivid memories. [Bob's eyes grew misty, briefly.] I remember how I used two bikes and an old leaf cart to build a funny-looking contraption I used for my paper route. It let me carry more papers than any other carrier in the city. For years I won the award for having the largest route. I used the money to buy groceries and hid them in the old refrigerator in the garage behind my father's beer supply. I would always volunteer to go get my father's beer, and that way he never found the food. I'd grab a quick bite to eat and be back in the house before anyone knew what I was doing.

Bob
(speaking with
obvious pride)

- Humor/Creativity

    Did you have any memories of playing?

What were your fantasies as a child? Did you have any imaginary friends?

What hobbies do you remember having?

Do you have any memories of being artistic, whether by drawing, painting, acting, dancing, singing, playing music, or in athletics?

One of my greatest triumphs as a kid was writing a poem that I got to read at my class graduation. Everyone heard what they wanted to in it; but only my English teacher and I really understood that it was about my family. I described how some of us in our class would go on to success and others would have more troubled, even tragic, lives. When I wrote the poem, I was picturing my mother as a high-school senior; and I was describing how alcoholism became her downfall.

Brian

* Morality

   Did you have any feelings of injustice connected to your house?

   Do you remember judging your parents' alcoholism or other inadequacies?

   Do you remember what values guided you as a child?

   Did you feel that life had any purpose as a child?

   Do you remember helping others in your family or serving people outside your family?

I was always trying to be helpful as a kid. In many ways, I was the main caretaker for my grandmother, whose arthritis made her almost a total invalid. She wasn't a particularly pleasant woman, but she was aware that she was a burden. She often told me she thanked God for sending her such a caring granddaughter. I always knew her appreciation was genuine, and it made me feel proud to be helping God take good care of her. . . . No wonder that I like being a nurse as an adult.

Sharon

2. Can you identify how you use any of these skills in your current life? Write a brief description in your journal of at least two ways in which you remain resilient as an adult.

Feeling Exercise

Take time to do the Feeling Exercise as described in chapter one (page 15).

Journal

For some of you, these will have been the most difficult exercises so far. If you found them overwhelming or impossible to finish, even after having spread them out over several weeks, you might consider discussing your difficulty with a therapist experienced in working with Adult Children of Alcoholics, increasing the number of ACoA Twelve-Step meetings that you attend, and/or asking someone in the program to work with you as a sponsor.

For those of you who feel ready to move on, the following questions may help focus your journal writing.

1. What was it like to do the Home Exercise?

2. How did you take care of yourself while you were doing these exercises? Did you need to take breaks in order to remember a little at a time?

We hope that you took care to choose the right time, the right place, and the right people with whom to remember the past. It may be hard to realize that you are free to take care of yourself during these exercises—that it is all right to make the work as easy on yourself as possible.

3. Can you remember some good times?

Good times are a part of life in even the most dysfunctional families, although they may occur less frequently than in functional families. This workbook is designed to chronicle the truth of your experience to the best of your recollection. It is not devoted to focusing only on the negative experiences in life, although there may be times when that's all you can remember and the weight of the darkness and pain seems to block out the light. The truth is that in most alcoholic families, even the most chaotic and abusive, there are moments of joy. As a child, these may have been the moments you clung to in order to survive.

Recovery involves acknowledging the warmth and joy that you experienced in your family as well as the pain and hurt.

Take this opportunity to refer to the Family Floor Plan and remember the pleasant, warm, joyous times that you associated with the house you grew up in. Write these down on the same floor plan and describe some of the events in your journal.

I always thought of myself as having a completely miserable childhood. But when I was doing the floor-plan exercise I came across the bathroom and remembered my mother giving me baths when I was a little kid. There were times when I guess she wasn't drinking . . . I don't know. I remember how much fun I had playing in the tub. She'd come in and sit on the toilet and read while I played. Sometimes I'd accidentally splash her on purpose to get her to play, and she'd splash me back. One time we were both splashing, she got soaked, the bathroom looked flooded. I was laughing so hard I was choking, and she was crying she was so happy. [tears rolling down his face] *Phew.*

Bill

4. Having identified the effects of trauma (hypervigilance, reexperiencing the trauma, survivor guilt, and psychic numbing) in your childhood, do you find shadows of these characteristics in your adult life? Describe what you see today.

5. What was it like to recognize some of the resiliencies you developed in response to the challenges of an alcoholic family?

★ Recommendations

Two books that help bring alive the trauma of living with an alcoholic parent are Suzanne Somers's *Wednesday's Children,* and *The Drama of the Gifted Child,* by Alice Miller. Although Miller's book never mentions alcoholism, most ACoAs find its message very relevant.

For those who have experienced sexual abuse, we recommend *Intimate Violence,* by Richard Gelles and Murray Strauss, and *Outgrowing the Pain,* by Eliana Gil.

Additional information about resiliency can be found in *The Resilient Self,* by Steven and Sybil Wolin. This book makes the important statement that tough times not only wound children but also strengthen them, sharpen their wit, and hone their creativity.

Chapter Six

Control

Many adult children of alcoholics have spoken in our groups of being terrified to loosen the control they exert over their lives. As a result, they rarely allow their emotions to emerge spontaneously, do not often permit themselves to become very vulnerable, and have difficulty relying on others in the group. This terror comes from believing that the ability to *appear* under control, no matter what turmoil may exist within, is the last barricade against complete chaos—a belief that stems directly from their childhood experience in an alcoholic family.

One group member eloquently expressed his relationship to willpower by saying the following: "I remember watching my parents fight, sometimes for days, about trivial things. One time my mother forgot to buy my father's favorite kind of pickles. He berated her unmercifully for not being able to remember what he had asked for. I, of course, heard all this through a child's understanding, but without understanding that my father was on a drinking binge. What I saw was two people who looked ridiculously weak. If only my father had not let the forgotten pickles bother him. If only my mother had concentrated enough to remember everything at the grocery store. I knew that, when I grew up, I would handle such trivial matters much better. I would have the strength and wisdom they lacked. I would remember *everything*. And I wouldn't let *anything* bother me."

What this person did not understand as a child is that the real issues had nothing to do with whether the right pickles were bought. His parents were arguing about whether they felt loved and taken care of by each other. They were angry about how out of control and arbitrary their lives had become. They were yelling at each other out of their pain and shame. But, through it all, their child was learning dangerous, and mistaken, lessons: Don't let anger happen. Don't let even the smallest detail fall through the cracks. Don't be weak and inattentive. Exercise willpower, but do it better than your parents were able to. The latter lesson didn't seem as though it would be that hard, because his parents had fallen so far short in the face of the most trivial and obvious challenges.

As a child, you probably had a lot of disturbing feelings to protect yourself against. Without defenses against these feelings, you truly ran the risk of being overwhelmed by them. By "overwhelmed" I mean several possible things. Without finding a way to control and contain the feelings, your fear may have paralyzed you, your sadness may have led you to withdraw into apathy, your anger may have caused you to hurt others, your shame may have caused you to lash out against yourself, or your very sense of self may have been fragmented and lost by the tidal wave of emotions crashing against it. The stakes for you were enormously high. When your parents were spiraling out of control, it was very important to have as much sense of control of yourself as possible. Even if this sense was an illusion, it was better than nothing—far better.

Given all the emphasis on control during their childhoods, it is no surprise that most ACoAs seeking treatment and entering recovery discover that control issues remain important in their current lives. Control is a problematic issue because almost everything ACoAs have learned about control and willpower was learned at the knee of a practicing alcoholic—who knew damned little about these two matters. As a result, children of alcoholics are often quite unrealistic about the proper uses of control and willpower. Like the alcoholic, their self-esteem often depends on having enough willpower to keep everything in life under control. For alcoholics, it is the effect of alcohol that they try to control by the sheer power of their will (rather than recognizing that they cannot drink without developing problems). For ACoAs, it may be their parents' drinking, or their own reactions to a parent's drinking, that they feel they should be able to control. The underlying problem is a distorted and unrealistic relationship to willpower; and both alcoholics and ACoAs eventually face a profound and thoroughgoing reevaluation of the proper relationship that humans must have to their will, if they are to be healthy.

Most ACoAs have tried so hard to avoid having anything in common with their alcoholic parent that the underlying similarities can be difficult to acknowledge. To help people see these similarities, we often talk about the subtle, but profound, distinction between "having an alcoholic parent" and *being* the child of an alcoholic.

Although it is important to be honest about whether a parent is alcoholic or not, some ACoAs get stuck focusing attention on someone else. For them, "having an alcoholic parent" points the finger outward and only serves to feed their disappointment and bitterness. We believe that the real value of such honesty about a parent's shortcomings has less to do with judging our parents and more to do with taking an honest look at the influences that have gone into making *us* who we are.

Being a child of an alcoholic points the finger inward. It focuses attention on oneself, particularly on the facets of your own personality that are reflections of the kind of crazy thinking and dysfunctional relationship to the world, the kind of immaturities and irresponsibilities that you have incorporated from your alcoholic parent. You don't have to be actively alcoholic to think about the world, or about yourself, as alcoholics do. You can rely on denial just as much as the alcoholic. You can have just as low self-esteem, just as much shame, and just as much blind faith in willpower as your alcoholic parents.

Alcoholics often have a very grandiose view of themselves. In addition to ignoring many of their blemishes, they also hold very high standards for how powerful they believe their willpower should be. For example, many feel they should be able to watch with ease as other people drink, simply by using enough willpower to abolish their own cravings. Although this is altogether unrealistic, such grandiose thinking is really quite attractive to their children, who are desperately trying to rise above being influenced by their family. (More precisely, these children are trying to rise above, or disconnect from, their own *experience* by sheer power of their will.) People in alcoholic families believe that they would be able to keep matters under control if they all tried harder, or found the right way to try. Rarely does anyone stop and ask whether willpower is truly the best strategy for solving their problems, or whether maintaining control is even the appropriate goal.

Several examples of how people can ignore the limitations inherent in willpower may be useful here.

None of us has control over gravity (although more than one person in California has tried to debate this with me). If we step off the edge of a cliff, we fall. The only way we have of getting away from the effects of gravity is to travel into space. Even then, we have not gained control over gravity. We have simply removed ourselves from its immediate influence.

None of us has control over the weather, although we have all probably tried to keep the rain away from a picnic by "thinking positive thoughts." The weather, just like gravity, is controlled by forces that are unaffected by any power that our will can exercise.

Likewise, none of us has direct control over other people's feelings. I may ingratiate myself in order to get you to like me. I may study your likes and dislikes and then cater to you. But, if you are put off by such ingratiation, I can't make you have a different reaction. Rather than controlling your feelings, the fact is that I am actually allowing myself to be controlled by you.

The truth is that none of us even has direct control over our own feelings. I cannot use willpower to make myself wake up in the morning feeling ecstatic. I cannot make myself get excited about a boring lecture. I cannot fall in love with a new flavor of ice cream if my taste buds are revolted by it. I cannot *force* myself to never feel anger at my spouse. The part of me that is trying to control my feelings is simply not the same part that is generating those feelings.

Our emotions have a life of their own. The great paradox for people who remain bedeviled by the alcoholic's distorted relationship to willpower is that we must simultaneously take responsibility for the feelings we have while acknowledging our inability to control them directly. Although this sounds contradictory, it is not. We can take responsibility for our feelings because they arise from somewhere within us—no one else put them there. And, although they are not the result of conscious choices, they are nevertheless ours, and of our own making.

A proper relationship to willpower comes from recognizing the parts of ourselves and the world that are under our direct control, as well as acknowledging the limitations outlined above. Among other things, willpower has a great deal to do with what we pay attention to. We can force ourselves to keep looking at unpleasant realities, or we can direct our attention away from them. In this sense, our will is like a doorway that can shut out awareness or open up to it.

This does not mean that willpower can *force* awareness to surface. It can only open us to the truth and invite it to come into the sunlight. We can use willpower to discipline ourselves continually to pull the doors of attention open to awareness. The more we practice this discipline, on a daily basis, the more awareness eventually develops. Our openness to such awareness is under considerable control, although the timing of when awareness emerges is not.

The above thoughts should be seen not as a complete, or even a short, course on the proper relationship that we should have to our willpower. Instead, think of what is written here as the course description found in a catalogue, designed to intrigue you. Also, do not think of yourself as being "under indictment" for having distortions in terms of how you think about control. We are merely inviting you to explore your current relationship to willpower with two thoughts in mind: 1) There are more effective ways to find a sense of security than trying to control the world; and 2) there are good and sufficient reasons for your having developed a dysfunctional relationship to willpower.

For readers not familiar with Alcoholics Anonymous, it might be useful to note here that the *very first step* many recovering alcoholics say they took in getting sober was to acknowledge their inability to control the effects of alcohol, then to explore how riddled their lives were by unworkable strategies for trying to control the world. Step number one of the Twelve Steps reads "We admitted we were powerless over alcohol—that our lives had become unmanageable." If this seems paradoxical—that alcoholics gain sobriety by acknowledging that they had lost control—it is because you do not yet understand the kinds of mistakes alcoholics make having to do with the issue of willpower. Alcoholics are confused by what can legitimately be controlled by human willpower and must reexplore from the ground up the rightful place of willpower in a person's life. This chapter has tried to help you understand that ACoAs often have to "work the first step" every bit as much as their alcoholic parents had to.

One place to begin is with the following exercises, which help you look differently at the relationship that you currently have to the power of your own will.

· · · · · · · · · **EXERCISES** · · · · · · · ·

What's wrong with being in control? Someone *has* to be, otherwise there'd be chaos. Besides I'm good at it. I'm a natural leader. I see things other people don't. If we don't try for perfection, we'll end up with mediocrity. There's no excuse for that!

Brian

When ACoA groups discuss control, people quickly begin seeing how this issue permeates their lives. For example, in one group, Sharon described how she had stood outside the waiting room on the first night the group met. This assured that she would be the first one up the stairs and into the room, which would allow her to sit in a chair near the door. That way she could rush out at the end of the meeting in case people wanted to be hugging each other. The whole group laughed with her as she revealed the complex way she had plotted out the whole scenario, just to keep her anxiety about hugging under control.

Bob smiled after Sharon told her story because he remembered how he had waited until everyone else chose his or her chair and he took the last one. He said, "I do this all the time. I wait until other people claim their space, and I take what's left. That way I keep people from thinking I'm too pushy."

The struggle for control is intimately linked to the need for safety. This struggle can take a wide variety of forms and may be occurring at the following times:

- when you **modify** your thoughts, speech, feelings, behavior

- when you **minimize** your thoughts, speech, feelings, behavior

- when you **direct** your thoughts, speech, feelings, behavior

- when you **restrict** your thoughts, speech, feelings, behavior

- when you **withhold** your thoughts, speech, feelings, behavior

- when you **manipulate** your thoughts, speech, feelings, behavior

- when you **repress** your thoughts, speech, feelings, behavior

- when you **master** your thoughts, speech, feelings, behavior

- when you **force** your thoughts, speech, feelings, behavior

- when you **change** your thoughts, speech, feelings, behavior

- when you **disguise** your thoughts, speech, feelings, behavior

The following exercises will help you explore how you control yourself through willpower, control others through your influence and manipulation, and struggle for control of the world around you. The exercises will also shed light on the relationship between your need to be in control and your experiences growing up in an alcoholic family.

This exercise helps you develop awareness of your relationship to willpower, the ways in which you strive to maintain control in your life, and the impact of this struggle on your life and those close to you.

Exercise 17: When, Where, How . . .

1. On a blank page in your journal, make a list of ten examples from your life growing up in your family when you tried to control yourself (your thoughts, your speech, your actions, and your feelings) or someone else (e.g., "I tried to get my father to stop drinking, so I poured his gin down the toilet and filled the bottle with water").

2. Below each example, write the result that you were hoping for (e.g., "I hoped that he'd stop drinking").

3. Then record what the actual result was (e.g., "He got mad at my mother and bought more booze").

Here's a part of Mark's list:

1. When Dad was drunk, Mom just sat and cried. I tried everything I could to get her to stop crying.

    I hoped she'd stop crying.

    She cried more. I felt useless and got frustrated.

2. Once I hit my father with a lamp to get him to take me seriously.

    At the time I really wanted to kill him. I was nine.

    I felt good when I hit him, but I got scared that I might've really killed him. . . . Of course, he didn't remember it the next day, so I told him he hit his head falling down.

3. Tried to get good grades in school.

    I wanted my parents to be proud of me and stop treating me like I was a burden.

    They barely noticed but just expected me to keep getting A's.

4. Ran away from home.

    I wanted my parents to be upset.

    They didn't notice for three days, so I went back home. To this day, I'm still furious about this.

This exercise explores the feelings you have when struggling to be in control and when you feel out of control.

1. Take a few minutes to think about a situation in which you feel the most *in control*.

2. Write a description of the experience, including how it feels to be in control.

I feel in control at work. I work in shipping and receiving. I am very organized. Everything has its place in the storeroom: the computer, the shipping labels, materials, boxes of various sizes. I have three men working under me. I have a routine, and as long as we follow it everything runs smoothly. I feel at the helm. I feel in place. I feel like I can handle anything that comes my way. I feel strong.

Mark

3. Take a few minutes to think about a situation in which you feel the most *out of control*.

4. Write a description of the experience, including how it feels to be out of control.

I feel the most out of control when talking to my wife about our relationship. I just don't understand her. I hate to say it because it's such a cliché, but she's so emotional. Everything seems to bother her. She's never satisfied. She tells me she wants to spend more time together, so I schedule some time for us. Then she uses the time telling me she's unhappy about something. She's got feelings about *everything* and complains that I don't pay attention to what she's saying. . . . I admit it. Sometimes my mind wanders. I feel in over my head when I'm with her—like I'll never be able to make her happy.

Mark

5. Continue the exercise by elaborating on your description of being *out of control* with a fantasy about what would happen, and how it would feel, if things con-

tinued to get further and further and further out of control.

If things just continued getting further out of control, I picture my wife getting more and more upset. Nothing I could do would satisfy her. She'd start to yell and scream at me. She might throw things and threaten to leave. If I took it further, she'd leave and I'd feel terrible. I'd feel like it was all my fault that she left. I'd feel alone, responsible, and hopeless.

Mark

Some of you will feel relief with this exercise; some will feel agitated and tense. And some of you will find yourselves stubbornly avoiding the exercise (especially part 5, which requires you to let your imagination run "out of control"). We commonly hear people in the groups complain that they cannot imagine getting further out of control, because they know that they won't let that happen. If you experience any reluctance with the exercise, remind yourself that its purpose is to increase your understanding of two things—the actual consequences of your efforts to maintain control and the fears that your control is designed to protect against. You will discover what these fears are through imagining what might happen when you exaggerate feeling more and more out of control.

Mark learned not only that his struggle for control was getting in the way of his marriage but also that its origins were in his childhood struggle to keep his mother from leaving the family. Ironically, his pattern of stoicism and placating behavior only made things worse, both with his mother a long time ago and with his wife today. At one meeting he startled the group with a powerful admission:

I can't believe what I wrote in my journal this week—I'm afraid my wife will turn into my mother. In the fantasy, I was feeling the same way I felt when I was a kid. I was always trying to diffuse the situation at home so my mother wouldn't leave. She'd stay for a couple of years. Then things would blow up and she'd leave. I always felt responsible. . . . What am I doing to my marriage? My wife keeps saying, "I'm not your mother!" I try to soothe

her feelings but really dismiss her as being too emotional—just the way I treated my mother!
Mark

The previous exercises focused on the how, when, and why we struggle for control. This exercise makes the leap from acknowledging this struggle to awareness of when and how humans are all powerless. In Alcoholics Anonymous, this awareness comes through "working the First Step."

Exercise 19: The First Step

1. Look over your answers to the previous two exercises. In your journal write,

    "I admit that I am powerless over _____" and fill in the blank with something, someone, a situation, etc., from your list.

2. Do this for ten different acknowledgments of your powerlessness. Really, we mean it, ten . . . at least.

Here's some of Mark's list:

1. When Dad was drunk, Mom just sat and cried. I tried everything I could to get her to stop crying.

    I admit that I am/was powerless over my mother's crying.

2. Once I hit my father with a lamp to get him to take me seriously.

    I admit that I am/was powerless over my father's drinking and how much it angered me.

3. Tried to get good grades in school.

    I admit that I was powerless to get my parents to notice my pain.

4. Ran away from home.

    I admit that I was powerless to get my parents to notice me.

While it was relatively easy for Mark to begin admitting his powerlessness over much of his parents' behavior, including their drinking, it was extremely difficult for him to admit his powerlessness over himself. He struggled with the idea that he:

- "should be able to control his anger."
- "should be able to control his pain."

After listening to the other group members' experiences with trying to control themselves, Mark had a flash.

> Wait a minute. I get it. I am powerless over feeling sad, but what I do with it, once I become sad, is up to me. I can either stay at the office and busy myself into oblivion or I can feel the sadness and reach out. I may not have control over *having* the feeling, but what I do with it is up to me . . . wow!

Exercise 20: Letting Go

Having acknowledged your powerlessness in at least ten circumstances, you are now ready for the next step in letting go of control. Bear in mind that we are not talking about giving up *all* notion of control, only the struggle to bring things *completely* under control, or to dictate to the world what *should* be under your control. Once you are able to acknowledge that you are powerless over something, however small, it is easier to begin defining what your actual limitations are. This exercise will help you take that step.

1. Look over the list of First Steps that you have created above. Choose one situation in which you struggle for control. In your journal, write a description of the many strategies you use in your struggle to control this situation.

Be explicit. It's quite likely that you're familiar with a whole pattern of behavior in this situation. You know the script, as you try over and over to bring things under control.

> Sure I know the script. I want to do something nice for my husband; I want to have a romantic dinner. I drop hints during the week preceding the big night. I kiss him

in the morning and tell him not to be late because I'll
have something special for him when he comes home. I
get all worked up throughout the day. I feel happy and
excited. I'm enthusiastic when I do the shopping and
sing as I work in the kitchen. I get everything ready. I call
him at noon to check on how his day's going. I call him at
four, then five, then five-thirty. At five-thirty there's an
edge to his voice, and I know he's coming home late. I
feel depressed.

I try to control our relationship by doing things for
him, for me, for us . . . even though I don't ask his opin-
ion about it.

Denise

2. Now, acknowledge your powerlessness by rewriting the
script to abstain from a specific controlling behavior.

In the example above, Denise described how she often esca-
lates efforts to make things work out with her husband by calling
him at work throughout the day. She rewrote the script between
herself and her husband by choosing to abstain from these phone
calls. She reported the following results to the group.

On Monday, it was easy. He came home at the usual
seven o'clock. I was busy all day with shopping and my
part-time job, so I didn't notice it much.

On Tuesday, it was hard. I thought about calling him
all day, but I wasn't going to let it get the best of me. I
kept saying to myself, "I admit I am powerless over my
husband's coming home from work on time." I kept
busy. I didn't call him. He came home at seven, but I
didn't feel as miserable as I usually do at the end of the
day, and he wasn't angry with me for bugging him. He
even asked me if I was all right.

On Wednesday I slipped and called him once, but
that was to relay a message and I didn't ask him when he
was coming home. He came home at six.

On Thursday I felt better. I wasn't so anxious. He
came home at six-thirty. Since I wasn't sure when he was
coming home, dinner wasn't ready till seven. He didn't
seem particularly upset. I wasn't particularly upset because I was busy working in the garden.

On Friday, I totally forgot about calling him. I had dinner prepared for six, and he showed up at six. We had a nice dinner. Amazing. I can't believe that by not trying to control things I feel better.

Denise

Feeling Exercise

Take time to do the Feeling Exercise as described in chapter one (page 15).

Journal

The questions below will help you reflect on your experiences with the exercises. As always, write your responses in your journal.

1. What was it like to list how you try to control yourself and others?

2. Did you find yourself minimizing the issue?

3. What is it like to acknowledge the disparity between the results you want and the results you get by trying to control yourself/others?

4. What are you most afraid will happen if you begin to relinquish control?

5. As you reflect back on these control issues, do they remind you of the alcoholic in your family? The non-alcoholic parent? Siblings? Grandparents?

6. What were your immediate reactions to reading about a First Step?

7. What was it like to do a First Step?

8. What was it like to begin abstaining from one type of controlling behavior?

9. What did you learn about yourself in the process?

I tend to be a bit rigid about having a tidy home. In the Letting Go Exercise I set a goal of letting my son's dishes sit in the sink until he noticed them. . . . Forget it. After two hours, I had to do them myself. I couldn't stand the tension of not having everything in its place. I couldn't relax and enjoy the evening until all the dishes were clean and put away.

It is still very hard for me to stop my controlling. What I eventually did was to turn it into a game. I bet my son that I could tolerate his dirty dishes longer than he could. When I kept losing, night after night, he took pity on me one day and came out to the kitchen to help me clean up. We were both laughing at what a sap I am, but we were doing the dishes together!

Marion

While Marion was still struggling with her need to control others and maintain order around her, she had developed a great attitude toward her journey. By learning to laugh at herself, she also became more understanding of other people's flaws.

★ Recommendations

The struggle for control is so pervasive for many ACoAs that our first recommendation is *Al-Anon's Twelve Steps and Twelve Traditions*, which explores the Twelve Step Programs' understanding of willpower and the dysfunctional relationships that people can take to self-control. For an examination of the ways an obsession with control can subvert and poison a relationship with ourselves and others, we recommend *A Struggle for Intimacy*, by Janet Woititz.

We also recommend three movies that nicely illustrate control issues. In the movie *Parenthood*, an ACoA (played by Steve Martin) is plagued by the feeling that his life is constantly on the verge of flying out of control. His wife states the simple fact that all parents must face, "Life's messy." The ACoA responds by saying, "I hate messy. It's so . . . *messy.*" A kindly grandmother comes on the scene and tries to give some perspective by saying that she loved the roller coaster as a child because it was so scary and exciting. Others liked the carousel, but that confused her. The carousel just goes around and around, too predictable. No, she liked the roller coaster. Of course, the ACoA just stares blankly at her, not beginning to comprehend what she is talking about but too polite to do anything but look as though he is agreeing. In *An Officer and a Gentleman,* with Richard Gere and Debra Winger, an ACoA strives for self-mastery in the military but finds he must stop controlling his emotions in order to love well. And *Rainman,* with Dustin Hoffman and Tom Cruise, illustrates the transformation of a man living under the illusion that having a lifestyle is the same as having a life, that with enough wit, lies, and con he can master his business, his girlfriend, and his childhood pain. Ultimately he meets his match in his autistic brother, the Rainman, who teaches him about the fragility of relationships, our need for each other, and humility.

Finally, John le Carré's novel *A Perfect Spy* provides a fascinating portrait of how one ACoA used the well-honed facade he had developed growing up with his alcoholic father to take on whatever identity his trade demanded of him. In the end, after his father died, the central figure in this story came face-to-face with the fact that he had no center within himself.

Chapter Seven

Codependence

As a child, you may have patterned so much of your life on your alcoholic parent's personality that you entered adulthood knowing almost nothing about who you really are, and with little sense of how to take your rightful place in relationships with other people. In order to fit into your alcoholic family, you may have thoroughly learned the habits of feeling overly responsible for others and changing who you are to please them. Or you may have learned a variety of compulsive behaviors in order to fill the void where a true sense of self should have been developing. These habits seep so deeply into your very sense of identity when you are a child that they can create a lifelong dependence on relationships, any relationship! This painful and compulsive dependence on approval from others (or on other compulsive behaviors) as your main source of safety, self-worth, and identity is called codependence.

ACoAs who are codependent have several characteristics in common. Although most people demonstrate these characteristics on occasion, you may recognize that they represent a clear and consistent pattern within yourself. To begin with, *codependents have the same distorted relationship to willpower seen in alcoholics.* Refusing to operate within the natural limitations of human will, codependents believe they are at fault when they cannot get another person to stop drinking, when they cannot keep other people happy, or when they cannot control their own emotions. As the following quote from the Big Book of AA says, ". . . Usually we did not leave. We stayed on and on." Such perseverance is often cloaked as virtue, loyalty, or martyrdom, but it usually stems more from a stubborn refusal to accept that some parts of the universe are eternally out of our control. Codependents are often locked into a willful, compulsive wrestling match with the world, determined to force events to comply with their will.

Some ACoAs never stop believing that they could have, even should have, found the right way to make their parents stop drinking. Many are still looking for the right thing to say, the right accomplishment or compliment to get their parents to love them more. And many get into relationships in which they continually take the responsibility for getting their partners to like them. If any of these patterns describe you, then you know the excruciating difficulty many ACoAs have relinquishing their illusions of control. Without this illusion, you may feel such vulnerability, such inadequacy, and such a terror that things will fly further out of control that the only relief is to try harder, once more, to keep your world together.

Codependents change who they are to please others. They mistakenly believe that they have the power to make others happy by becoming whomever they think the other person wants. But they also presume that they must sacrifice their own identity in order to have intimacy. You may be aware of a myriad of subtle ways in which you continually modify what you think and what you feel in response to what others think and feel. Some ACoAs talk of always allowing other people to set the tone of their relationship. It becomes more important for the other person to be happy than for the codependent to be happy.

Why would anyone get to the point of *presuming* that they had to abandon who they really are in order to be acceptable to others? Who would *presume* that every relationship they are in has to revolve around the other person? What does it feel like to *presume* that life must continually be lived on other people's terms? The second and third of these questions are more easily answered than the first. Children of substance abusers *presume* that they must accommodate to others more than others must accommodate to them. And it feels normal. Understanding codependence involves understanding why this is so.

A mythical archetype exists for understanding the relationship between alcoholics and codependents—the myth of Narcissus and Echo. In this myth Narcissus, our prototype for the self-centered person, refused to respond to any show of affection. The one person who eventually moved him was Echo, who had no voice except to repeat what others said first. Echo was the ultimate victim of the "Don't Talk" rule. The only things she could say were reflections of others. She had no identity except for what she borrowed from others. Echo fit in perfectly with Narcissus, who responded to no one unless she was a copy of himself. The two were a match made in heaven (or hell). The chemistry was right.

Myths are not frivolous stories. They are the narrative fabric of another time's psychology. What makes them important is that human needs for relationship and the tension within each of us between our needs for dependence and independence have changed very little over the last few millennia. Narcissus and Echo still continue falling in and out of love. One difference today is that, when they want to get out of the cycle of unsuccessful relationships, each is finding a fellowship that is remarkably useful: AA for Narcissus and Al-Anon for Echo.

But what happens to the personality of a child who must grow up in Narcissus's home? What happens to the normal childhood needs to have the world revolve around you and to have something else to revolve your world around?

Despite the literature that exists on the "child within," children are not the epitome of wisdom and competence. We all began life with some very stark, paradoxical, and intensely felt needs, and maturation involves finding more effective ways of dealing with these feelings. Most pertinent to the issues of codependence are the needs children have to be the center of attention and independent (unconditional validation of their unique existence) but to be completely taken care of at the same time (absolute security and dependence). "Love me for who I uniquely am," but "Let me live under your wing and take my identity from you, whenever I need to." Raising kids can be like trying to referee a hockey match, with the opposite teams both living within the same child. The war between their need to be dependent and their need to be independent spills over into almost everything they do and every interaction they have with us.

In fact, raising children is so difficult that most people eventually adopt a standard for themselves of becoming "good enough parents." And, from the child's standpoint, good enough *is* good enough. Although sobriety is not a guarantee that parenting skills will be present, it is a prerequisite for good-enough parenting. The effects of chronic intoxication on parenting skills is as predictable as it is tragic. The authors of the Big Book of Alcoholics Anonymous understood the cause of this impact over fifty years ago when they wrote of the alcoholic "Selfishness—self-centeredness! That, we think, is the root of our troubles." Well, if that is at the root of their troubles, it is at the very *heart* of the troubles many of their children have.

When there is good-enough parenting, a child's need to be the center and to have her unique developing capabilities validated eventually matures into self-esteem and a healthy sense of entitlement. And the need to trust and depend upon others, to revolve your life around them, matures into a healthy capacity to appreciate and empathize with others. Both of these needs—for independence and for dependence—are part of a healthy personality. In their mature forms, they coexist with little tension. Our logical mind may not quite understand how such paradoxical needs can coexist comfortably, but our heart knows how to make it happen.

When children must interact with parents who are overly focused on themselves, whether through chronic intoxication or other obsessions, they quickly learn that their need to be the center is quite problematic, if not an outright danger. When Narcissus is confronted with people who are different from himself (i.e., independent), he is unable to make a connection with them. He only connects with people when he sees aspects of himself in the other person. If Narcissus's children express a need to be independent, they pay the price of losing the connection to their parent. But it is intolerable for children to lose the bond with their parent too early. As a result, the children of Narcissus often deny their impulse to become independent. They deny their unique qualities. They forsake their drive for autonomy. They lose contact with who they really could be. And they do all this in order to maintain the vital bond with their alcoholic, self-centered, Narcissistic parent.

On the other hand, children's normal need to find someone

upon whom they can depend and revolve their life around is quite acceptable to Narcissus. The more children become Narcissus's reflection, the more bonded he is to them. There is no encouragement to let this need mature into its healthy forms (appreciation and empathy for others). Instead, it remains in a stark, all-or-nothing childhood form.

The experience of codependence is the experience of denying our own need to be the center and never letting our need to be dependent mature into its healthy adult forms. If we take our lead from the myth, we might say that codependence arises from disowning our normal narcissistic needs and failing to allow our normal echoistic needs to mature. Both needs—the need to be the center (to feel entitled) and the need to have someone else to revolve around (to serve)—are normal. It is part of the human condition to recognize that we must all find a way of letting these needs mature enough to feel comfortable with both of them. Codependence is one of many ways in which we experience the human condition gone wrong.

We can now understand the futility of trying to define which behaviors are codependent and which are acts of true generosity and altruism. It is not the act in and of itself, but rather the spirit within which the action is taken, that determines whether it is codependent. This means that two people can perform precisely the same action, and it is codependent for only one of them. Two people can cancel their plans to go to a movie in order to fix dinner for an ailing friend, but only one may have the *experience* of feeling compelled to take this course of action. She may feel impinged upon, without any sense of choice. She hides her disappointment about missing the movie and attempts to look more willing to be helping than she actually feels. Underlying is a feeling that she is not being true to herself, even as she feels good about being so "helpful" (largely because the friend will like her for the generosity). The other may feel that the sacrifice is freely chosen, comfortable, and an expression of her deepest values. Her sense of integrity may be enhanced.

Of course, complicating many ACoAs' efforts to explore their experience of codependence is the fact that denial can keep them from being aware of their deeper experiences. One group member insisted that what makes him happy is to make other people happy. Although I believe that this was true for him, as far as it went, it was not the whole truth. Underlying his belief that all he wanted was to make others happy was a desperation that he only occasionally experienced. When he did experience the desperation (usually when he was unable to keep others happy), it was an overwhelming whirlpool pulling him down into despair. As soon as the whirlpool experience faded, he acted as though it had never happened. He denied its significance. Denial can leave people feeling thoroughly altruistic when they are actually deeply codependent. The surest way to tell the difference is to look to see if there is peace in their lives. Altruistic people know peace; codependents only know the calm between storms.

It is imperative that we do not destroy the reality of generosity and altruism while we are trying to understand codependence. I believe that people do sacrifice for others in healthy ways. I believe that it is possible even for a person to give up her own life, perhaps for a child. And, in the sacrifice, their integrity may grow. If we deny the possibility of such selflessness as a virtue, we have done ourselves a disservice.

But, the converse is also true. It is imperative that we continue exploring the experience of codependence that so many people in recovery have discovered within themselves and found freedom from. If you grew up in a family with an addicted parent, it is likely that you grew up with an adult who had limited capacity for truly mutual relationships. It is likely that you learned to sacrifice your own identity to keep a strong connection with him or her. It is likely that you have experienced codependence.

There is nothing you can *do* to stop being codependent if you are doing it to impress someone else or to look good to yourself. But there is nothing you need to do, if you are acting from a place of integrity. It is not defined by your behavior. It is who you are, and it is defined by the attitude that your behavior emanates from.

· · · · · · · ·   **EXERCISES**   · · · · · · · ·

I'm a nurse, and I'm good at it. I feel great when I'm taking care of my patients. I'm always willing to go the extra mile for them. . . . I have a lot of friends, but I always seem to be taking care of them, listening to them, buying them presents, calling them. I feel as if I never leave work. Sometimes I wonder, "When is someone going to take care of me?"

Sharon

Because codependence is so intimately connected to growing up in an alcoholic family, recognizing your own codependent characteristics is an important step along the path of recovery. The exercises below help identify your codependence.

On the following Codependence Questionnaire check how thoroughly each statement applies to you.

Exercise 21: Signs of Codependence

The Codependence Questionnaire

	Never	Seldom	Occasionally	Often	Usually
I am very proud of my self-control.	___	___	___	___	___
I base much of my self-esteem on getting others to be in relationships with me.	___	___	___	___	___
I feel responsible for meeting other people's needs even when my own do not get met.	___	___	___	___	___
I tend to deny my own needs and feelings.	___	___	___	___	___
I am afraid that people will leave me.	___	___	___	___	___
I change who I am to please others.	___	___	___	___	___
I have low self-esteem.	___	___	___	___	___
I feel driven by compulsions.	___	___	___	___	___

I drink/use drugs
more often than I
should.

I get afraid that
things will get out
of control.

People see my false
front more than they
see the real me.

I have stress-related
medical problems.

> I wasn't surprised at all that I scored in the "often" or
> "usually" category on virtually every question. I knew I
> was a caretaker, but I never realized how pervasive it is. I
> can't tell you how many times my supervisors have said
> to me, "Sharon, you're a gem, but you have to think
> about yourself!" *I always took it as a compliment.* I just
> feel so good when I'm taking care of other people. Be-
> sides, I just can't see being any other way.
>
> > Sharon

Sharon's comments illustrate two attitudes that we commonly
find in our group members. First, ACoAs often justify their codependent behavior as altruism ("I just feel so good when I'm taking
care of other people"). But the truth is that they feel compelled to
serve others. Their codependence is at the center of their self-
image and not a choice ("I just can't see being any other way").

The following exercise helps personalize the characteristics
you have identified, then takes a closer look at the impact of codependence on your life.

**Exercise 22:
Personalizing
Codependence**

Part 1: Codependent Acts

1. On the left side of a page in your journal, list three situations in which you have changed who you are to please
   others.

For example, Sharon wrote:

"It is really difficult for me to just say outright what restaurant or movie I want to go to. Whenever I go out with my boyfriend, I always agree to his choice."

2. On the left side of the page (underneath the first three) list three situations in which you have felt responsible for meeting other people's needs at the expense of your own.

Again, Sharon wrote:

"I always end up with the extra work on my shift, but I don't really mind too much. I have more experience than the others, so I can get it done faster. . . . But I know it's unfair, if I let myself think about it."

3. On the left side of the page (underneath the others) list three ways in which your feeling good about yourself has been wrapped up in the approval or behavior of someone else.

Sharon's response:

"I used to base how good I felt about myself on how successfully I avoided any reproach from my alcoholic father. No matter how I tried, he always found some way of criticizing me."

4. On the left side of the page (underneath the others) list three ways in which you find yourself thinking, acting, or feeling compulsively.

Sharon's response:

"Last week when one of my patients died, I came home and cried for an hour. Then I got up and cleaned my apartment for four hours. I scrubbed all the tile in the bathroom, the kitchen, and the hallway. I packed up all my recycling, vacuumed, and did four loads of laundry.

"It's funny. All the time I was cleaning I kept seeing images of my childhood."

5. On the left side of the page (underneath the others) list three things you've done or said to yourself in which you

have denied your parent's (or someone else's) drinking and its impact on the family.

Sharon's response:
"I always thought that once my father died everything would settle down in my family. It's been ten years since he died, and my family is just as screwed up."

Part 2: The Intentions

Frequently, there are surface justifications for acting codependently. If we look closer, however, we often find hidden agendas compelling our actions. This part of the exercise identifies the hidden motives and feelings that underlie your codependent behavior.

For numbers 1–5 of the first part of this exercise, in the middle of the page, *write down the intentions behind each action.*

For example, Sharon recorded the following as her intention for always letting her boyfriend go to the restaurant or movie he prefers:

"I want us to have a nice evening. I don't want to stir up any conflict. Besides, I'm not very picky when it comes to what I eat; so why shouldn't I just let him choose. I do have preferences about movies, but by the end of the week I don't have the energy to argue about a movie."

Part 3: The Results

Now write on the right-hand side of the page what the results were.
Sharon wrote:
"Last week Marty chose to go to a really fancy restaurant. We go dutch all the time, and I'm really tight for money right now. I didn't have the energy to argue. I didn't want to make a scene. Besides, he works hard all week, too, and deserves a nice time. It was okay with me. I just ordered soup and salad and told him I wasn't hungry. I made up for the expense by skipping lunches for the next week.

"I can't believe what I did. I was willing to starve myself and go to a restaurant I didn't want to just because I was afraid of what could happen if I said something. . . . That's just what I did as a kid. I was the peacemaker in the family. If there was a problem, 'go to Sharon, she'll take care of it!'"

Sharon discovered that her characteristic caretaking was not as altruistic as she had thought. By becoming more aware of the subtle ways she discounts her own needs in order to take care of others, she was able to see how defensively she lives. By reacting always to her fears of *what might happen,* rather than *what is* happening, she inadvertently ends up sabotaging the possibility of having a good time.

In the next few weeks, Sharon began noticing these habits in many of her relationships, not only outside the group but within the group as well. Over the next several weeks she timidly experimented with changing her behavior. She was still afraid of being reproached for being "selfish," but she found support among the group for stepping out of the role of taking care of everyone.

Feeling Exercise

Take time to do the Feeling Exercise as described in chapter one (page 15).

Journal

Having identified and personalized your codependent characteristics and your motives for acting codependently, we encourage you to respond to the following questions in your journal:

1. What was it like to explore the motivations for your codependent behaviors?

2. Did you find yourself defending, justifying, or rationalizing the value of these behaviors? If so, what were your arguments in defense of yourself?

3. What was it like to acknowledge the contrast between what you hope for in acting codependently and what actually results?

4. Did you have a hard time being honest with what you perceive as the results?

5. In what ways did you criticize yourself for having co-dependent tendencies? Are you guilty of pathologizing yourself instead of simply understanding yourself?

★ Recommendations

Of the many books that have been written about the complex phenomenon of codependence, we recommend the following: *Facing Codependence,* by Pia Mellody; *Co-dependent No More,* by Melodie Beattie; and *Women Who Love Too Much,* by Robin Norwood. Although written for professionals, *Diagnosing and Treating Co-dependence,* by Timmen Cermak, M.D., has been useful to some ACoAs as well.

Films that deal with the loss of one's identity in a relationship include *Hannah and Her Sisters,* with Mia Farrow, and Woody Allen's *Zelig,* which is a marvelous portrayal of a human chameleon who takes on the identity of whomever he is around.

Chapter Eight

Anger

Very few people come out of alcoholic homes feeling comfortable with anger, because they rarely saw their parents deal maturely with their anger. For some ACoAs who watched their family deny anger for years, anger does not seem to exist; for others who watched their family use anger as a weapon against one another rather than finding ways to resolve their conflicts, anger seems to seethe relentlessly. For some, anger is the only emotion they can freely express because anger was all that their family knew; for others, expressing anger seems like suicide because they watched family members be abused for expressing their anger. For some, anger covers up their pain; for others, the pain seems to cover up anger. For most, even small expressions of anger by others are reacted to with fear. Sometimes the fear borders on terror, but their controlled facial expressions would never let you know that.

Whether through the laws of evolution or the providence of God, humans share the capacity with other animals to respond to the world with anger. Anger is a natural, healthy, and probably even a necessary emotion for living in this world. It is a message from deep inside that tells us we are being threatened in some way. We ignore this message at our own peril.

As soon as I made this point in one ACoA group, Estella quickly challenged me. "But anger leads to violence, and we can do better than smashing each other on the head whenever we don't get our way." Apparently, Estella's experience had taught her that anger has only one possible outcome. She had never witnessed her parents respect each other's anger, listen to it, or struggle through their anger to a feeling of greater intimacy with each other. These outcomes remained inconceivable to Estella.

Because emotional or physical violence was usually experienced when people in their families were angry, it is hard for many ACoAs to understand that expressions of anger (just like expressions of sexual feelings) can contribute to intimacy. As much distance can be created between family members by hiding anger as by expressing it destructively. Closeness depends upon being able to be honest about feeling angry and then having these feelings heard and responded to, rather than merely counterattacked. In this way, anger becomes one of the engines that drives people closer and closer to each other.

However problematic anger might be in an ACoA's life, recovery means accepting that it is normal to experience anger. Recovery means "letting go" of your efforts to legislate anger out of your life. Recovery means "letting go" of trying to exterminate anger in others. Instead, we are left to search for ways to deal with anger that enhance our lives, not that drain life from us. The first steps in changing your relationship to anger are often to acknowledge its presence, rather than deny its existence, to interrupt your mind's tendency to react to anger in old ways, and to find ways to communicate your anger without spewing it out onto other people. The existence of anger cannot be denied during recovery, but its expression can be modulated.

In chapter 5 (Survival) we mentioned how the stress and trauma of alcoholic homes intensify all feelings and create a black-and-white world. As a result, anger often has only two faces—it is either absent or it is expressed as rage. As youngsters, you may well have seen the same all-or-nothing behavior modeled by your intoxicated parent. Many children in alcoholic homes experienced periods of tension and quiet desperation, when everyone was just trying to hold things together in between drunken episodes. During these periods, people tried to suppress any irritation, and discord was avoided whenever possible. Unfortunately, these periods alternated with periods of intoxication, when the disinhibitory effects of alcohol permitted deep reservoirs of anger to burst forth from their parents like geysers of hot fury. As a result, children became even more convinced that anger is a destructive emotion and should remain hidden.

Of course, no one description of "ACoA experience" applies to everyone. Many other children in alcoholic homes experienced parents who could not control their anger *unless* they felt the artificial sedating effects of intoxication. Their parents were able to find freedom from their disappointments, unrealistically high standards, or irrational resentments only by dissolving these feelings in the soothing balm of mother liquor. As a result, some ACoAs view the times when a parent was intoxicated as among their fondest memories. It was only then that a parent's chronic irritability was absent. As different as this experience may have been from ACoAs who witnessed violent outbursts of anger, the lesson is the same—anger must be avoided for life to be comfortable.

The point of commonality for all children of alcoholics is that their experiences teach them that people cannot be trusted to modulate their anger effectively. Its intensity rarely seems to match the transgression or disappointment that triggers it. It does not seem to have shades of gray. It either is, or is not, present.

And when anger is present, it means danger. The reasons for this danger are many, and they vary from one ACoA to another. In some cases, a parent used anger as a weapon. In their intoxication, anger was used to bully people into submission. In other cases, the anger often escalated under its own momentum until objects were destroyed and people were beaten or shamed. Anger may have led to withdrawal, as a parent used the anger as an excuse to leave the house and go to a bar, or to leave the home by divorce. Anger also feels more like a weapon when parents are so self-centered in their fury that they lose all sense of how their ravings and threats are being experienced by others. Children feel isolated in their experience of being a target for the anger, with no way of reaching their parent. There is no chance that the person punishing them is able to consider pleas for mercy. The telephone line to the governor has been cut, and no possibility of a pardon exists. No wonder that children in alcoholic homes fear being victim to their parent's out-of-control anger.

Even when anger has never erupted into violence, there are real reasons for those around an alcoholic to fear this possibility.

The most fertile ground for generating violence seems to be when anger is combined with feeling impotent to affect the world. This explosive combination exists in most alcoholics, and it is a wonder that the disinhibition of drinking does not lead to more frequent violence. (Other drugs that disinhibit without simultaneously providing the sedating qualities of alcohol, such as crack cocaine, do in fact lead to more frequent, and more intense, violence.) Impotence can be thought of as the negative way of perceiving being out of control, unable to effect any changes in what is happening to one's life. The following bears repetition: Even when anger has not erupted into violence, many ACoAs come to fear the threat of violence whenever someone gets angry at them.

It takes a lot of experience with a mature parent for children to begin learning effective ways of dealing with anger. First, healthy parents teach that anger is only one point on a wide continuum ranging from mild annoyance and irritation to murderous rage. Second, they teach that it is possible for a parent to be mad at you and to love you at the same time. Usually, this means that the parent is able to reject your *behavior* without rejecting *you*. Third, healthy parents understand that it is normal and acceptable for you to be mad, even furious, at them from time to time. Again, this is easier when *you* are helped to make a distinction between *what* your parent has done and *who* he or she is.

Given what chapter 6 said about control, it should not be surprising that many children of alcoholics try to deny their anger. Unfortunately, these efforts to deny the existence of anger or to banish it from your life can only lead to burying the feeling alive. It can only lead to a charade, an *appearance* of being very accepting and nonjudgmental. This charade is undertaken to help—to help oneself and to help others. There is no wish to harm others by the deception. And often, the fact that a deception is occurring is beyond your awareness. After all, the most effective deceptions are ones that involve self-deception as well. As a result, many children of alcoholics enter their adult life quite unaware of the amount of anger toward their families that lies in wait, below the surface, out of sight.

The most persuasive reason for people who have grown up in an alcoholic family to reconsider the way they relate to anger is when their current relationships are not working. Sometimes the unresolved anger leaps out with unexpected intensity at a spouse or one's own children. Sometimes ACoAs create emotional distance from others when they refuse to acknowledge their anger.

Intimacy is blocked by unresolved anger because anger cannot be banished from our lives without becoming a dark shadow that relentlessly follows us. In Jungian theory, the "shadow" is made up of all those facets of our personality that we find too uncomfortable to own up to. The shadow that we all possess also possesses us. When people deny anger its rightful place, they experience the dark side of their disowned anger in two ways: First, they have no choice but to be "nice" to others. Their own feelings count for nothing. But they find that the feelings remain alive no matter how long they have been buried, and they continually find cracks and back alleys to squeeze through. A remarkable number of ACoAs have spoken of how they get enraged at their own young children when they are out of control. When anger is expressed in inappropriate outbursts, or indirectly through criticisms and judgments, it is always more confusing and painful for others to bear.

The second way that ACoAs experience the shadow of their anger is in the pervasive fear of conflict that puts its stamp on their lives. Fear of conflict is a result of all the negative experiences you have actually had that revolved around anger. It is often a reasonable, rational fear, if the whole of your experience with anger is looked at, although it might seem grotesquely out of proportion to a specific current event.

Fear of conflict is more than an abstract idea. For many ACoAs, it is the terror they feel when not pleasing others. It is the awful sense that you are about to be criticized—and being criticized feels like rejection. It is the fear that someone is going to leave you. It is the twisted bowels and constricted throat that you feel when you have to approach someone else with a complaint.

Finally, there are those ACoAs who are consumed by their anger, who abuse others as they were abused. Their anger has turned to bitterness that tries to exact revenge—not to communicate. Anger is purposely used to alienate and distance others. It is used to punish. In the language of self-help programs, they have become "rage-oholics." Their highly destructive use of anger obliterates any chance for intimacy, although they may develop very intense, usually short-term, relationships.

It might seem paradoxical, but those ACoAs who remain

most rageful often have a problem, not with anger but with their pain and grief. As heartfelt as their anger may be, it is usually covering the real problem. It has become easier to feel rage than to touch upon their pain, which may feel bottomless. If you identify more with difficulties controlling your anger than with difficulties accessing it, you may well find that your most important issues have to do more with the unresolved hurt you feel.

It would have been nice if I had learned during childhood that my experiences regarding anger were teaching me more about intoxication than about anger itself. For many adults who grew up in alcoholic homes, understanding that sober anger is an entirely different emotion than drunken anger is very late in coming. But, whether late in coming or not, it is still an important distinction to make. Because until anger is integrated into one's life as a normal (albeit still frightening) emotion, the ability to accept oneself fully remains aborted, and life continues to be lived behind a mask—a placid persona—that hides us from the world. The ability to develop truly *mutual* relationships, which are the source of that precious experience called intimacy, is stunted.

If you do not like what we are suggesting about the proper role of anger in your life, let yourself feel annoyed at us. Or even irritated by us . . . Perhaps a little mad at us. Maybe angry at us . . . But let yourself feel whatever your reactions are, without pretending that you can decide how you should feel about things.

· · · · · · · ·   **EXERCISES**   · · · · · · · ·

I know I've got a problem with anger. I tend to keep putting things off and putting things off until I feel like exploding—and then I clamp down on it really hard. I can't get angry. If I get angry, I know I'll explode or be violent. I've never been violent in the past, but I just know that's what will happen.

Bob

For many ACoAs, anger is a beast. The beast may be nightmares of past rage and terror witnessed in their family or the unexpressed rage imprisoned within themselves today, or both.

Most ACoAs who begin to confront their relationship to anger approach it with the dread of opening Pandora's Box. This caution is understandable. The power of anger in alcoholic families often has the potential to erupt into violence in its many forms: emotional, verbal, physical, sexual.

Through the exercises below, we invite you to explore:

- how anger was dealt with in your alcoholic family
- your relationship to anger, both in the past and today
- your ability, or inability, to express anger
- how your anger affects you and those around you
- how your inability to express your anger affects you, and those around you
- how you are affected by other people's anger
- the relationship between your feelings of anger and your self-esteem.

Exercise 23: The Anger Graph

Because many ACoAs have a black-and-white relationship to anger, both their own and other people's, it will be useful to explore the wide range of feelings that often get lumped into one category called "anger." The first part of the exercise will help you increase awareness of the *range* of emotions that actually make up your "anger scale." The second part will help you identify how anger was expressed in your family. And the third part will help you consider alternative ways to express anger that may not have been in your family's repertoire.

1. Label a new page in your journal "Anger Graph." Draw a vertical line in the middle of the page. On the top write the word that represents the mildest form of anger you can imagine (e.g., *annoyed*). On the bottom write the word that represents the most extremely volatile expression of anger you can imagine (e.g., *murderous*).

2. Now place as many words along the Anger Scale as you can think of. Make the list according to how you experience these words and the feelings associated with them.

You may be helped by referring to your Weekly Feeling Exercises in each chapter, the Feelings List in the Appendix of the workbook, and/or other dictionaries.

Not everyone will agree on the placement of any specific word. Some people put *mad* right in the middle of the graph; others put it either a bit above or below. When you've finished, you will probably have as many as twenty or more angry-type words. Take the time to finish this before continuing.

Bob's Anger Graph looked like this:

annoyed
|
irritated
|
upset
|
mad
|
angry
|
furious
|
enraged
|
murderous

3. In the space to the left of the line, record how your family acted when they experienced the different feelings on your graph. Feel free to use colored pencils for a more dramatic effect. Finish this before continuing.

For example, when your mother felt irritated, she withdrew. When she was angry, she pouted. When she was furious, she yelled.

4. In the space to the right of the graph, list alternative ways of expressing and coping with these angry feelings; i.e., rather than expressing my rage by screaming and

yelling at someone abusively, I could *take time out and think about the situation before attacking someone verbally* (write: take time out or go for a walk) or *I could let them know how I feel* (write: tell them).

Or, when someone else is rageful, rather than standing there and taking it I could say, *"I will not be yelled at! If you can't talk respectfully to me I am leaving!" and leave* (write: confront and leave).

Bob's completed Anger Graph looked like this:

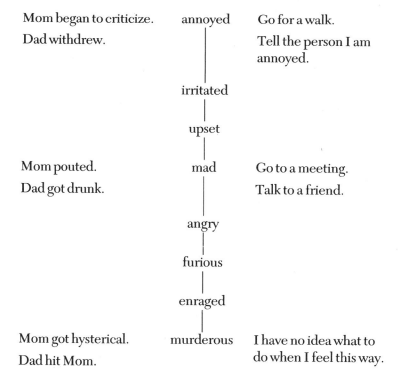

Mom began to criticize. Dad withdrew.	annoyed	Go for a walk. Tell the person I am annoyed.
	irritated	
	upset	
Mom pouted. Dad got drunk.	mad	Go to a meeting. Talk to a friend.
	angry	
	furious	
	enraged	
Mom got hysterical. Dad hit Mom.	murderous	I have no idea what to do when I feel this way.

Working on the Anger Graph helped me remember millions of times when my parents blew up and got into the worst kind of fights. My father was a mean-spirited person. He'd pick on your weakest points—and he knew them all. He knew my mother was self-conscious about her hair being curly so when he was drunk and mad at

her, which was often, he'd call her "Brillo Top." She'd
pout, then after a few minutes she'd come charging back
into the room with a newspaper and slap him across the
face. Once she knocked him out of his chair, and he split
open his head!

When I was writing this I had to stop every so often.
The memories were so vivid, I started getting stomach
cramps. I haven't had those since I was a kid. That's
amazing. I remember the family doctor saying I was the
youngest kid he ever met who had an ulcer. I worried
about everything. I never told him what was going on
at home.

Bob

Like many ACoAs, Bob struggled all his life with feeling that
he had to contain his anger. Having grown up in a family where
alcohol led to his parents' spilling out their anger in violent and
unpredictable ways, Bob learned the wrong lessons that we hear
ACoAs voice over and over again:

- Anger is destructive. Hold it in. Nothing good comes
  from being angry.
- If I get angry, things will only get worse and explode, because no one else can be counted on to be in control.
- If I get angry, I'm bad.
- If I get angry, I'm like my parents; and I *never* want to be
  like them.

Bob never learned that anger can be helpful in telling you
how strongly you feel, how strongly you feel hurt, and how deeply
you feel about someone. Bob, like so many people who grew up in
alcoholic families, never learned that anger can be expressed in
nondestructive ways that can help people understand one another better. He never saw his parents channel their angry energy
into *constructive* arenas. Readers who are interested in pursuing
further how energy can be used constructively should be sure to
look through the Recommendations section for additional resources.

The dysfunctional relationship that many ACoAs have to anger is often a result of experiencing anger only in its most extreme and destructive forms (at the lowest end of the scale). In order to help deepen your awareness of the ways anger was expressed in your family, we encourage you to use the following exercise to remember a typical angry scene more vividly.

Exercise 24: The Scene of Anger

Use your journal or a large sheet of paper with crayons, Magic Markers, or colored pencils to draw a typical family scene in which someone got angry. Place the scene as accurately as possible in the part of your house where it occurred. Focus on one particular episode in order to recall as many concrete details as possible.

Take your time. It isn't necessary to create a piece of art, but it is useful to give your heart enough time to react to your drawing. Represent who was present in the room, the emotions expressed, or not expressed, who did what to whom, and how you and others present reacted at the time.

If you don't remember a time when someone *got* angry, draw the scene when you knew people were *angry but weren't expressing it*.

> I had a hard time with this. I know other people grew up in families where there was violence when their parents got drunk; people got hit and ended up in the hospital. It just never happened in my family. No one ever got angry in my family. No one raised their voice, no one as much as swore at each other. But you could still *feel* the rage.
>
> It was like living in a nuclear reactor. It just kept getting hotter and hotter and hotter with no KABOOM!
>
> Marion

One reason Marion gave herself for not feeling accepted by the group was that her very restrained family made her different from the others. After completing the exercises for this chapter and sharing her experience with the group, she was able to see that she felt just as debilitated, just as controlled, just as terrified as everyone in the group when we talked about getting angry or being in the presence of someone who was angry.

The following exercise, in which she began to explore her own anger, opened the door for Marion to begin feeling more a part of the group.

Exercise 25: The Face of Anger

The Anger Graph helped you see the *range* of feelings that often get lumped under one term—*anger*. This exercise helps personalize these feelings by creating a self-portrait of you and your anger.

1. Draw at least three portraits of your anger illustrating a word on each end of the anger graph, as well as one near the middle (e.g., *irritation, rage* and *mad*). You can draw your face or an abstract, symbolical illustration with the color, shape, and power of your anger.

Remember, this is not a piece of art to be viewed by anyone else—so give yourself permission to express the depth of your feeling without being an art critic.

2. After completing the portraits of your anger, answer the question in your journal: Whom am I angry at and why?

Feeling Exercise

Take time to do the Feeling Exercise as described in chapter one (page 15).

Journal

The exercises above will have undoubtedly evoked many memories, further reminding you of what you survived growing up in your alcoholic family. The following questions will help you reflect on your experience while doing these exercises.

1. What was it like to create your anger graph?

2. If your experience was similar to those of many of our group members, you had many more words for the extreme ends of the graph and very few for the middle part. What do you make of this?

3. When you were remembering how your family expressed the different degrees of anger, what painful events were you reminded of?

4. Looking back at your Anger Graph, what words describe how you've felt at some time in your life?

   • Which have you expressed?

   • Which have you expressed but minimized?

   • Which have you felt but not expressed?

   • Do you find yourself able to feel anger only at certain people in your family and not at others? Why not?

I thought for sure I wouldn't be able to get in touch with any anger. I have a really hard time sticking up for myself, and I can count on one hand the number of times I've gotten angry. I started out drawing a portrait of myself with an oval head and circle eyes. Then I began remembering what it was like to draw as a child. I could see myself drawing, alone in my room. I could feel the silent tension in the house. I wished someone would scream. I almost scribbled all over the page the way I did when I was seven or eight—and I got angrier and angrier and angrier. I was furious with my parents. I drew myself with a purple face, a red tongue and horns growing out of my head and fire coming out of my nose.

Marion

5. Look at your self-portraits of anger. How does it feel to see the intensity, or lack of intensity, of your anger?

6. What are you afraid will happen if you begin to get in touch with even greater degrees of intensity of anger? If you tried to express more intense anger?

⭐ **Recommendations**

Two books that address the question of "What do I do with all these feelings of anger and rage?" are *The Dance of Anger*, by H. G. Lerner, and *From Anger to Forgiveness*, by Earnie Larsen.

Several films illustrate the consequences of people's inability to communicate and transform the energy of anger and rage into a positive experience: *Ordinary People,* with Mary Tyler Moore; *Rebel Without a Cause,* with James Dean; and *Do the Right Thing,* directed by Spike Lee.

Chapter Nine

Shame

Shame is one of the most painful emotions that humans experience and one of the most serious problems that people from alcoholic homes must face. Its seriousness comes from the extent to which shame can invade every corner of our lives, how it attacks our very being, and how it is often hard to label and talk about.

Shame takes many forms. It lies beneath the feeling that you constantly have to apologize for yourself. It lies beneath the feeling that you have been contaminated by your family and are defective. It lies behind the feeling that you must keep your inner life hidden from the rest of the world in order to be acceptable. It creates the feeling of being "less than" other people. It robs you of feeling that you have a right to exist. It lies beneath feelings of being stupid, inadequate, undeserving, "not normal," and a thousand other harsh judgments ACoAs make on themselves.

Just as with anger, it is important to understand that shame is a natural, normal experience. All children instinctively feel shame, primarily when they are forced to accept their limitations and boundaries. In the beginning of his book *Healing the Shame That Binds You,* John Bradshaw explicitly acknowledges the important role that shame plays in healthy human interactions. This can be illustrated by pointing to how we all feel about someone who is "shameless." Their shamelessness makes it impossible to trust that they will observe the rules and honor the bonds that are necessary for community to exist among people. Healthy shame helps us maintain healthy boundaries. It occurs when we violate boundaries, perhaps by telling an off-color joke in an inappropriate setting. It is good that we feel shame when we recognize that the joke was too explicitly sexual for a young listener, for example. Although painful, this shame is a useful signal about proper boundaries.

Being incapable of shame is not healthy, but neither is it healthy for your life to be controlled by shame. When shame controls your life, your spontaneity is destroyed and you are left feeling fundamentally unacceptable. Bradshaw calls the experience of being bound by shame "toxic shame." Toxic shame goes beyond being a feeling that we have violated boundaries and becomes a state of being. We experience toxic shame when we feel that our very *being* is a violation, when we cannot imagine being accepted by others.

Whereas healthy shame lets us know that we are limited, as all humans are limited, toxic shame makes us feel fundamentally inadequate, and not fully human. Healthy shame is a useful signal about something we have done; toxic shame is an indictment against who we are at the very core.

Children of alcoholics are often confused about what is healthy shame and what is toxic shame. Such confusion is natural because their parents were equally confused, often laboring under the burden of their own shame to such a degree that it began to infect the identity of everyone in the entire family. The experience of shame becomes "toxic" when it is experienced in isolation, when it is so frequent and so intense that it is overwhelming, and when it is transmitted from one generation to the next—all of which is inevitable in an alcoholic family.

Shame is an isolating experience. We feel shame when we are "outside the circle," when we feel excluded or abandoned, and when we do not belong. Alcoholic families usually become disconnected from friends and neighbors, often in disgrace. Children sense this disgrace and feel it as their own fault. You may remember feeling embarrassed to have friends over to your house, or even the experience of having a friend whose parents would not let their child spend the night in your home.

Shame becomes overwhelming when it is too frequently and too intensely experienced, and when it is misused. Although shame does teach us about boundaries, it can also be misused to control us, to keep us quiet. Children can be shamed into not telling other family members about a parent's drinking. Shame can be used to keep children from talking to friends, neighbors, or teachers about the drinking or violence in their homes. You may remember being shamed for accusing a parent of drinking too much ("How could you say that about your mother?"). Shame can also be used to keep a child from telling anyone that a parent is sexually abusing her, for fear that even greater shame will come if the secret is broken.

And shame is toxic when it is inherited, when it is passed from one generation to the next. Shame is transmitted to children when parents are so overwhelmed with their own shame that they begin to blame others for their unhappiness. In their intoxication and defensiveness, alcoholic parents become convinced that they must drink to get away from the excessive demands of the world, including their own kids. You may remember being told by your mother to be quieter, so that you wouldn't upset your father. You knew enough to decipher the message: "Be good so you don't make your father start drinking again." Or you may remember being blamed directly by a drunken parent that you made their life miserable. When such blame hit the mark, you were inheriting the burden of your parent's shame. You were feeling toxic, isolating, overwhelming, inherited shame.

One reason healthy shame does not overwhelm children is that it is usually accompanied by the comforting presence of an accepting adult. The five-year-old who wets his pants in kindergarten feels the embarrassment of not getting to the bathroom on time, but he is gently soothed by a teacher who understands his sense of having fallen below expectations. Shame becomes overwhelming, and toxic, when no one is there to see a child's shame, to understand, and to comfort it. You may have trouble remembering anyone offering comfort to allay the shame you felt from your parent's drinking because very few children in alcoholic families ever receive such comfort.

Once shame threatens to overwhelm us, we naturally begin to protect against it. You may have distanced yourself from your feelings and become "shameless" (several drinks helps this process along quite nicely). You may have distanced yourself from your family, or from people in general. In their efforts to protect against shame, ACoAs are often left wearing a suit of armor between themselves and the outside world. But because the very existence of this armor only intensifies the feeling of being separate from the world, their defenses against shame contribute to a very negative, self-reinforcing spiral. Defenses against shame lead to feeling more separated from the world, which increases your shame, which in turn increases the need for defenses, which only separates you further . . .

Unfortunately, sometimes it *is* healthiest to remain outside the circle of a dysfunctional family. Sometimes it is best to lift yourself out of your family, even if this means the bond with your addicted parent is lost. Even when this is the healthy course, being outside the circle often brings the experience of shame. Most of us need considerable support and validation from people we respect before we can take a stance outside the circle of our family. When this support is not available, the loss of bonding with our parents may feel as though it threatens our very survival. It is often unclear whether it is more sustaining to remain in a dysfunctional family, or not. Such decisions are difficult. They are truly dilemmas, for they have no solution that is completely satisfactory. No matter which way we decide, there is loss. These are not decisions that young children should be forced to face. And yet they are made on a daily basis by millions of children in America every day, sometimes every hour.

Another common defense against shame is often called "the Committee" by children of alcoholics. The Committee refers to a dialogue between internal critics that has become stereotyped and repetitive. For example, "You should have known that she wasn't going to like that shirt. When you put it on, you knew that it didn't go with those pants. Your color sense is lousy. You should pay more attention to what other people wear. You neglect your clothes too much, etc."

This incessant brain chatter is constantly demanding the perfectionism necessary to avoid feeling shame. Most ACoAs complain that the Committee is far too harsh and critical, constantly commenting about how they could do everything better. Or, if they have done things well enough, then they should have been able to do them more quickly. One person reported completing a project perfectly and ahead of schedule. Instead of relaxing, complimenting himself, and enjoying the experience, he complained that he should have been able to perform with less effort. It had drained him more than what would be necessary if . . . if what? If he had been a totally enlightened saint?

Very few of us are ever going to qualify for sainthood. Of course, many ACoAs immediately recognize that their Committee says that *they* should qualify. Or, if they never qualify, at least they should get closer than they are. Or, at the very least they should be trying harder to qualify. Or, at the very, very least they should be able to understand what all these damned self-help books are saying about accepting their limitations and no longer try to be a saint. As you can see, the demands of these internal committees are driven by fear. They can never relax, because the smallest chink in their master's armor can lead to the worst shame attack. Perfectionism is the other side of shame.

The exercises that follow will help you begin looking at how shame has had a pervasive impact on your life. It may not need to be said, but recovery from excessive shame requires help from others as much as any part of your recovery does. You can't get out of isolation on your own.

• • • • • • • EXERCISES • • • • • • •

> I always feel as if I've done something wrong. I walk around as though I'm carrying this five-hundred-pound weight around my neck. I apologize for everything. When I pass a police car on the highway, I'm sure I'm going to get a ticket even though I'm driving below the speed limit. I feel like people are always judging me, and at any moment someone is going to publicly reveal all my faults, all my sins, everything I've ever done that was wrong.
>
> Denise

The exercises below will help you explore the spiral of guilt and shame that binds, blinds, and stifles many people who grew up in alcoholic families. The first exercise focuses on the negative messages we've internalized from the comments, criticisms, and judgments of our parents. The second exercise develops a clearer awareness and understanding of the ways in which shame can be a defining experience in your life.

Given the depth of feelings that tend to emerge when ACoAs explore shame, we especially encourage you to use Twelve-Step meetings, your group, your therapist, or trusted friends while doing these exercises. Recovery from toxic shame requires more help from others than some of the other steps in recovery.

Exercise 26:
The Committee

The following exercise helps cultivate deeper awareness of your Committee and the many ways in which it affects your self-esteem, your relationships, and your peace of mind.

1. In the following week, pay close attention to times when you:
   - internally note your inadequacies
   - judge these inadequacies harshly
   - hold yourself up to impossible standards.

2. For each day of the week, perhaps at the end of the day, write in your journal the internal dialogue that watches and judges you, the critical phrases and names it uses against you, and the impossible standards it holds up to you.

3. Choose several incidents and write down all the Committee's criticisms you had to endure. We really mean it. Commit them to paper, in the form of a list. For this part of the exercise some people carry a little notebook around with them and write down each phrase as it happens.

   If you are like most ACoAs you may need more than one sheet of paper.

You were right. I needed more than one sheet of paper. I started on Monday and by lunch already had half a page. When I woke up, I criticized how mousy my hair is. I looked at myself in the mirror and called myself ugly for the size of my thighs. I harassed myself for eating a do-nut on the way to work and not eating a good breakfast and degraded myself for not maintaining my car well enough. By the time I got to work I was a wreck. I wasn't just getting down on myself, I felt downright depressed. I had a hard time working because I felt so bad.

I do this every day. I've just gotten so used to it that I don't usually notice it. I wonder, do I really need to be this hard on myself?

Denise

Denise was becoming acutely aware of how her self-criticism was linked to her low self-esteem. She had difficulty continuing with the exercise because, the more she paid attention to her internal dialogue, the more depressed she became. Unfortunately, this was a necessary step in becoming more conscious of the ways she was carrying her family's destructive legacy of shame. In time, with the help and feedback of the group, she did begin to separate from her family's debilitating vision by defining herself in a more nurturing, compassionate light.

This exercise will help you explore three forms of shame: **Exercise 27: Shame**

- The shame associated with having an alcoholic parent

- The shame associated with the alcoholic's behavior, including the shame of incest, family violence, growing up in poverty, public drunkenness, arrests for drunk driving, incarceration, your parents being out of control, growing up in a foster family, or being adopted

- The shame associated with your parent's judgments and criticisms of you

1. To explore the shame you may know from having an alcoholic parent or parents, make a list in your journal of at least ten words that come into your mind immediately associated with the word *alcoholic.* One way of compiling this list is to fill in the blank:

    "An alcoholic is (a) _____
    (b) _____, etc."

2. Every alcoholic family has its own brand of chaos, its own secrets and it own emotional violence that generate the experience of shame in children. To explore the

shame that grew out of your parent's alcoholic behavior, make a list of ten actual family incidents that you feel ashamed of.

These may be passive experiences, such as incest, verbal harassment, and constant negative messages; or they may stem from something you actively did, such as stealing to feed your siblings or lying to cover for your parent.

3. To explore the shame associated with parental criticism we would like you to look over the list of judgments and criticisms you have made in Exercise 26: The Committee. Repeat each phrase out loud to yourself and listen closely to your tone of voice. Listen carefully to the exact words used in your self-judgments. Some people have found it beneficial first to say the phrases out loud into a tape recorder and then play them back several times to listen carefully.

4. Next to each judgment, criticism, harassment, and unreasonable standard, write the name of the people whose voices lurk behind them. Try to identify the original source of the voices that make up your Committee.

Bob responded to this exercise by saying, "At first, when I was making the list of judgments for the Committee exercise, I felt a bit stupid. Then I realized that, by calling myself stupid, I was doing exactly what the exercise was about. I laughed. Then, I can't believe it, I criticized myself for judging myself. It was like a roomful of mirrors. I wanted *not* to judge myself and then did." (laughs) When Bob named the original authors of his Committee's judgments, he was left with the following list:

"Stupid!"	Dad
"Idiot!"	Dad
"You took the wrong turn. Can't you drive?"	Dad
"Not good enough."	Dad
"There you go again, being lazy!"	Dad
"Lazy never got anyone anywhere."	Dad

"Success is 99 percent perspiration, 1 percent
inspiration. So where's the sweat?"   Dad

"You'll never amount to anything."   Dad

"Don't yell, young man. You're just like your father." Mom

Like many recovering ACoAs, Bob was discovering something
he already knew. The voices of his unrelenting self-criticism
and the deep shame he carried with him were predominantly
those of his parents; 90 percent his father's voice and 10 percent
his mother's voice.

Bob's healing, like Denise's in the previous exercise, came
from his gradually detaching from his parents' view of him. This
view had been internalized as a negative self-image. When he began defining his self-worth through the values and relationships
developed in recovery, he was relieved of much of his shame. Including himself *inside* the circle of the recovering community
gradually moved the Committee within his head off center stage,
out into the periphery of his mind, where its judgments had far
less power over him.

Feeling Exercise

Take time to do the Feeling Exercise as described in chapter one
(page 15).

Journal

To help you reflect further on the above exercises, answer the following questions in your journal:

1. Did you make a full list of your self-criticisms, or did you
   stop short by rationalizing that "I know all the stuff I feel
   bad about. I don't have to do this!" What excuses did you
   use for not following through with the exercise?

2. How did you feel when you named the original voices of
   your self-criticism?

3. What does it feel like to recognize this source of your pain?

I'm starting to feel a little angry. Usually I shut off my anger. I just distract myself by saying "Well, my parents didn't have such a good childhood, either. My grandfather was an immigrant and an alcoholic." Then before I know it, I'm not angry anymore.

I feel angry now. I was just a kid—a little kid. What did I know about life? It just pisses me off how hard my father was on me. And my mother never challenged him!

Bob

Bob discovered one of the common ways in which many ACoAs avoid their feelings about their parents. He distracted himself from feeling angry toward his parents by rationalizing how difficult a childhood they had had. Although it is true they had difficult childhoods, that has little to do with whether or not Bob was or wasn't angry with his parents when he was a little child. Another thing Bob discovered was that his shame and his rage were two sides of the same coin, minted in his father's judgments.

4. What is it like to acknowledge the strong feelings you associate with the label of alcoholic, especially when you're talking about your mother or father?

5. Was it difficult to let the Committee's actual words come up?

6. In reflecting on your feelings of shame, whom in your family do you identify with the most?

7. What do you make of this?

My mother. She was a wreck. Whatever criticism my father gave me, he gave my mother twice as much. No wonder she never stood up to him. He was a tyrant. When he'd drink, he'd get nasty and threaten to take us away from her. She was always crying. I can remember it as if it were yesterday. She's sitting in the kitchen, crying, repeating over and over and over to herself, "I'm no good. He tells me I'm no good. I can't do it."

Denise

In this session Denise discovered for the first time how similar *her* feelings of shame were to her mother's. An important next step for Denise's recovery will be to separate her own sense of shame from what she inherited from her mother.

★ Recommendations

Your exploration of how guilt, shame, and feelings of responsibility can be transmitted across generations can be deepened by the films *The Man in the Gray Flannel Suit,* with Gregory Peck (based on the book by Sloan Wilson) and the Holocaust survivor story *Sophie's Choice,* with Meryl Streep. We also recommend the short story "Young Goodman Brown," by Nathaniel Hawthorne, which illustrates the conflict between externally imposed values and responsibility and the voice of one's inner guide and nature in a Puritan community.

Many ACoAs have found John Bradshaw's *Healing the Shame That Binds You* extremely useful. Bradshaw draws upon a wide range of sources to view shame as both a normal human emotion and a potentially poisonous force that spans generations. This theme is further developed by Merle Fossum and Marilyn Mason in *Facing Shame: Families in Recovery.*

Chapter Ten

Mourning

Recovery inevitably brings ACoAs to greater awareness of the tremendous number of losses they have suffered over the years. Allowing yourself to feel the emotional impact of these losses and grieving for what "might have been" often require a distinct period of mourning. This chapter helps you to take this mourning seriously and begin moving through it rather than getting mired in the grief.

Some children of alcoholics *physically* lose their parents. Alcoholics disappear for days or come home hours later than expected. You may remember the fear of waiting, not knowing if your parent was coming home again. Other times, prison separates children from their parents, who may have been convicted of driving under the influence, illegal drug possession, or other crimes. Parents also leave the family permanently through divorce or because Death claimed another premature victory.

Some children of alcoholics *emotionally* lose their parents. A parent's body may still be at home, but her mind is absent when she sits completely engrossed in the artificial life shining out of a television, slumps into a stupor on the back porch, or lies unconscious on the floor. Others become emotionally unavailable because their lives have deteriorated into endless arguments with the other parent or have declined into obsession, dementia, and terminal self-centeredness.

And most children of alcoholics lose large portions of their *own childhood.* You may be left with few memories of your childhood, either because the only memories are too painful to recall or because childhood was so terrifying that you disconnected from your experience much of the time. Perhaps your childhood was aborted by having to take on too many adult responsibilities at an early age in order to keep the family going. You may remember having put away playfulness a long time ago, in favor of practical survival.

Sometimes the loss is hard to feel because it was *always* there. In this case, the word *deprivation* would be more accurate. Deprivation is more fundamental than loss. It cuts into the very definition of who we are, leaving us unsure if we were ever worthy of being cared for. It forces us to live in a world with narrow horizons, with no idea of what "normal" childhood is like for other people. Feelings of deprivation seem to rip at the fabric of your soul, whereas loss merely breaks your heart.

Children experience so many losses when a parent is overtaken by chemical dependence that the grief can be too much to bear. Later in life, they often fear that if they were to take the full measure of their sadness, they would be overwhelmed by its depth. Buoyed by the delusion that they can control how sad they feel, many ACoAs push this grief onto the back burner of their lives. There it sits, simmering; but at least it no longer threatens to overwhelm. There it sits, sometimes festering, needing energy each day to keep the lid on tightly.

Some ACoAs are primed to begin mourning as soon as they find a safe group to unload their burden of tears. The safety they need is that of having the depth of their losses understood by others, and the shedding of their tears respected. Such safety is often difficult to find. Your friends who did not grow up with a chemically dependent parent are often unable to comprehend the pervasiveness and depth of the loss you feel. And friends who are from chemically dependent families may still be so busy denying their own losses and keeping their own sadness at bay that they are not able to listen to your pain. Worse yet, unrecovering ACoAs are likely to see your tears as signs of weakness.

Other ACoAs need to become more aware of the sadness that lurks within them before their mourning can begin. Many have a complex codependent belief system (chapter 7) which has caused them to suppress, and eventually repress, their grief. We are *suppressing* an emotion or a thought when we consciously fight against being aware of, or expressing, it. Most people have experience with trying to choke back their tears so that others do not see them, or so that they do not have to be experienced. We are *repressing* emotions and thoughts when we have gotten so good at keeping them out of awareness that we no longer know that this is what is happening. The entire process works so well, we are unaware that it is taking place. Not only is the grief "gone," but the efforts needed to keep it away are also out of sight.

Other ACoAs harbor more grief than they realize because their losses were traumatic enough to produce the dissociation from self described in chapter 5 as psychic numbing. Once psychic numbing has developed, when any grief begins to well up toward awareness, your mind can suddenly mistake the current situation for times when the grief was so great that it overwhelmed your capacity to tolerate it. In response to the threat of being overwhelmed, reflex fight-or-flight, all-or-nothing defenses spring into action. Then, in the midst of what had felt like a normal conversation, you may find your emotional life constricting. You get confused inside. You can't remember what people were talking about. You no longer know what you are feeling. Maybe you start feeling nothing at all. The rupture between yourself and your immediate experience (the welling up of grief) has temporarily returned. Psychic numbing does not have to be present all the time to be effective. It merely has to be available whenever sadness (or any other feeling that once threatened to overwhelm you) begins to stir into your consciousness.

Therapists often encourage people to express the grief that they feel (or that they almost feel, are about to feel, or would feel if they let themselves). But this is not because tears are any magic elixir. Rather, it is more because so much energy is wasted keeping the tears inside. The purpose of mourning is to stop wasting this energy.

An ACoA who is still fighting back her tears is like someone rushing through an airport carrying a heavy suitcase. The weight of the case becomes so great that her hand begins to cramp and turn white. Rather than pause and rest the hand, she hurries faster to get to her car before her hand falls off.

Would it seem strange to someone who has carried her suitcase far too long if I took every chance to encourage her to put it down for a moment? Would she wonder why I think it is important for the suitcase to be on the floor? Would she feel that I was afraid she was too weak to carry the load all the way to the car without stopping? Would I offend her by suggesting that she stop, rest for a moment, and let her hand recover? Would I have to explain that I have no particular interest in the suitcase being on the floor, but rather in her taking better care of herself?

Allowing yourself to mourn is like pausing to put the case down, then painfully unfolding your fingers from the handle. The muscles gradually become flexible again as the cramps are massaged out of them. The blood flows back into fingers that have been like a desert, parched for life-giving oxygen.

Each tear that flows when you mourn is evidence that something was lost, a concrete clue that begs to be noticed. Each tear is a memory sent up from your past, a living moment that pleads to be taken seriously. Each tear is the physical embodiment of an emotion. How you choose to treat these tears determines the pace of your recovery. How you treat them determines how long you have to carry that suitcase.

You can make the mistake of treating your tears precisely the way a drunken parent might treat a crying child. You can be oblivious of them. You can be aware that they are present but ignore them. You can denigrate them as weak. You can shame them into submission. And, you can base your self-esteem on your ability to keep them under control.

Or, you can pursue recovery by dismantling your denial and acknowledging the reality of your grief—and the tears that wash that grief away. You can step out of their path and allow them to pass by, loosening your throat and letting the tears seep from your eyes out into the world. You can listen with your heart, and with your soul, to the barely audible whisper that comes from each tear. Each delivers an important message. Paying attention to what each one is saying to you means that its message has finally been heard. And that tear will not have to come again.

If there is an answer to the question many ACoAs ask, "Why

do I have to have these tears," that answer is contained in the messages those tears carry. As you listen closely to the answers they give you, you will be spending a few moments resting from the burden of denial and rigid control. It is this burden that does far more harm than a few drops of moisture ever could.

In the end, some ACoAs still resist their grief by insisting that they have accepted their parents' chemical dependence and no longer feel any loss. Maybe this is so. But my understanding of acceptance is not that it *stops* feelings. On the contrary, acceptance is more often the *beginning* of feelings. If you find yourself trying to use acceptance as a way to avoid emotions, you have probably entered one of the most vicious whirlpools of disguised control.

Acceptance of loss means that you are no longer fighting against the reality of loss. You are no longer negotiating with the finality that what was lost, *was lost*. Accepting loss means allowing your emotions to react to it, rather than holding the emotions off just in case that loss may not be as real, or as permanent, as it seems.

Recovery begins when we *stop* doing the things that hold back our grief. Once we stop resisting the grief, nature provides us with just the right number of tears needed to wipe our own particular slates clean.

· · · · · · · **EXERCISES** · · · · · · ·

When I think of what I went through as a child, a tidal wave of sadness engulfs me. Five years ago, I started to have nightmares. I dreamed I was a little girl dressed in white. But then I would see blood everywhere, on the walls, on the floor, on my clothes. It was about that time I started to remember being molested by my father. I couldn't get angry, I only felt sad. I felt like I was going to die with the weight of that sadness.

Susan

The following exercises help you become aware of your family's myths about grief, sadness, and loss, the barriers that keep you from mourning, and how willing you currently are to explore your grief, sadness, and loss. They will help you see how you have, *or have not*, coped with the losses in your life.

Once again, we encourage you to be in contact with trusted friends and relatives while working through this chapter. Most of us need support during times of mourning.

The first step toward mourning is to explore your family's myths about sadness and loss. Family myths are conveyed in old sayings ("Smile at the world, and the world smiles back at you"), in direct commands ("Stop bawling!"), and in harsh statements ("You don't have a thing to cry about!" or "Things could be worse"). Underlying each message is the unspoken reality "I can't stand it when you cry."

Many family myths about grief convey a message of denigration: "Only babies cry!" or "Tears are a sign of weakness." The underlying message here is "I won't love you if you cry." Such myths are often transmitted through a prominent story from the family's history. For example, "Don't start crying—remember what happened to Uncle Joe?" Whether or not you know that Uncle Joe was hospitalized once for depression, a serious warning has been issued. Crying is dangerous.

Exercise 28: Family Myths about Grief

1. Remember those incidents during childhood when you learned your family's myths about sadness, grief, or mourning. The lessons may have been taught explicitly, as we described above, or learned simply by observing others.

2. Record these memories in your journal.

3. Then, list the messages about sadness, grief, and loss that your family passed on to you.

Mark described the following memory:

I was seven years old. It was my birthday. My parents invited a few of their friends over for dinner. They told me the party was for me. I thought some of my friends would be coming. My mother said we'd have dinner soon, after the grown-ups had a few drinks.

Tears welled up in Mark's eyes as the memory became more vivid.

> I waited. I was hungry. All the grown-ups were drinking. Seven o'clock passed; eight o'clock passed. I went into the kitchen, where my father was mixing some more drinks. I asked him when we were going to have dinner. "Soon," he promised. I stood very still and started crying. No sound, just tears.

Sobbing quietly, Mark continued,

> "Don't start crying on me young man," my father shouted. "Only sissies cry." And he walked out. I don't remember if I ever had dinner that night.

Mark had an incredibly hard time talking about his childhood. In the spirit of his family tradition and the military career that he had pursued during the first decade of his adult life, he tried to be strong. Being stoic to Mark meant "never wearing his heart on his shirtsleeve." The unfortunate result of his stoicism was that it disconnected him from other people emotionally. It wasn't until the eighth week of the group, when we discussed mourning, that Mark began to feel as though he belonged. Up until that point, he had still been controlled by his father's admonition that "Only sissies cry."

Exercise 29: Barriers to Mourning

The second step toward mourning is to identify ways in which you have internalized your family's myths to protect against feeling grief, sadness, and loss. These protective barriers are automatic at times, but they can also be used intentionally. Mourning begins as soon as you let down the barriers.

This exercise identifies the variety of ways in which you prevent yourself from feeling grief, sadness, and loss.

Some means that ACoAs use to protect themselves from mourning are listed below. You may notice a similarity to the Tools of Survival from Exercise 16 in chapter 5.

- numbing out and disconnecting from their experience

- minimizing their feelings

- withdrawing from being in contact with other people

- preoccupying themselves with obsessive thoughts and compulsive behavior
- denying sadness
- being "rational" instead of emotional
- not caring about themselves—apathy
- being too mature, enlightened, or recovered to have negative feelings

1. Use your journal to describe the ways in which you protected yourself from, avoided, or controlled your feelings of sadness, loss, and grief when you were a child.

2. Now describe the barriers within yourself that keep you from feeling sadness and loss in your current life.

> I'm still using the same barriers I used as a kid—I disappear. When I even get close to feeling sad, I just disappear. I cut off the conversation and leave, or I space out emotionally. I did it as a kid when my parents were hitting each other, and I do it now. It's absolutely automatic. I don't think I have any control over it. Even as I'm talking about it now, I feel myself beginning to fade.
> Susan

In this group session, Susan was able to see how she had developed the ability to become invisible and protect herself from feelings of sadness. A moment later she laughed and acknowledged that it was the same way she protected herself from her anger, and she wondered how often she faded away while she was there in the group.

By talking about her disappearing in the group, Susan was able to begin recognizing the exact moment when she began to disappear and, over time, with the group's support for her to state her feelings out loud, she was able to make progress toward staying present with her feelings in the moment and begin sharing her grief rather than hiding it.

This final exercise focuses on the losses you have experienced in ways that help old feelings of sadness and grief finally come to the surface. It has three steps: the first involves *listing losses*;

Exercise 30: The Willingness to Mourn

the second, *describing the losses*; and the third, *sharing your experience* with at least one other person. If you are willing to explore the grief, sadness, and loss you have identified, you should continue with the next exercise now. If you are unsure, consider reading the exercise first and waiting a day or two before beginning.

Listing the Losses

In your journal, list five important losses caused by your parent's abuse of alcohol or other drugs. For example:

- a parent who was emotionally distant because of drinking or drug use
- death of a parent, directly or indirectly due to alcohol or drugs
- abandonment by a parent because of drinking or drug use
- a promise that was broken or "forgotten" because of a blackout
- divorce

Then list five common childhood experiences that you never had as a result of your parent's alcohol or drug use. For example:

- never having a birthday party
- never having a holiday feast that wasn't disrupted by drinking
- never feeling safe at home
- never seeing a parent with a good work ethic
- being unable to sleep through the night without being woken up by the yelling of drunken parents

Mark's list included the following:

Losses

1. "When I was three or four, my mother's drinking got worse. I remember once having the distinct feeling that

I was in danger when she picked me up. I started wiggling too much, and she spanked me."

2. "My father made the promise while he was drunk that I would get a full-size bike for Christmas. When I looked under the tree on Christmas morning, there was no bike; and no one seemed to have any sense that I might be disappointed. I never mentioned the bike, and it was as if the promise had never happened. Now I understand that he never remembered making the promise."

Childhood Experiences I Never Had

1. "I don't know what it's like to not be afraid of my parents."
2. "I can't remember a decent birthday party."
3. "I don't remember my mother ever hugging me past the age of four or five. In fact I don't even remember her ever even touching me. She said I was too old."

Describing the Losses

Now describe one of the experiences in detail, including how you felt physically, how you reacted emotionally, and how the experience affected your relationship to the person involved.

I was always afraid of my parents. I remember flinching one time when my mother scratched her head because I thought she was going to hit me. The woman visiting from next door looked startled at my reaction. My mother hurried me out of the room. I also remember when my third-grade teacher reached out to raise my hand as the winner of a spelling bee and I nearly tripped over a chair trying to get out of her reach.

Mark

Sharing the Losses

Now it is time to share some part of your story with another person. Choose carefully. Ask a trusted friend, a therapist, a veteran member of the Twelve-Step Programs, or an understanding rabbi, priest, or minister to help you. All they have to do is listen.

Give yourself a minimum of ten minutes to share. Use the notes in your journal, if this helps. And feel free to postpone this final step if it still feels too threatening.

Feeling Exercise

Take time to do the Feeling Exercise as described in chapter one (page 15).

Journal

In this chapter you have explored your family's myths about grieving and the ways in which they continue to create barriers to mourning the losses you experienced in an alcoholic family. Now we encourage you to reflect in your journal on the following further questions:

1. Can you describe the impact that avoiding your feelings of sadness and grief continues to have on your current life?

2. Do you have difficulty loving deeply because you are protecting against the inevitability of being hurt in intimate relationships?

When I don't have strong feelings about someone, I can act normally around them. But, if I start to feel warm or close to someone . . . or start to have sexual feelings, I panic. I feel so vulnerable, I start thinking about how painful it will be when things fall apart. I fantasize about being happy but then worry about getting cancer or some horrible accident happening to the person I care about. It's way too painful. It's easier just not to get involved.

Susan

3. What is it like to acknowledge the depth of pain you feel about the losses you described in detail?

4. Did you write about losses with a sense of detachment and aloofness, or were you able to experience the losses as you remembered them?

5. What did you learn from sharing your story with another person?

Susan had been one of the most active members in her group. I was concerned about her silence during this session. With five minutes left, I asked how she was doing. Holding back her tears, she said,

"All right, I guess." Then she said, "Jacques . . . can you give me the name of a therapist I can see individually? I think it's time for me to get into therapy."

Susan made an appointment with the therapist I recommended that week and completed the remaining eight weeks of the group. For six solid months, twice a week, she cried and cried and cried. And then she stopped. . . . Healthy mourning is a time-limited experience.

★ Recommendations

The mourning that heals wounds inflicted by an alcoholic family may require far more time than it takes to complete this workbook. To help you continue grieving your losses, we recommend three books: *How to Survive the Loss of a Love,* by Melba Colgrove et al.; *On Death and Dying,* by Elisabeth Kübler-Ross; and, once again, Harold Kushner's *When Bad Things Happen to Good People.*

Several movies may also be helpful. *Ordinary People,* with Donald Sutherland and Mary Tyler Moore, is an extraordinarily sensitive and rich drama about loss, as the entire family grapples with a son's death. Also, *Batman,* with Michael Keaton and Kim Basinger, and *The Fisher King,* with Robin Williams, help explore the struggle to cope with grief and mourning.

Finally, *Woman in the Mists,* by Farley Mowat, is the story of

Dian Fossey and the mountain gorillas of Africa. Although Mowat does not highlight Fossey's history as a child of an alcoholic, the book chronicles how her inability to grieve losses took her to fascinating ends of the earth, but also led to horrible loneliness and what appeared to be bouts of alcoholism. And a precious little book, if you can find it, is Richard Zybert's pictorial essay on the disintegration of his family, *Notebook on Time.*

Chapter Eleven

Healing

The chapter on healing follows the chapter on mourning for a reason. The sequence is intentional because it duplicates the process of healing. Until ACoAs are willing to notice their wounds and care for them, healing is not possible. It is only when you empathize enough with your own fate to grieve for *your* losses (as opposed to focusing excessively on what others have lost) that the healing process begins. The first half of this workbook has been devoted to releasing the healing forces within you. The second half is now devoted to nurturing and strengthening these healing forces directly.

Healing your mind, your heart, and your soul is as mysterious as planting a seed and watching it grow into a flower. None of us can take credit for the existence of the seed, and certainly no one has direct power to *make* seeds sprout and grow. Nor must we understand the mechanisms of DNA, enzymes, or photosynthesis to be excellent gardeners. All the above have been taken care of by forces (nature/God) outside of our control, and beyond our understanding. Our job is merely to maintain the day-to-day conditions that promote the seed's greatest growth.

Gardening takes both presence of mind and responsibility. Presence of mind means that we pay attention, that we notice when weeds are choking the flowers and when the soil is too dry. Responsibility means the *ability* and *willingness* to respond to changing conditions that affect the flowers' day-to-day needs.

Responsibility requires discipline, in the sense that you must become a disciple of the flower (from the Latin *discipulus,* which means "learner"). To be good gardeners, we must let the flower teach us what is needed on an ongoing basis. Gardeners enjoy the whole "process," as opposed to going to a floral shop and purchasing the end product to enjoy for a few days.

Healing and recovery require the same presence of mind, the same responsibility, and the same enjoyment of the process (and not just the final product, or goal) seen in gardening. Just as gardeners till the soil, pull weeds, fertilize, and water, people in recovery must attend to a variety of tasks in an ongoing, disciplined manner. These tasks are the same for those who have been in recovery for twenty years and those who are beginning their healing today (just as both the beginner and the master gardener must attend to the same needs presented by a growing flower). In order to allow your healing to proceed at its maximum pace and to its maximum extent, you need only maintain your focus on three practices, making them routine parts of your day-to-day life. The "work" of healing involves the following three disciplines:

1. Honesty

People in recovery are disciples of honesty, especially about themselves. Denial is treated like weeds. It is a normal part of daily life, but necessary to notice and uproot on a regular basis. The fellowship of Alcoholics Anonymous emphasizes "rigorous honesty," especially when taking an inventory of your strengths and defects and continually monitoring ways in which you wrong other people. The underlying belief here is the same in psychotherapy—there is no truth that is so ugly that more harm is done by bringing it to the light of day than by hiding it in the shadows of one's soul. This may *sound* praiseworthy, but it is quite difficult to live your daily life according to this belief. People who practice great honesty in their day-to-day affairs generally make the most progress in recovery, and they experience the most healing.

2. Welcoming Feelings

Just as gardening is never done well with clean hands, honesty is more than just an intellectual pursuit. People who are in successful recovery are not only honest about what they think; they are also honest about what they *feel*. Emotional honesty is only achieved by developing a receptive, inviting relationship to one's feelings. I call this relationship "welcoming feelings." The word *welcoming* implies not only awareness of your feelings but also *experiencing* them as well. They are taken in as honored guests and allowed to rumble around in your chest, grip your bowels, or heat up your groin. In order for healing to proceed, feelings must be admitted unconditionally into your awareness and experienced in their full depth and intensity. And they are welcomed for no other reason than that they exist, they are yours, and they deserve to be allowed into the light of day. This is quite different from letting yourself feel angry, for example, in order to "get through it." No feeling is truly honored if it is only tolerated.

3. Entering Community

One group member, Brian, insisted for several weeks that he could never allow himself to cry in front of the rest of the group. When I asked him if it was easier to cry when he was alone, he said yes but then acknowledged that he didn't cry then either. I believe Brian's life shifted subtly, but profoundly, the day that he first allowed himself to cry in the group. In mourning his father's death, Brian experienced for the first time that it was actually *easier* for him to feel his pain in the presence of the supportive group members than it had been during the week, when he worked the mourning exercises alone. People in recovery leave their isolation. Attempting to recover "on your own" is one of the surest ways to limit your growth. *Healing is about changing how you relate—to the truth, to your feelings, and to others.* It is when this last element is included that healing has its greatest depth and lasting power. It is only when ACoAs bring their recovery into the world of other people (by being honest with others about what they feel in the moment) that it reaches full bloom. For many people, the first community they feel comfortable joining involves Twelve Step meetings; for others it involves the leap of faith needed to enter psychotherapy, or to explore their relationship to a Higher Power. In the end, no one recovers alone, because part of the wound ACoAs experience is their disconnection from others.

With the advent of recovery and therapy groups specifically

geared toward youngsters and adults from alcoholic homes, a new era of connection with one another has opened up. Support for recovery has never been greater than it is today. No matter how mired you may feel in problems that were spawned during your childhood, your life can be improved. That is the experience of millions of ACoAs who have come into recovery together, and that is the message of hope they can deliver to you.

Your healing will occur in a predictable series of stages.* As ACoAs practice the disciplines of Honesty, Welcoming Feelings, and Entering Community, they pass through the same stages seen in recovering alcoholics. Before healing begins, most ACoAs are hunkered down in a *Survivor Stage*. Just as some alcoholics keep drinking to avoid going into withdrawal and feeling worse (physically, emotionally, or spiritually), many ACoAs spend years keeping their denial intact in order to feel safe. The most common comments by ACoAs who still have one foot in the Survivor Stage are "I don't see what good can come from opening this all up again" and "I'm afraid if I let myself begin to cry I'll never stop." I am reminded of Tom Wingo in *The Prince of Tides* when he said, from his survivor stance, that feeling sad would never bring his father back to him. His psychiatrist agreed, but she added that it might bring *Tom* back to himself.

It is common for people to be wrenched out of the Survival Stage when they are no longer able to tolerate, or cover up, their pain. Called "hitting bottom," this critical moment places people at the threshold of recovery. Sometimes a series of stresses makes the pain too acute to be ignored. At other times, people gradually become "sick and tired of being sick and tired." In either case, the choices that people face when they hit bottom are to try their failed strategies even harder, to become apathetic and die, or to step across the threshold into recovery—to begin reopening themselves to the truth, to their feelings, and to other people.

There are two hallmarks of the stage of healing—*Identification*—that lies across the threshold. The first involves denial, which begins to disappear—sometimes explosively, and some-

---

* The following stages of recovery stem from the work of Herbert Gravitz and Julie Bowden (see Recommendations section).

times in painstakingly slow increments. The second hallmark involves a shift in your very sense of identity, as a result of dismantling your denial. For the alcoholic, the Identification Stage means accepting the label of being an alcoholic. For the ACoA, it means acknowledging not only that your parents were chemically dependent (which points the finger primarily outward) but also that you are the *child* of an alcoholic (which points the finger inward).

There is healing magic in the label "adult child of an alcoholic—ACoA." When you accept this label, you are literally taking on a new identity. By acknowledging that you are an ACoA, you give yourself the freedom to reinterpret your past, reviewing events more realistically, without the blinders of denial. You acknowledge the lifelong importance of your childhood experience. But you simultaneously acknowledge that you are an *adult* now. You are not just a child anymore. You have the power to make connections that never existed in your family—connections with other ACoAs in recovery. When you accept the identity of being an ACoA, entrance into the recovery community becomes possible.

Once you comfortably identify yourself as an ACoA, you will be ready to enter the *Core Issues Stage.* The Core Issues Stage is a time when ACoAs ferret out all the ways that the distorted relationship to willpower learned from their alcoholic parent continues to affect them. In this third stage of recovery, the intense control that ACoAs exert over themselves and the rest of the world is gradually relinquished. Their constant protection against chaos and unpredictability is gradually relinquished. They begin to look for people whom they *can* trust. And they begin to connect with their deeper experience instead of putting most of their energy into maintaining "normal" facades.

When the Core Issues Stage nears completion, many people in recovery discover that they are entering a new phase of life, called the *Integration Stage.* I hesitate to describe this stage, and the next, because so many ACoAs are prone to feel ashamed for not having arrived at them yet. Many attempt to achieve these goals by *understanding* them, then trying to imitate them. Unfortunately, putting on a "better" facade is still the same process as putting on any other facade; it's more of the "same old same old." In the Integration Stage, people no longer put on facades in order to appear different from who they are. Their guiding principle becomes their own sense of integrity, not what someone else might think.

In deciding whether to tell someone about their anger, for example, ACoAs in the Integration Stage look inward to see whether communicating their anger increases, or decreases, their sense of integrity. If expressing their anger is intended primarily to hurt another person, this violates their own sense of integrity, and they will remain silent. Conversely, if they are remaining silent in order to please others, this violates their sense of integrity, and they will speak. The Stage of Integration is a time of looking inward for guidance and using one's sense of wholeness as the gauge. It is important to understand that no one "figures out" how to get into this stage. The intellect is inadequate to achieve integrity by itself. The Stage of Integration requires experience with your emotions and with trusting others. It *happens* to people when the time is right. And the time is never right for people who are trying to rush their recovery.

Recovery often begins when people acknowledge and embrace the powerlessness that exists in all of our lives. It culminates in the *Genesis Stage,* when people can embrace the power that *does* exist for us all. Before the Genesis Stage, people in recovery are often justifiably afraid of exploring feelings of power. In fact, they are to a large extent recovering *from* the problems created by their distorted views of what should rightfully be under their power. Allowing themselves to feel powerful again often feels like backsliding. They feel as if they are regressing to the point that old problems are reemerging.

But the human condition contains both areas of powerlessness *and* areas of great power. During the Genesis Stage, people are clear enough about the natural limits to human power that they can exercise the power which is legitimately theirs. They are no longer seduced into thinking that they can control everything, just because they can control some things. For example, during the Genesis Stage, an ACoA may take the initiative to sponsor a new Alateen group. At the same time that he feels entitled to start the meeting, he recognizes his powerlessness to make people attend.

The Genesis Stage is a time of initiative, creativity, and empowerment. It is a time of generativity. The concept of serenity, described as the culmination of recovery in AA, is a part of Genesis. It is a time when ACoAs feel fully entitled to be whoever they are. There is little fear, and few things are forced. Life is lived with vitality, because it is lived within its limits. The past is in its place, and no longer has power over the present.

One paradox of recovery is that those who focus too much on completing the journey never achieve their goal, whereas those who learn to enjoy the journey itself no longer need to reach their destination for the journey to be a success. And, as a result, those who focus primarily on the journey itself are most likely to find themselves at their destination. The best advice is to focus your attention on practicing honesty, welcoming feelings, and entering community; and let the milestones of Identification, Core Issues, Integration, and Genesis arrive at their own pace.

· · · · · · · · **EXERCISES** · · · · · · ·

> When I left home, I told myself I'd never depend on another person as long as I lived; and I never did, even through three marriages.
>
> Then ten years ago, my little sister told me she was in therapy. I couldn't believe that she could talk to a stranger about our family. When I told her I didn't think she had any problems, she said she was an expert at fooling people. Then two years ago my brother said *he* was in therapy, and asked why I wasn't. It took me another year, but I finally called someone. I was so scared, and so smug, and intellectual. It took me a year before I figured out how to use therapy, but now I have more hope than I've had since the days I ran away from home as a kid.
>
> Susan

During the eighteen weeks our groups meet, a subtle transformation begins to take place. As a result of the honesty and feelings members share with one another, the group starts to feel like a healthy family. The following vignette illustrates the healing that occurs:

When Estella came to the group she immediately claimed the chair closest to the door. Week after week, she sat almost motionless with her coat on and her purse in her lap. Her dark eyes focused on each person speaking and occasionally she would nod her head in acknowledgment. When she did speak, her voice trembled with fear. It seemed that she could bolt out of the room at any minute.

During the discussion of guilt and shame, the atmosphere in the group was almost luminous with a sense of openness and vulnerability. Mark commented on how at that moment he felt as if he were in a church.

Silently, tears rolled down Estella's cheeks. One by one, group members noticed and turned their gaze toward her. At first no one was sure what to do. Slowly her tears gave way to a muffled sob. Estella raised her hands to her eyes and cried.

No one interrupted. For ten long minutes, the group held Estella in their silence without trying to fix her, stop her tears, or change the subject. In the moment before the group was to end, Bob reached over and touched her hand. "Thank you," she said, "to *all* of you."

The next week, Estella took off her coat for the first time.

Estella had grown up in a family where violence erupted quickly and without warning. Because her alcoholic father was unable to keep a steady job, the family often had to leave town on a moment's notice. As a result, Estella lived in a constant state of readiness to be uprooted. Removing her coat after so many weeks of being on guard was a profound expression of her trust that no one in the group intended to harm her. For Estella, this was the beginning of a healing transformation that changed her life.

The exercises in this chapter explore where you are in the healing process. The information, insight, and understanding you gain from these exercises will help you evaluate what Twelve Step Programs and therapy may contribute to your recovery.

Exercise 31:
The Stages of Recovery

The stages of recovery that we have described in this chapter are: *Survival Stage, Identification Stage, Core Issues Stage, Integration Stage,* and *Genesis.* In real life, people often find that they straddle more than one stage at a time. In this exercise you will explore the stages you are in at this point in your life. *Take approximately fifteen minutes to review your journal responses in the exercises up to this point in the workbook.* Use the journal to record your responses to the following questions:

1. What stage of recovery does most of your writing reflect?

I've read a zillion recovery books this last year, so I thought I should be in the Integration Stage. But after going back through my journal, I honestly think I'm still in the Identification Stage. I'm really just beginning to have feelings about my father's drinking and to look at how codependent I am. I'm a perfectionist; I'm miserable at taking care of myself; I work so hard, I'm always on the verge of exhaustion; I have an ulcer; I smoke like a fiend; I've always believed that if you just put more effort—what you call willpower—into anything, you can fix it. . . . And, if you haven't noticed, I'm a bit judgmental and critical.

Susan

2. What other stages of recovery did you find illustrated in your journal?

Susan described the following incident in which her Survival Stage had reemerged:

After reading about ACoAs for a year, my sister insisted that I try this group. I felt completely calm when I came for the evaluation session, until Jacques asked me what I hoped I would get from the group.

Suddenly I felt sadness well up and I started crying. I was totally surprised to hear myself talk about how lonely I felt. And I cried the whole time I talked about my father's drinking. After the session I felt better, at first; but I was really overwhelmed and scared by the depth of my sadness. I put off joining the group with the excuse that it was too expensive and I didn't have the time.

Now I see that I went back into my survivor mode for a month. I tried to deny that my tears in Jacques's office had any significance. But I could not push away the

loneliness and sadness I felt. At last I called to join the
group because I knew that I had to face the truth about
my family if anything was going to change for me. . . .
My sister and I had a good cry when I told her about how
I was really feeling and that I had decided to join the
group.

3. What circumstances most often lead to your slipping
   back to old ways of thinking, feeling, and behaving?

I had the most trouble when I lived with my family.
Every time I walked through their front door I disap-
peared into a fog. It takes me weeks sometimes to have
my feelings when I am with them.

Gail

Exercise 32: Aids to Recovery

The practices of Honesty, Welcoming Feelings, and Entering
Community constitute the practical work necessary for healing
and recovery. This exercise explores how you can use both Twelve
Step Programs and therapy as vehicles for integrating these important disciplines into your day-to-day life.

Twelve-Step Programs

At this point, we assume that you have attended several ACoA
meetings. If you have not attended a Twelve-Step ACoA meeting
yet, it is recommended that you do go to one and review Exercise 3 in the first chapter before continuing on.

Write your responses in the journal.

1. How do you feel about Twelve-Step meetings?

At first I thought it was a roomful of losers who just
didn't seem to have a very good handle on life. They
seemed *so* wounded that I didn't belong there.

I started noticing that most of the people at one
meeting were obviously well dressed. I know it's snob-
bish, but I felt more comfortable with people who I think

are like me. . . . Then I actually started to listen to people talk, and it became clear that we had a lot in common.

Susan

Susan reacted like many people who come to the meetings with preconceived ideas and attitudes. We all have judgments about who we are like and who we are different from. We tend to feel more comfortable with people we sense a kinship with and uncomfortable with those whom we see as the "other." By being honest about her reactions, Susan was able to use her feelings of kinship, regardless of how superficial, to help her listen. Once she listened to what was being said, she began to hear her own life history in the voice of virtually every person at the meeting.

2. What are your thoughts and feelings when everyone introduces himself with, "Hi, I'm Bob; I'm an Adult Child of an Alcoholic," and the group responds with "Hi, Bob!"?

3. How do you feel about the lack of cross-talk (the rule that prohibits people from commenting directly on one another during the meeting in order to create a safe, noninteractive environment)?

It drove me crazy. The first meeting I went to, a woman talked about how depressed she was, and how she had thought about killing herself. I couldn't believe that no one said a thing! Everyone just let her talk. In my head I'm screaming, "Go to a therapist! Get some Prozac!" I was very agitated, digging my fingernails into my hands, thinking "Somebody do something!"

Susan

Susan's first emotional response to the sadness and depression of the woman who spoke at the meeting was to try to rescue her. The intensity of her need to fix the woman's depression caused her to judge the program harshly. She assumed no one cared. By leaving the meeting early she didn't see the four or five people who went up to the woman later, hugged her, and exchanged phone numbers.

4. How do you feel when the rules of the meeting are not maintained by the secretary or the members?

5. What do you fear most about going to meetings?

My real fear is that I'll stand up and speak. . . . I've been in the program for about a year but have not spoken at a meeting yet. Speaking means that I'm letting people into my life more. It means that I am really joining the meeting. Even after a year in the program, I'm afraid to put both of my feet into the room.

Sharon

Sharon was still avoiding the practice of Entering Community, fearing that it would overwhelm rather than support her.

6. What negative experiences have you had in a Twelve-Step meeting?

7. What positive experiences have you had?

8. What do you think about the focus on a Higher Power?

Most ACoAs have found that their particular religious traditions are quite compatible with the Twelve Steps. In fact, the practices and disciplines important to your religious/spiritual tradition may be of tremendous benefit in recovery as well. For example, many religious and spiritual traditions encourage the following:

- a rigorous honesty with oneself

- a relationship to a Higher Power, God, or a teacher

- an interdependent relationship to a supportive community

- a contemplative, meditative process

- an inner journey

If you have any fear that the Twelve Steps conflict with your primary spiritual practice, we encourage you to talk to someone within your tradition about these concerns.

9. What religious experiences have made it difficult for you to relate to a Higher Power?

10. Do you think the idea of powerlessness is used to avoid responsibility?

I used to think people who cried in meetings were weak. Now I'm starting to see how these judgments are really my own struggle with being in control. There is a big part of me that would really like to cry, too. This is really scary stuff.

Bill

11. What is hard about reaching out to someone and asking for a sponsor?

It was a matter of trust for me. I didn't want to let someone have any influence over me. And underneath that, I was afraid I'd be judged.

Denise

Denise had been in a program for nearly two years before she considered getting a sponsor. When she asked around for names of good sponsors, three people had positive things to say about Doreen, a long time Program member who was ten years older than Denise. She watched Doreen at meetings for several months before she finally got up the courage to ask her to be her sponsor.

Doreen invited Denise out for coffee, where they talked for two hours about what Denise was looking for in a sponsor—and what Doreen could offer. They made a mutual agreement to talk once a week on the phone and to have coffee together after their regular Thursday meeting. . . . Denise was taking another step to enter the recovering community.

12. How do you feel about the Twelve Steps?

13. Which step do you have the most trouble with? Why?

14. Which step do you find the most comforting? Why?

Psychotherapy

Many people have preconceived ideas about therapy, therapists, and people who use therapy. "Preconceived ideas" is a polite phrase for prejudgments, or even prejudice. Although not everyone in recovery needs to be in therapy, the right therapist *has* aided many people in their healing. In order to decide whether therapy could be beneficial to you, you need to be aware of the judgments and feelings that may cloud your thinking. We encourage you to respond to the following questions:

1. List in your journal all the reasons why you *can't, shouldn't, or won't* get into psychotherapy. If you are in therapy now, list the reasons you used to delay getting started, or that make you think of quitting from time to time.

    Here's part of Susan's list:

    1. Too expensive.

    2. They just tell you what you want to hear.

    3. Therapy's only for sick people.

    4. If I'm really honest, I'm afraid I'll be judged and analyzed.

    5. I'm afraid I'll start crying and I won't be able to stop.

    6. I don't want to tell a stranger my deepest fears; I'm afraid they'll be used against me.

    7. I can do this myself.

2. Circle the reasons on your list that are based on fear. Identify whether the fear is about any of the following:

    - fear of feelings
    - fear of the unknown
    - fear of becoming dependent on your therapist
    - fear of discovering something ugly about yourself
    - fear of being vulnerable
    - fear of how friends or family will react

3. Circle the reasons based on your distorted relationship to willpower, such as:

  • I should be able to do this alone.

  • I don't need anyone.

  • Therapy is for sick people.

4. Now look at the reasons that are left. Are any of them based on ignorance of how therapy works?

5. If you have had negative experiences in therapy, list the things you found disappointing, hurtful, upsetting, painful, irresponsible, unethical, or criminal.

6. If you are in therapy, complete the following three lists:

  A. In what ways are you being less than honest with your therapist?

  B. What feelings are you keeping out of the therapy?

  C. In what ways are you avoiding being closer to your therapist?

**Exercise 33:
Recovery Planning—
Your Self-Esteem List**

Recovery Planning is an exercise developed by Sharon Wegscheider-Cruse for her workshops for ACoAs and co-dependents. The exercise has four steps.

  • The first step is to identify ten relationships or activities that have a direct impact on your sense of well-being.

  • The second step is to focus on one of the categories and identify behaviors associated with it.

  • The third step is to define a very small behavior and plan how to modify it during the next week.

  • And the fourth step is to act on your plan in a way that assures success.

The troubles you are likely to have with this exercise will be either aiming to make too many changes within the span of a single week or discounting the importance of changes that are small enough to be accomplished within one week. The purpose of this exercise is to begin the process of "chunking" change down into humane, manageable pieces. Once you can find steps that are small enough to take with predictable success and then string enough of these steps together day by day, your progress along the path of recovery will be steady and sure.

1. Begin a Self-Esteem List by listing, on the left side of a journal page, ten areas of your life that have a direct impact on your sense of well-being and self-esteem.

In the sample that follows, Bob listed the following ten activities and relationships as those having the greatest impact on his sense of well-being:

health	work
friends	wife
relaxation	house
exercise	having fun
creativity	relationship with God

You may list some of the same things but will undoubtedly identify others that apply more to your life. Give yourself a few moments to identify those areas that truly have meaning for you and have an impact on your self-worth.

2. Next, choose one of the categories to work on during the upcoming week and list *at least* five specific behaviors associated with the category you have chosen.

Be sure that the area you choose is one that you are inclined to deal with during the next week. Bob chose to work on his friendships. He tends to isolate himself and avoid friendships by working too much and keeping himself busy with tasks at home or the office. He listed the following kinds of behavior associated with his friendships:

• playing poker
• going to the movies

- going out to dinner
- inviting friends over for dinner
- helping a friend with some task
- inviting out-of-town friends to visit for the weekend

3. Now choose *one* of the listed behavior patterns and develop a plan to modify it in a way that will enhance your self-esteem during the next week.

Bob chose to work on "inviting a friend over for dinner." He decided to invite his friend Nathan and his wife, Gloria, over for dinner because he'd been to their house several times without returning the invitation, and he realized he hadn't seen them for some time.

Before you take the final step, ask yourself one more time, "Is this plan simple enough that I am guaranteed success within the next week?"

Bob thought about this and realized that there was a chance he would begin feeling nervous about calling his friend. His way of handling this anxiety was to promise that he would send a written invitation by the end of the week if he had not gotten around to calling them.

4. Once you've confirmed that it will be easy to complete your action in the following week, the only thing left is to put your plan into action.

Bob reported the following experience with the exercise:

My friend Nathan was not able to come over for dinner this week. But I still felt successful, because my goal was to reach out to him and his wife. I felt good about inviting them; and he sounded sincere when he asked me to call next week when his schedule settles down. So I already have my plan for next week. I'm going to continue letting him know that I want to get together.

Bob

In each of the following chapters we return to this Recovery Planning exercise to review how the previous chapter's recovery plan worked and to plan the next actions to take. The goal is primarily to get into the habit of planning actions that support your sense of self-worth and assuring that your plans are realistic enough to guarantee success! Over time, you should be able to make progress in each of the ten areas you have listed.

Feeling Exercise

Take time to do the Feeling Exercise as described in chapter one (page 15).

Journal

The following questions can help you further explore where you are in your recovery:

1. Look back over your responses to the questions on the stages of recovery. Did you struggle with a false sense of humility and hesitate to acknowledge the work and healing you have accomplished? If so, why do you imagine that you do this?

2. In what ways did you overestimate your recovery? Why do you imagine that you do this?

3. When you were exploring how you feel about the Twelve Step Programs, did it feel like a betrayal to acknowledge anything negative? Describe these feelings.

4. Have you found yourself using the program for reasons other than for what it is intended—i.e., to get dates?

5. If you have had a positive experience in psychotherapy (either individual or group), describe how the experience has been beneficial to you in your recovery and healing.

The success of psychotherapy can depend on a number of variables including: the therapist's training, theoretical perspective, clinical experience, and understanding of the problems of adult children of alcoholics and alcoholic families; the timing in your life; your motivation and capacity to tolerate the experience of therapy; your resources (financial, emotional, social, spiritual); and the match between you and your therapist. An ACoA may have a frustrating experience in therapy if the match isn't right, if the therapist asks you to do things you don't feel comfortable with, and if the therapist seems to be at odds with your understanding about the importance of having grown up in an alcoholic family. Unfortunately, there is no sure method for finding the right therapist. We have included a book in the recommendations below that may prove helpful.

6. Describe how it felt to list the specific areas and behaviors that are central to your self-esteem. If you had trouble developing a plan for modifying your behavior, describe the difficulties you had.

7. If you carried out your plan but found ways to downgrade this accomplishment, describe the reasons you gave yourself for dismissing your success.

★ Recommendations

The number of books devoted to healing is almost overwhelming; however, a great deal of material is repeated in each. If you have not already read some of the original works in this area, we strongly recommend *Al-Anon's Twelve Steps and Twelve Traditions* and *Alcoholics Anonymous* (the Big Book). We also suggest the following:

A Time to Heal, Tim Cermak

The Courage to Change, Dennis Wholey

Becoming Your Own Parent, Dennis Wholey

Guide to Recovery, Herbert Gravitz and Julie Bowden

When Talk Is Not Cheap or How to Find the Right Therapist, Mandy Aftel and Robin Lakoff

Films that detail the path of recovery from alcoholism and drug addiction include: *Clean and Sober*, with Michael Keaton, and the TV movie *The Story of Bill Wilson*, with James Woods.

Chapter Twelve

Honesty

Healing begins with honesty. When you practice honesty in all your affairs, your awareness is less distorted by your judgments. For example, you may begin to see your parents' alcoholism differently when you no longer condemn them on moral grounds. And you can gradually accept the realistic limits of willpower when no longer condemning yourself as inadequate. Like much of recovery, total honesty is a goal that is only occasionally attained, and it is rarely sustained. But it is a pivotal part of recovery and can be the beginning of real wisdom. Honesty greatly facilitates healing by weeding out the unrealities and distortions that choke the truth.

The discipline of honesty often develops slowly. It violates many of the rules governing alcoholic families—rules that support denial and view speaking the truth as betrayal. But once honesty achieves momentum, it can expand exponentially throughout your life. When this happens, you begin to identify more with your healing than with your wounds.

Strong forces work against being honest. Fear is one of the first in line.

Many ACoAs are intensely afraid that there is something festering at their very core. You may be so convinced that you would be disgusted by what lies unknown within yourself that you avoid looking closely. Fear is a potent enemy of the truth. It pits your drive for self-preservation against the willingness to be honest with yourself.

Shame and pride are also potent enemies of the truth. They are twin horsemen that appear to be on opposite sides, but their horses share the same stable. Shame averts your gaze from the truth because it fears being shunned by those you love. And pride hides from the truth by putting on false displays to capture your imagination and leading you to believe that perfection is in your grasp. It is painful to watch these powerful horsemen race through the countryside within people, trampling the terrain before they are able to appreciate its natural state. They are both so pompous; one greater, and the other less, than anything that is humanly possible.

Fear, shame, and pride often combine into that chorus of voices described earlier as the Committee. In a sense, the Committee is a classic example of the "superego" running amok. For ACoAs, the Committee often speaks with the voice of a drunken parent. For example, when Bill described details of his alcoholic family, he quickly added, "But I'm probably blowing some of this out of proportion." I stopped Bill and asked what he had been thinking just before he uttered his disclaimer. "I thought that I was just trying to get people to feel sorry for me," he replied. When I asked if he recognized the voice his Committee used when it threw this thought at him, Bill did not hesitate; it had the same tone of voice his alcoholic mother had when she accused him of always feeling sorry for himself. The Committee is not so much a strict conscience as it is echoes still reverberating from the past.

In a sense, those ACoAs who were able to anticipate their parents' critical attacks were in the best position to cut them off at the pass. But, in the process, the voices got inside and became reflexes. Their existence no longer depended upon contact with the parent. The Committee became part of them; and, although people cannot extinguish their Committee, they *can* detach from it. That would mean being aware of when it is present and wasting no energy trying to control it.

For many ACoAs, the idea of no longer trying to control and exterminate the Committee seems counterintuitive. They have spent much of their life trying to quiet the Committee's voice. To allow it free rein might feel as dangerous as dropping your hands in the middle of a boxing match.

Boxing with the Committee is like boxing with a shadow. The

Committee gains most of its power by your efforts to control it. Shadows cannot hurt you, but continually jumping out of the way of a shadow can. You must also work to *observe* the Committee *without* judgment, if you are to find freedom from it. It is an echo. It is not you. It does not tell you much of importance about who you are today. Repeat, it is an echo. Let it be. And then move on.

Honestly observing yourself without judgment does not mean that you force yourself to stop making judgments. It means that you find a new place to stand to watch the judgments go by. It means that you detach from the Committee.

Within Twelve-Step recovery, self-observation without judgment lies at the core of the important concept of detachment. Unfortunately, detachment is one of the most misunderstood program skills. Virtually every Genesis group has a couple of members who think they are practicing detachment when they are unknowingly still involved in trying to control their feelings. For example, Marion reported that her husband had returned to drinking after nine months of sobriety. When other group members asked how this was for her, Marion sighed shallowly and said simply that she had detached from the whole thing. When I pointed out that this did not give me a very clear idea of what she was feeling, Marion seemed surprised. "Why, I'm not feeling anything. I let go of my anger."

Marion believed that feeling agitated about her husband's return to drinking would show a lack of recovery. She judged her feelings as being inappropriate and used her "detachment" to get rid of them. Unfortunately, the idea of letting go of feelings is more properly understood as *allowing* them to exist. We are called upon to let go of our efforts to *control* them. Detachment is a discipline of getting out of their way, largely by acknowledging their presence while not feeling compelled to act on them. We can detach from our judgments about them. We can detach from our efforts to control them. And we can detach our sense of identity and self-worth from the feelings we have. When detachment is practiced in a healthy way, people experience a return of their vitality. Feelings are free to flow through your life, without the hindrances and obstructions of being judged and attacked.

In working through the following exercises, Marion told the group that she was beginning to make some progress in detaching herself from her Committee's control. When it harangued her for feeling angry at her husband's relapse, she was able to step back and say, "I'm feeling angry, *and* the Committee doesn't want me to have this feeling. It is trying to shame me for feeling angry." Marion's victory was twofold. She acknowledged the anger, which was real. And she felt an unexpected sense of peacefulness as she watched the Committee flail about with decreasing success as she progressively detached from its judgments.

Healing begins with honesty. And honesty stems from looking at the world clearly, without the distortions of our judgments. With time, and practice, the discipline of honesty can become a way of life—the way of recovery.

· · · · · · ·   **EXERCISES**   · · · · · · ·

> I'm amazed at the way I judge myself. It's like I've got a nonstop, twenty-four-hour-a-day video camera that never blinks. It watches *everything* I do. I'm so used to it I almost never notice how pervasive it is.
>
> Denise

Cultivating clearer awareness can be instrumental to your recovery. The exercises below work toward further detaching from the judgments, and the Committee making them, that cloud and diminish your mindfulness.

Exercise 34: Practicing Mindfulness

This exercise guides you through a simple meditation called mindfulness practice. Many of you may have had experiences with meditation techniques through religious or spiritual groups. Some of you will even have an intrinsic sense of this practice naturally and find the experience familiar. For those of you who think about skipping this chapter because you've had some previous experience with meditation, we encourage you to give this a try regardless of your previous experience.

1. Set aside at least twenty minutes.

2. Find a quiet place where you won't be interrupted or disturbed.

3. Sit in a comfortable position that you can maintain without shifting or moving for the entire twenty minutes.

We recommend sitting upright, with your back straight and
erect, rather than lying down. (People tend to fall asleep when
lying down.) If you sit in a chair, it's best to keep your legs straight
rather than crossed to avoid the discomfort of blocked circula-
tion. You can place your hands either in your lap or on your legs,
palms upward or downward as you wish.

4. Once you've found a comfortable position, close your
eyes and sit quietly, without moving.

5. As you sit quietly, begin directing your attention to the
sensations in your abdomen, focusing on the changes as
you breathe.

Breathe naturally without forcing the breath one way or the
other. Notice that as you breathe in, your abdomen expands. As
you breathe out, your abdomen contracts. Notice all the fluctuat-
ing sensations as you breathe in and then out.

Allow your awareness to rest on the sensations of the breath,
without force, without strain, without struggle. Notice the sensations as they flow from the in-breath (reaching fullness) and then
to the out-breath (reaching complete expiration). Then the cycle
repeats itself. Follow this closely without interruption.

You may find that, although this is a simple process, it is not
necessarily easy. When sitting quietly it is normal for a variety of
thoughts (images, memories, internal dialogue), feelings (pleasant, unpleasant, and neutral), and sensations (sights, sounds,
smells, tastes, and tactile sensations) to interrupt awareness of
your breathing. These interruptions may be very subtle, but you
will probably find your awareness intermittently wandering to
one or another of them.

6. Each moment you notice your awareness momentarily
focusing on a distracting thought, feeling, sound, or
other sensation, simply note the thought as a thought,
the feeling as a feeling, the sound as a sound, or the sensation as a sensation—then return your attention to the
sensations of breathing in and out.

If you find yourself all of a sudden "waking up" and realizing you have been daydreaming or distracted for some time by thoughts, memories, or feelings, just notice your waking up and redirect your attention back to the sensations of the breath.

It is unnecessary to chastise or criticize yourself when your awareness wanders. In fact, at this moment, the thought, judgment, or criticism can become the object of your awareness like any other thought that has occurred to you. Note it as a judgment—the product of your restless mind—and then return your attention to your breathing.

7. Repeat this practice on a daily basis for the following week, and longer if you wish.

If you are inclined, increase the time gradually to an hour. The cultivation and development of awareness builds momentum. We encourage you to give it a try on a regular basis. Remember, if you have a hard time committing to regular practice, ten minutes occasionally is better than nothing consistently.

Exercise 35: Recovery Planning (continued)

1. Describe what happened with the recovery plan developed in the last chapter.

2. If you completed the plan, record how it felt to be successful.

3. If you did not complete the plan, record what got in your way.

4. Finally, formulate the next plan for changing one of the types of behavior associated with an area that has an impact on your self-esteem. Feel free either to continue working on the same area or to switch to a new area on your Self-Esteem List (chapter 11, exercise 33). After listing the specific kinds of behavior associated with this new area, choose one and develop a recovery plan to modify it. Keep your plans small. If you did not complete your last plan, be especially careful to keep this next one even smaller and easier to complete. Record the plan in your journal.

Feeling Exercise

Take time to do the Feeling Exercise as described in Chapter one (page 15).

Journal

After practicing the mindfulness meditation above each day for a week, we encourage you to respond to the following questions.

1. Did you have any fears about meditating?

> I was a little concerned at first. I was afraid you were going to ask us to do something I wouldn't feel comfortable with. We do meditations and guided imagery at church, so I was familiar with just sitting quietly. But I was afraid you'd ask me to do something I couldn't or didn't want to do. *Hmmm*—that feels familiar. I wonder what that's about.
>
> Denise

By paying attention to her reactions to the instructions for the meditation practice, Denise recognized familiar fears of being forced to do something she couldn't or didn't want to do. Although at the moment she was unable to discover just what felt so familiar about this feeling, her willingness to wonder about it will contribute to understanding her reaction at a later time.

2. What was it like to sit for the first time?

> First it took me a few minutes to find a comfortable way to sit without fidgeting. Then, after just three breaths, my mind started wandering from one thought to the next and back again. I'd be paying attention to my breath and then grab onto some worry or feeling or plan about the day and then ten minutes later I'd jerk myself back. I'd try to start over again with my breath but found myself judging how flighty my mind is instead. Then I remembered what you said about making the thought or the

judgment the object of my attention and it became
easier not to get sucked into berating myself. I noticed
the same old judgments and let them pass as excess
thoughts.

                                               Denise

Denise discovered that although it may sound simple, just
paying attention is not an easy task. Her mind was used to jumping around from one thing to another. After a month of practicing
mindfulness, however, she was able to stay present with her
thoughts and feelings just a bit more than at the beginning and
was encouraged to continue practicing.

  3. Was it more or less difficult than you expected?

Much more difficult . . . Absolutely! I thought I would
be able to stay focused right from the beginning. But the
more I tried to focus, the tighter my head felt. I think I
was trying to force it too much. After a few tries I gave up.
                                               Bill

Bill found himself quickly dissatisfied with his meditative sitting and asked me why he was having such a hard time. He described how he tried and tried to force his mind to stay put; but
the tighter he squeezed his attention to hold it still, the more it
jumped around. The more he tried to control his mind, the more
it became agitated. Finally, Bill gave up and just sat without trying
to meditate "correctly." Gradually, his mind calmed down and he
began sitting more easily.

  4. How was the experience different at the end of the
     week?

It's a bit easier. I don't drift off as often, and when I do I
catch myself quicker. Funny, I haven't been as self-
critical lately. When I make a mistake I notice it, but I
don't dwell on it as much as I used to.
                                               Denise

Denise took naturally to practicing mindfulness and had begun to notice some positive effects more quickly than most. She
accomplished in a week what takes most people a month or more.
As a result of her ability to keep a focus on the momentary
changes in her breath, she became less obsessed or possessed by

any given thought or feeling throughout the rest of her day. And when her self-critical side did come up, she didn't automatically latch onto the criticism and continue obsessing. She just noticed the thought, recognized it, and maintained her sense of balance.

★ Recommendations

For more information about the meditation practice, we recommend two books: *The Experience of Insight,* by Joseph Goldstein, and *Zen Mind/Beginner's Mind,* by Suzuki Roshi.

The film *Koyaanisqatsi,* directed by Godfrey Reggio with a music score by Phillip Glass, is an interesting cinematic meditation.

Two pieces of Al-Anon literature relate to this chapter's topic: *One Day at a Time in Al-Anon* offers daily meditations for the entire year, and the *Blueprint for Progress: Al-Anon's Fourth Step Inventory* is an important exercise in self-observations without judgment.

Chapter Thirteen

Honoring Feelings

Healing begins with honesty; but it only grows when you begin relating more honestly to your feelings. In chapter 4 we introduced the idea of welcoming feelings into your awareness more directly and fully. We now extend this idea to welcoming your feelings into the *world*—honoring them enough to act on them.

Giving voice to your feelings, needs, and ideas is an integral part of recovery because it honors your inner life enough to bring it out into the world. Traditionally, assertiveness involves techniques such as making "I" statements, giving information about your needs, repeating your desires rather than explaining them, and not taking "no" for an answer without reasserting your needs. But assertiveness involves something more fundamental than these techniques. It involves a willingness to make yourself more vulnerable, not less. And it requires the same detachment from your internal Committee practiced in the preceding chapter, except that now the detachment is from trying to control other people.

Assertiveness is an attitude that you take toward communicating—giving voice to inner experiences. It has nothing to do with getting other people to do what we want them to do. A common misconception is that assertiveness is measured by whether or not you get someone in a complaint department to give your money back when you return merchandise. Assertiveness has nothing to do with controlling, especially controlling others. When codependents believe that their success in assertiveness must be measured by getting others to do their bidding, they are still focusing on other people's behavior to judge their own self-worth.

You can be very successfully assertive even in situations in which you do not begin to get your way. For example, saying to parents that they are only welcome in your house when they have not been drinking is very successfully giving voice to your true feeling, whether the parents respond the way you want them to or not. In such situations, being assertive leads to feeling good about your own sense of integrity and behavior, although at the same time you may feel sad or angry at having your wishes disappointed. *Asserting yourself to others rests upon the same detachment that permits people to observe their feelings, needs, and desires without judgment.*

At times, assertiveness is an internal matter. For example, I may be encouraged by someone to carry a teddy bear around for a week to nurture my inner child. When I imagine doing this, I begin to feel embarrassed. But I think that I'm not supposed to feel embarrassed and try to banish this feeling.

My honesty is in jeopardy here. If I practice the discipline of honesty, I will treat my feelings of embarrassment as a fact, neither good nor bad. Next, if I am practicing assertion, I will not deny my embarrassment to myself. I will not bargain with myself, because that means deviating from being honest. Just as I will not let a store manager talk me into being satisfied with merchandise that I do not like, I sometimes must assert feelings to myself in order to keep them from being ignored.

This same attitude toward communicating feelings exists in relationships. In the above case I may decide to say to my friend that I am feeling embarrassed at the thought of carrying my teddy bear everywhere for a week. When the response is "Oh, you shouldn't feel embarrassed about that," assertiveness would lead me to say something like "Well, you may be right, but that does not change the fact that I *do* feel embarrassed." Perhaps you can imagine how the conversation might proceed from here:

Friend: "But you have a right to nurture yourself."

Me: "You are right; I do. But I still feel embarrassed at the thought."

Friend: "That's letting your shame-based family system still control you."

Me: "You may be right, but I still feel embarrassed at the thought."

Friend: "I feel fine about doing it; you should try it."

Me: "I'm glad you feel fine, and maybe I *should* try it. But I still feel embarrassed at the thought."

Friend: "Just make yourself do it, and the embarrassment will go away."

Me: "I *could* try that. And maybe I will someday. Right now, I feel too embarrassed."

Honoring feelings means giving them a voice both within yourself and in the outside world. It begins with being honest with yourself about your feelings in order to be honest with others. And it requires a detachment from how others react to your feelings, which is easiest to maintain when you remind yourself that the ultimate goal of asserting your feelings, needs, and thoughts is to experience the benefit of giving them a voice, not to change other people.

When I repeatedly tell my friend about embarrassment at the thought of carrying a teddy bear around for a week, I am having to trust that he will not denigrate me. I have to trust that he will not reject me because I am feeling something *he* doesn't, something he doesn't think *I* need to feel, or something that threatens him. I have to trust that he is capable of allowing differences to exist within our relationship.

At the same time, I must trust in my ability to detach from trying to control how others see me, because sometimes other people cannot tolerate differences. My friend might actually criticize me for my embarrassment. Can I trust that I am able to withstand such rejection without falling apart, being devastated, or talking myself into believing that my embarrassment is unimportant or does not actually exist? Can I trust myself to survive when others do not see and respect my vulnerability?

When ACoAs learn to welcome their feelings and then to honor them by giving them a voice in the world, the rewards can be astounding. After the following exercises, one group member spoke of feeling "light and calm, as though I were floating through the day. I almost felt disoriented by how easily I was moving through the world. The thing I kept coming back to was the realization that I had spoken honestly to my father for the first time in my life—directly and honestly."

Healing begins with honesty, and it grows with honoring your feelings.

· · · · · · · · **EXERCISES** · · · · · · · ·

I've always had a hard time being assertive, especially with men who are in authority. I'm *always* the one given extra work after our shift is done because the boss knows I won't say a thing about it.

Marion

Assertiveness is the process of stating your feelings and needs—clearly, succinctly, and without artifice or hostility. Being assertive is the culmination of a process that begins with gaining awareness of your feelings and needs, experiencing and naming them, and then giving them a voice.

Many ACoAs find voicing their needs a risky business, fraught with memories of old wounds and shielded against by layers of self-protection. The exercises below explore the barriers that block your assertiveness. Knowledge of your specific barriers will equip you better to begin experimenting with being assertive in your daily life.

This exercise focuses on the *reasons* you give yourself, both today and in the past, for not being assertive.

Exercise 36: Barriers to Being Assertive

1. Make a list in your journal of at least ten reasons you have had in the past, particularly in your childhood, for not expressing your needs.

   Notice whether you find yourself using similar justifications and rationalizations as you did with the exercises in chapters 3 and 5.

Here's part of Marion's list:

1. I was afraid someone in my family would go crazy.

2. I was afraid my mother couldn't handle my needs.

3. I thought my mother would fall apart.

4. I was afraid something terrible would happen.

5. I was afraid if I asked for something I wouldn't be loved.

2. Now reflect on your life today and list ten reasons that you currently use for not being assertive.

Exercise 37: I Have the Hardest Time Being Assertive When . . .

This exercise focuses on *the present-day situations and relationships* in which you tend to retreat from acting assertively.

Across the top of a journal page, write the words "never," "seldom," "occasionally," "often," and "usually." Then place each of the following phrases under the proper column.

"I am (never, seldom, occasionally, often, usually) able to ask for what I need _____."

at work	with my children
with coworkers	in restaurants
with friends	when choosing a movie
with close friends	while shopping
with acquaintances	in school
with authority figures	when buying a car
with my father	with salespeople
with my mother	with my therapist
with my lover	with my minister/priest/rabbi
with my spouse	with my sister
with my grandfather	with my brother
with my grandmother	in my group

Marion thought a great deal about her life and her relationships and admitted that she had the most trouble being assertive
with her father, less with her brother and mother, and the least
with her sisters. She also realized she had a hard time being assertive with her husband, her boss (who is also a man), and her
male therapist. She has the easiest time with her women friends.
After some thought, Marion ventured a guess about her difficulty
with men: "They're all my father. It's as though I see him in all the
men I know. Amazing. I never realized how I do that."

Here's Marion's list:

| "I am able to ask _____ for what I want /need . . ." | | | | |
Never	Seldom	Occasionally	Often	Usually
my father	my mom	my older sister Tara	my sister Cia	girlfriends
my boss	my brother	my children	my cousin Sara	
authority figures	my husband			
the phone company	in a restaurant			
the bank	at the laundry			
	mechanics			
	at the grocer			
	salespeople			

Now that you have identified the situations and relationships in
which you have a difficult time being assertive, you are ready to
visualize *what it would look and feel like to take a first step toward
giving voice to your needs.* The following exercise creates an image of your acting assertively, then explores your willingness to
take a first step toward that image.

**Exercise 38:
One Small Step**

1. Review your responses to the previous exercise.

2. On a page in your journal, make a list of the people
    and situations in which you have a difficult time being

assertive in descending order of difficulty, tension, and anxiety.

At the top of the list will be the situations and people you have the most difficult time being assertive with and at the bottom, those you have an easier time with.

3. Look over this list and choose one of the items toward the bottom.

4. Underneath the list you have just created, describe the way you tend not to be assertive in the relationship or situation you've just chosen.

Here's Marion's example:

> I go to my favorite restaurant once a week. I order the same thing: a well-done steak, french fries, and a Coke. It's a treat I give myself, and I really look forward to it. I'm from Texas and we like our meat burnt. Unfortunately, Californians don't know what "well done" really means because every single time, it's too rare and I just can't bring myself to ask the waiter to take it back.

5. Now describe how you could act more assertively.

Remember, assertiveness does not mean acting rudely, with anger, or aggressively. People do not feel humiliated or deprecated when they encounter healthy assertiveness. It *does not* mean acting in any way that would cause harm to anyone. It simply means being clear and direct about what you want.

Here's Marion's vision of acting assertively:

> The next time the waiter brings me a steak that isn't done enough, I know I'll be scared. I'll probably break out in a sweat, but I could politely ask him to come over. I'll show him the steak and describe in more detail what I mean by "well done." At this point I know my voice will be quavering, but I'll ask the waiter if he could take it back to the kitchen and have it cooked some more.

Marion was able to visualize how she might act assertively as well as how she would probably feel in the process. She continued to visualize her new option on a daily basis and, even though we had not suggested that she actually carry out her new vision, after a week she found herself feeling less and less anxious at the prospect of asking for what she wants at her restaurant.

The following week when she went back, she ordered her usual well-done steak, french fries, and a Coke. When the waiter turned to go to the kitchen, Marion got his attention again and nervously explained exactly what she meant by "well done." The waiter was surprised. He asked, "Isn't that the way you always get it?" Marion felt herself shrinking. It was all she could do to say that the steak had always been undercooked for her taste. When the steak arrived, it was perfect. There was no need to ask for it to be taken back.

Marion's only comment to the group was "It was so easy that I can't believe I ate meat that was half cooked for all those years when all I had to do was ask for something else."

6. At least once a day, remind yourself of the image you have of acting more assertively in the situation you chose. What would it take to get you to begin putting this image into action?

Most of our group members find themselves having a difficult but not impossible time envisioning assertive ways of acting, especially when they've chosen something from the bottom of their list. Some people end up frustrated, sabotaging themselves by choosing something from their list that is too emotionally charged and threatening. If this has happened to you, you may want to pay special attention to the process of "chunking things down" in the exercise we call the Self-Esteem List (chapter 11).

1. Describe what happened with your recovery plan from last chapter.

2. If you completed the plan, record how it felt to be successful.

3. If you did not complete the plan, record what got in your way.

Exercise 39: Recovery Planning (continued)

4. Finally, formulate the next plan for changing one of the types of behavior associated with an area that has an impact on your self-esteem. Feel free either to continue working on the same area or to switch to a new area on the Self-Esteem List (chapter 11, exercise 33). After listing the specific kinds of behavior associated with this new area, choose one and develop a recovery plan to modify it. Keep your plans small. If you did not complete your last plan, be especially careful to keep this next plan even smaller, thus easier to complete. Record your plan below.

Feeling Exercise

Take time to do the Feeling Exercise as described in chapter one (page 15).

Journal

After having explored your barriers to acting assertively and visualizing an assertive response to an old situation, we encourage you to take the time to respond to the following questions in your journal:

1. What was it like to list your barriers to being assertive?

2. What was it like to acknowledge the specific situations and relationships in which you have difficulty being assertive?

3. Did you learn anything about yourself in this chapter's exercises? Describe what you learned.

4. Do you have any sense of what you are afraid you might do if you became more assertive?

5. If you asserted yourself in a familiar situation, as Marion did, describe what the experience was like. What were the benefits, and the costs, of being more assertive?

★ Recommendations

Taking the step from a lifetime of fear and self-protection into a more assertive stance toward the world is an emotional and spiritual risk that tests our integrity and strength. Two movies illustrate the struggle to honor your feelings: *Guilty by Suspicion,* with Robert De Niro, and *Grand Canyon,* with Mary Mc-Donnell.

Two books are also particularly useful: the classic *When I Say No I Feel Guilty,* by Manuel Smith, Ph.D., and *How to Say No to the One You Love,* by Peter Schellenbaum.

Chapter Fourteen

Entering Community

Children raised in dysfunctional families often experience more pain than comfort when depending on others. Many ACoAs learned early in their lives to depend primarily on themselves. They hide their vulnerability from others. They have little or no experience that families and friends can make their burden lighter to carry, rather than merely add to that burden. As a result, many ACoAs feel anxious when they have to rely on others' good will. They have difficulty entering into community.

This difficulty can be seen most clearly in the spiritual life of adults from alcoholic homes, for spirituality stems largely from the experience of being one part of a far greater whole. Many of you may feel great anger toward God for allowing you to be trapped in alcoholic families and for failing to answer your childhood pleas for help. You may fear your spiritual impulses. Or you may have no sense of your spiritual life and no willingness to open to it.

The relationship with your parents provided your first lessons about whether or not the universe can be trusted. As an infant, you were introduced to the experience of being one part of something far greater by your relationship with your parents. When this vulnerable relationship is comforting and good, it can shepherd you into trusting relationships with others and with the wider world. When this relationship is the source of too much incomprehensible pain, it can push you away from trusting anything else.

Spirituality is, first and foremost, an *experience*. It is the experience of feeling intimately connected to a universe that dwarfs us as individuals. Many people have such an experience in places of great natural beauty—the seashore, a redwood grove, in the mountains. Others have it when holding a newborn baby. During such times there is a sense of belonging, of completion, and of meaning.

All people experience a longing for meaning; and those who have been traumatized have the greatest need for this longing to be satisfied. Spiritual experiences involve the meaning of your relationship to the whole, whether to the whole of life on earth, the universe, or to powers that suffuse and exist beyond this universe. Spiritual concerns are ultimate concerns. As our spirituality matures, our experience of the whole, of which we are only one infinitesimal part, also changes. As spirituality matures, our sense of what is of ultimate concern evolves. Spirituality is the search for deepest meanings, through deepest relationship.

When Alcoholics Anonymous developed, there was a profound awareness of how most alcoholics become spiritually bankrupt, foundering upon the rocks of pride and "self-will run riot." It is the quintessential alcoholic attitude to believe that a person must rely only upon one's self if self-esteem is to be regained. Believing that one needs help, or even that help is available, is anathema to the remarkably self-centered universe inhabited by alcoholics and other drug addicts. Words such as *surrender* and *humility* characterized AA from the beginning. And AA was a spiritual program from the outset, and at its very core. It understands that part of the *dys-ease* of being alcoholic is being so self-contained and isolated that normal human limitations must be denied. This is tragic. It is illusory. It cannot be done. As the best history of AA is titled, alcoholics can recover only by accepting that they are *Not God*. We are only part of the whole.

The good news is that, although normal human limitations cannot be denied, they can be transcended. By accepting the reality of limitations, people are more likely to open themselves to more healthy relationships with others, and with the whole. Just as "I" must accept that the conscious part of my mind is unable to control what feelings exist and emerge into awareness, so I must accept that relationships cannot be controlled. I am unable to deal with relationships on my own terms. Dealing with relationships on my own terms is not truly being in relationships. If I am dwelling in an attitude that focuses exclusively on my efforts to control and manipulate a relationship, "I" am not dwelling in the relationship. Sobriety requires giving over some control of the relationship to others. It requires a dependence on others to treat me benevolently. It requires accepting that the relationship is an entity that is larger than either of the people making up the relationship. No *one* person can create or maintain the relationship on his or her own. Attempts to do this are, by definition, not being in relationship.

This concept of being one part of a large community is so difficult to comprehend that AA does not ask people to *comprehend* it. Instead, the organization takes a spiritual approach, which requires only that we accept and experience this perspective rather than analyze and understand it. The second and third steps throw down the gauntlet before prideful self-sufficiency. "[We] came to believe that a power greater than ourselves could restore us to sanity . . . [and we] made a decision to turn our will and our lives over to the care of God *as we understand Him* [italics in original]." These steps are no less important for adults who grew up in chemically dependent families to ponder than for the alcoholic.

Like their alcoholic parents, many ACoAs rebel at the spirituality that Twelve Step Programs unabashedly promote as an avenue to free people from their addictions and compulsions. Most have very understandable reasons for rejecting anything that even hints of spirituality. Some had their earliest images of God heavily contaminated by childhood experiences, and they resolved never to expose themselves again to anything so scary or malevolent. Especially because children *do* often develop their first image of God from the way they see their parents (sort of a "super" parent figure), this could be quite a scary image if the parent you used as a basis for God is alcoholic. For others, parents' rejection of religion, or use of overly restricting religiosity, affected their own sense of what spirituality has to offer. Unfortunately, families stressed by alcoholism and other drug addictions rarely provide their children with thoughtful models of how to relate to spirituality.

Fortunately, ACoAs in recovery often reach a point where honesty about their feelings and the willingness to experience feelings for their own sake lead them to acknowledge that the universally present spiritual impulses course through them as well. What is the proper stance to take toward these needs, from the perspective of recovery? Grant them the same legitimacy you give to all other feelings—and detach from them.

Detachment from spiritual impulses—what does this mean? It means nothing less than trusting that they have a right to exist. It means releasing them to follow their own course, even when this causes you to begin entertaining thoughts that do not fit with your self-image. Perhaps you have never been one to believe in God. Perhaps you have denigrated people who seek direction from a Higher Power. Detaching from your spiritual impulses means allowing them to exist and develop. Despite all your experience, which has often taught you (especially as a child) that others cannot be relied upon, recovery calls upon you to try it again anyway. You take a leap of faith.

If this entire chapter seems like pressure to believe in a god, I can understand this misperception. When group members raise this objection, I reduce the topic to one simple exercise involving the Serenity Prayer: "God, grant me the serenity to accept the things I cannot change, courage to change the things I can, and wisdom to know the difference." Eliminate the "God" in the beginning if you wish; it makes no difference. The exercise I suggest is that you move away from trying to *understand* what this prayer means, or how it works. Instead, focus on how you think your life would feel *if,* somehow, you were able to live in complete accordance with the prayer's request. What do you imagine it would feel like to have great clarity regarding what is under your control, what is not, and acceptance of these realities? Concentrate on your image of what your life would feel like if you fully integrated this perspective. Form as detailed a picture as you can. And, if you like what you imagine, ask the universe (whether that means your unconscious, God, or something entirely nebulous) for the *willingness* to let this perspective develop within you. Don't ask for the perspective to develop. Simply ask for the *willingness* for it to develop. Ask frequently and consistently. That's all.

In doing this, you will be relinquishing a *self*-centered relationship to the universe and opening yourself to something different. This attitude paves the way for entering community more effectively on every level—with family, friends, your local community, the web of all life which supports you and gave you birth, and perhaps even with a Higher Power.

• • • • • • • **EXERCISES** • • • • • • •

I remember the first time I felt a relationship with a Higher Power, God, whatever you want to call it. I was sitting in a hotel room in Los Angeles. I'd just given a presentation at a national nursing conference. It went great. But I was beating myself up over one minor error. I couldn't forgive myself. I was getting more and more depressed. I couldn't take in how well the talk went. I got nauseous. Hour after hour, I felt more and more miserable.

Finally, I realized I had no control over what was happening. I couldn't think myself out of this; I couldn't forgive myself. So I said to God, "I give up. Take this . . . it's yours!" In that moment all the depression, the criticism, and the pain began to vanish.

Sharon

Honest discussions of spirituality can be difficult because they require intense vulnerability on everyone's part. The following exercises explore experiences that may have contributed to, or interfered with, your spiritual awareness.

Exercise 40: The Experience of Transcendence

In the opening to this chapter, we described the experience of transcendence that people often have in places of great physical beauty—at the seashore, when holding a newborn baby, or when feeling the presence of God, for example. Transcendent experiences have a host of notable qualities, such as a deep sense of belonging, of being complete, and of meaning. Others describe a profound sense of calm, total absence of fear, feeling that everything is just as it should be, a great sense of connectedness and fitting into the scheme of things, and comfort with the immensity of the world. Time moves very slowly, if at all. Death seems to have no sting. Gratitude and awe seem to suffuse your feelings.

Transcendence is experienced differently by everyone. The same adjectives do not always apply. And the word *transcendence* may not be one that you have ever used to describe your experiences. The following exercise helps you identify and explore such experiences in your own life. (No examples from the group will be given in order to avoid narrowing your imagination.)

1. Begin a list of times when you most experienced the constellation of feelings we have called transcendence. Do not think in terms of spirituality or religion, but rather in terms of the basic feelings outlined above.

2. When you have listed as many events as you can, choose one that most stands out in your memory. Use your meditative practice to recall this memory as vividly as possible, including all the sights, sounds, physical sensations, and emotions you can remember.

3. Describe how it felt to meditate on the experience of transcendence.

A spiritual history records the experiences, insights, and relationships that have both contributed to and impeded your spiritual awareness and your relationship to a Higher Power. A spiritual history may include guidance from, or disappointment in, others, as well as moments of profound doubt, intense sadness, joy, or times when you reached into unknown depths for something greater than yourself. It may also include moments of intense challenge to your feelings, philosophy, and beliefs.

Exercise 41: A Spiritual History

Helpful Lessons

1. List the major positive events in your spiritual history.

Here's some of Sharon's list:

1. Age Five: I asked my mother what happened to dead people. She said they went to heaven. I spent all day thinking about what it would be like to be in heaven with my grandparents.

2. Age Ten: Watched a baby bird being born from an egg. Absolutely amazed by the gift of life.

3. Age Thirteen: Felt alone and depressed a lot that year. Spent hours and hours sitting by a stream watching the water.

4. Age Fourteen: In school we read the American Transcendentalists, Thoreau and Emerson. Profound effect on how I thought about life.

5. Age Nineteen: In a car crash. One pure moment of clarity and peace without fear. Felt a reassuring presence. Started going to church but the words didn't convey the feeling I had experienced. I preferred just to sit in a quiet park.

6. Age Thirty: Mom died. Life was black. I thought about killing myself. Depressed for a long time. Remembered my experience in the car crash.

2. Choose one of the events, relationships, or insights you have listed above and describe it in detail. If you have difficulty putting the experience in words in your journal, you might try other ways to express it: drawing, dance, etc.

Spiritual Nightmares

Unfortunately, some of us have been wounded spiritually. This exercise helps you remember and identify the harmful experiences that have hindered, distorted, repressed, or made you feel disillusioned about your spiritual development.

1. In your journal, make a list of the events you can describe as your spiritual nightmares.

Here's a part of Bill's list:

1. I'm seven. I'm lying on my back looking up at the sky with the grass swirling around me. I smell the

grass and the warm, moist earth beneath me. My father yells, "Git in here an' do something useful. Daydreamin's no good for nothin'." He was drunk.

2. When I was fourteen, my parents put me in a Catholic boarding school. All I remember from the first two years at that school was the face of this one Sister yelling at me, calling me stupid and bad. She hit the back of my hand with a ruler every time I gave a wrong answer. I got so scared, I couldn't think. I began to believe I was retarded. If God was speaking through her, I decided I didn't want to have any part of religion.

3. When I was having trouble in junior college, the counselor discovered that I have a learning disability. I'm dyslexic. I know the Sister didn't know better, but I still don't want to have anything to do with religion. . . . I'm an architect now, and to this day when someone passes me a ruler I jerk back my hand.

2. Now list the negative thoughts, judgments, preconceptions, and feelings about spirituality or religious life that you maintain to this day.

Bill wrote:

I do not forgive that teacher. And I do not forgive any religion that would submit kids to that kind of degrading experience. . . . I will not let myself even think about whether God exists; I hate him with such a passion for letting those things happen to me.

Transcendent experiences cannot be ordered to appear. They *happen* to us as unexpected gifts. The best we can do is to put ourselves in situations in which such experiences are more likely to occur.

Exercise 42: Putting Yourself in Good's Way

1. Make a list of places, events, and situations where the experiences of connectedness, belonging, and calm are most likely to happen for you.

Here's Estella's list:

1. Hiking
2. Walking on the beach, especially at sunrise
3. Jogging
4. Symphony concert
5. Empty cathedrals

2. Choose one item from your list and make a conscious effort to place yourself in this situation.

3. If you felt any qualities of transcendence, record them in detail. If you were not gifted with such an experience, record how it felt to open yourself to these feelings.

Estella wrote:

It was hard, but I forced myself to get out onto the beach before the sun came up. It was so cool that I had to lie down against one of the sand dunes. When the sunlight began to brush across the dunes, I watched hundreds of birds wake up and begin their day. It felt good to know that they are there whether I am watching them or not. They have been there for centuries and will be for centuries after I am gone. . . . There was a nice calm in knowing that.

Exercise 43: Recovery Planning (continued)

1. Describe what happened with your recovery plan from last chapter.

2. If you completed the plan, record how it felt to be successful.

3. If you did not complete the plan, record what got in your way.

4. Finally, formulate the next plan for changing one of the
    types of behavior associated with an area that has an im-
    pact on your self-esteem. Feel free either to continue
    working on the same area or to switch to a new area on
    the Self-Esteem List (chapter 11, exercise 33). After list-
    ing the specific kinds of behavior associated with this
    new area, choose one and develop a recovery plan to
    modify it. Keep your plans small. If you did not com-
    plete your last plan, be especially careful to keep this
    next plan even smaller and, thus, easier to complete. Re-
    cord your plan below.

Feeling Exercise

Take time to do the Feeling Exercise as described in chapter one
(page 15).

Journal 📖

Having recorded your spiritual history, we encourage you to respond to the following questions in your journal:

1. What was it like to chronicle your spiritual history?

2. What would it be like to share these very personal events
    in your life with others?

3. How has it been difficult to integrate these experiences
    into your daily life?

4. What was it like to write about your own spiritual night-
    mares?

It was very painful. I didn't sleep well for a few days. I
still feel this pit in my stomach like when I was a kid. I
can't believe how petrified I feel. . . . I am very thankful
that you ended with the exercise inviting us to experience a connection with my Higher Power today. I took
my kids to the zoo and just devoted the day to making
them happy. When I went in to check them before going

to bed, I felt my eyes tear up for the first time in a long time. They are the most precious things I could ever have; and when I take the time to really look at them, I feel that they are enough, just the way they are.

Bill

⭐ Recommendations

The following books offer a wide range of perspectives for exploring spirituality and your own experiences of personal transcendence:

Being Peace, Thich Nhat Hanh

Genesis: Spirituality in Recovery from Childhood Traumas, Julie Bowden and Herbert Gravitz

No Man Is an Island, Thomas Merton

Pilgrim at Tinker Creek, Annie Dillard (a modern-day *Walden Pond*)

Siddhartha, Hermann Hesse

The Way of the Sufi, Idries Shah

Waking Up, Charles Tart

Western Spirituality, edited by Matthew Fox

What is Religion, John F. Haught

Who Needs God, Harold Kushner

Films of spiritual transformation, the search for meaning, and inspiration include:

Mother Teresa, directed by Ann Petrie (1987)

Ossian: American Boy-Tibetan Monk, directed by Tom Anderson

The Power of Myth, Conversations with Joseph Campbell, directed by Bill Moyers

Field of Dreams, with Kevin Costner

Chapter Fifteen

Play and Spontaneity

Play and spontaneity are important to recovery because they involve healthy ways of relinquishing control and trusting that the outcome will be pleasant. We devote a full chapter to these topics because ACoAs are often ambivalent about cutting loose and having fun. You may already be aware of ways that you try to maintain control, even when playing. The price is a loss of spontaneity and a dampening of your vitality.

There are at least four very good reasons why you might have learned to distrust being playful and spontaneous:

First, the more violent, abusive, and traumatic your childhood was, the more difficulty you will have relaxing your vigilance enough to be playful and tolerating the experience of being out of control that lies at the core of being spontaneous. If you came to expect that danger always lurks just around the corner, it is probably hard to let your guard down and be spontaneous. And, if you learned to "leave your body" whenever emotions started getting too intense, you are likely to have trouble playing.

Second, the more you had to abort your childhood in order to take on your parents' responsibilities, the harder it is to feel good about being frivolous later on in life. As Estella explained:

I was the one who had to call the ambulance and tell the police what had happened when my father almost cut his finger off with the broken glass. My sisters were crying hysterically. My mother was sitting on the bed nearly paralyzed with fear and anger. And my father had passed out. If *I* had allowed myself the luxury of having my feelings, I probably would have run out of the house to get away from everything. But *someone* had to take care of things. *Someone* had to keep her head.

Third, you may not have had very good models to teach you healthy play and spontaneity. If people in your family were spontaneous and playful only when they were drunk, you probably came to associate spontaneity with dangerous unpredictability, and playfulness with irresponsibility.

Fourth, there is that cousin of shame—embarrassment. You may be familiar with the embarrassing discomfort that rises up when you let your guard down. Such embarrassment stems from a variety of experiences that children with chemically dependent parents have. You may have been mocked by a drunk parent simply for being smaller and weaker than the adults. Your parents may have played too competitively with you when they were intoxicated. Or you may have been publicly embarrassed by a parent's drunken behavior.

When members of a Genesis group enter the room for the meeting devoted to play and creativity, they are often feeling very anxious. Some are eager to let the child within them play. But others experience more fear than they have felt at previous meetings. When they find that the chairs have been removed for this meeting, their fear shoots up like a skyrocket. What is going to be expected of them? One member, Bill, immediately moved over to stand in the corner. When asked what he was feeling, he replied, "I'm just going to watch for a bit to see what you have planned." Fears of being out of control and embarrassed had flared into a firestorm for him.

We quickly assure people that the reason for devoting a meeting to play is not to embarrass anyone. Our goal is to help people face the degree to which their spontaneity has been blocked. No one gets points for *forcing* themselves to participate, because "acting spontaneous" would be a facade that hides their real issues about play. The goal is to see more clearly both how you defend against playfulness and to have some experience with abandoning yourself to play.

I must admit that I feel some nervousness myself each time I ask people to take off their shoes, and then put a Sesame Street aerobics tape on my daughter's Fisher-Price tape recorder. Just how silly are people going to think I really am? I use this fear to put me in touch with the reluctance that group members might also be feeling. Invariably, by the end of the ten-minute workout I am breathing more freely, my spontaneity has been released, and the fear has subsided. We play group games throughout the meeting (charades, tying and untying human knots, imitating animals, etc.), but we also continually observe how the invitation to play is resisted or given in to.

Many ACoAs use the metaphor of the "child within" to recapture the ability to play and nurture themselves. The child within can be thought of as the part of your identity that you learned to ignore, even to denigrate, *in precisely the same way you were ignored and denigrated as a child by your family.* Making friends with your inner child can mean giving that part of yourself a second chance. A potentially profound shift occurs when you stop trying to control what your needs are, in favor of becoming more honest about whatever they may be. This is part of the new relationship with self that recovery guides us toward.

Making friends with the child within is *potentially* a profound shift. However, there are two ways this powerful recovery tool can be used against you. Many ACoAs have been their own "parents" for far too long already. You may find that taking care of your inner child feels like one more responsibility to be shouldered. When an ACoA is taking care of his/her inner child, what part is doing the caregiving? Often it is the same unhealthy part that has always been doing too much caregiving! Sometimes it is more important for adults from chemically dependent families to find someone else to depend on—a Twelve-Step home meeting, a therapist, a sponsor, their Higher Power—and not to keep trying to take care of everything themselves.

Another way the metaphor of an inner child is misused stems from the fact that being a good parent is a lot harder than any child ever suspects. The "inner child" primarily wants to be indulged; but healthy nurturing involves a balance between indulgence and setting boundaries. It is possible, in the service of indulging your inner child, to be hurtful to others or to excuse irresponsible behavior, neither of which contributes to your recovery.

For example, one group member, Gail, promised to bring cookies for the last meeting. When she arrived without the cookies, she blithely reported that her inner child had wanted to stay in bed that morning, and so she had nurtured herself rather than "compulsively" take care of the rest of the group by forcing herself to get up and bake. Gail's reasons sounded good, and she used all the right words; but . . . she was mistreating both the group and herself. She not only disappointed the group but she also tried to keep them from having any negative feelings toward her by claiming the right of eminent "inner child" domain. In other words, she had simply indulged her inner child, not truly nurtured it.

The movie *Parenthood* illustrates the difficulty ACoAs have with spontaneity, and it provides a marvelous vision of recovery. Steve Martin plays an ACoA who cannot comprehend what his grandmother means when she says she prefers the excitement of a roller coaster to a carousel ("Nothing happens; it just goes around and around"). Later, while watching his own children in a grade-school play, Martin feels increasingly tense when the play falls into chaos. Suddenly, he begins hearing the ratcheting noise of a roller coaster climbing up the first hill. As his emotions swoop downward and veer around one turn after another, he gets pale and nauseated. He is holding on, feeling somehow responsible for the "disaster" happening on the stage. Then, he looks at his wife sitting next to him and sees her laughing at all the confusion, as though none of this is very serious, just the kind of thing that invariably happens with kids. Martin looks confused, then begins to realize that it's out of his control. It's *all* out of his control, but that does not mean that anything bad will necessarily happen or that he is responsible. He relaxes, begins to enjoy the ride, and the nausea disappears.

Healthy playfulness and spontaneity are two more steps on the path of recovery.

· · · · · · · ·   **E X E R C I S E S**   · · · · · · · ·

My wife tells me that I'm too stiff and could loosen up a
bit. I think I could loosen up *a lot*; but . . . whenever I
start to get the least bit playful, I shut down and get serious. I'm no fun at parties. At home with the kids, I'll relax
and open up a little bit. I'll get a little playful with our
son, then boom! I'll criticize something he's doing. He'll
cry. I get pissed and yell at him. He storms off. My wife
looks at me. I feel like a jerk . . . It's just like what happened when I was growing up.

Brian

In the week before the play session, group members talked
about their fears.

"I'm afraid you'll change the rules in the middle of the game,
and I'll feel humiliated in front of the group," Bill admitted.

"I'm afraid we'll be forced to do something physical, and I
won't be as good as other people," Gail said. "I know I'll be hard
on myself. I'm afraid I'll get flustered and cry in front of the
group."

"I'm afraid I'll feel like the outsider," added Sharon.

Once the fear was acknowledged, Bill, Gail, and Sharon told
of painful memories of how play had gone wrong in their families. Bill described how his father got drunk at a bowling party on
his thirteenth birthday. Gail told about how her father insisted
she play one on one with him in the backyard basketball court
whenever he was drunk, even though she was only five feet four
and he was six feet two and a college all-American. Sharon's ex-
tended family got together for a party every Friday night, and the
majority of the adults got so drunk that the police were often
called by neighbors. Sharon hid from the police in the kitchen
closet.

The following exercises help you explore your playfulness by
writing a fairy tale and visiting a playground and a toy store.

1. In your journal, write a short story about a child who
doesn't know how to play. Then, as a result of some

**Exercise 44:
The Magic of Play**

magic, the child becomes more spontaneous and playful.

Think of a child reading your story while you write it. Use as much imagination as possible, creating a new world or universe populated with interesting creatures and people.

    2. Now illustrate your fairy tale with crayons or colored pencils.

You may want to use a larger piece of paper than your journal. This is not an exercise in creating an artistic masterpiece; it is an opportunity to let the child in you dream, draw, and create.

**Exercise 45:
Child's Play**

    1. Visit a local playground and sit for half an hour just watching children play. Notice what kinds of activities they find pleasurable for their own sake: the rush from swinging, the thrill of going down a slide, climbing a jungle gym, jumping rope.

I did it. I went to a playground around the corner from my apartment, but I felt very self-conscious. I was sure I'd be seen as a trespasser and had a story all ready to tell someone if they asked me why I was there. I did watch the kids playing, though. I can't seem to remember my playing as a child. I was always helping my mom in the kitchen.

Susan

Susan was so self-conscious that she found it difficult to relax and enjoy watching the children play. What she did remember was how rare it was just to play. She remembered how frequently she was held accountable, to be the "big girl" in the family, act responsibly, and learn how to do the household chores. For Susan, "Idle hands are the devil's workshop," one of her mother's favorite sayings.

2. During the next week when you are by yourself, try some of the activities you saw the children doing. Keep at it for at least fifteen minutes.

Avoid choosing activities that involve intellectual development, goals, or competition (e.g., checkers, Scrabble, Nintendo, or most sports). Instead, choose more basic, sensate experiences like drawing, finger painting, dancing to music, climbing, wading in puddles—the sort of things three- to five-year-olds enjoy.

> I was surprised at how much easier this was than I thought, although I felt a little awkward at first. Once I got into it I really liked the big slide. For a brief moment, I totally forgot I was an adult and it was as if I were one of the kids. But when the fifteen minutes was up, I popped back into being an adult and then I felt a bit sad.
>
> Brian

Like Brian, you may find your efforts to recapture childhood tinged with many negative feelings. During the play session, Brian recalled how often he felt like an outsider as a child. He grew up always feeling different and fantasized that his real parents would find him and take him home. He even fantasized about being taken away by extraterrestrials. When we sat down toward the end of the meeting, Brian suddenly felt deep sadness and remembered the times · when he would sit in the playground—afraid to go home when his mother was drinking.

3. Now ask someone else to take part in some of the children's activities with you. At some point, try one of the activities that is really messy.

Now that you have watched children playing and tried some of their activities, it is time to give yourself a gift.

Exercise 46:
The Kid in the Toy Store

1. Find a toy store in your area. Spend at least half an hour browsing there.

    As you are browsing, notice which toys catch your

interest. Notice whether any particular toys bring back memories of your own childhood. Notice which ones you immediately smile at with a sense of recognition and remembrance, which ones you look at with desire, which ones you instinctively reach out to touch and hold.

If you are unable to get yourself into a toy store, try the children's section of a bookstore.

2. Buy yourself at least one toy. Try your very best to get whatever you want, without trying to figure out what would be best for your recovery. That turns it into work. Get something you want to play with.

3. In the next week free up at least one hour to play with your new toy.

I found this darling little doll just like the one I had as a kid. It was the first thing that caught my eye and I immediately knew I wanted it. It was a bit expensive, but I figured it had been a long time since I had a new doll. So I bought it.

And then I felt guilty. It's amazing. I thought I'd worked through all that guilt, but it popped right back up again. I started hearing voices telling me how many groceries I could buy with the money. How tight money is right now. How I really should keep to my budget. I almost returned it. When I finally got home, I cried for an hour.

Gail

Like Bill's visit to the playground, Gail's gift was colored by feelings from her childhood. The doll reminded her of the poverty that ruled her family. In Gail's family, money was tight partly because her father spent a lot of it on alcohol but also because they were extremely isolated in their community and would not reach out to others for help. When Gail's mother bought her a small gift for her birthday, Gail always knew that the money could have been used for more practical things, like clothes or food. She couldn't do anything about her father's drinking, but she took back her presents and saved the refund money for food when they needed it.

It took Gail a long time to feel that it was all right for her to keep the doll. She did return it once but then retrieved it. The doll, her doll, was a powerful symbol from her childhood. It stood for her willingness to let something precious into her world.

Exercise 47: Recovery Planning (continued)

1. Describe what happened with your recovery plan from last chapter.

2. If you completed the plan, record how it felt to be successful.

3. If you did not complete the plan, record what got in your way.

4. Finally, formulate the next plan for changing one of the types of behavior associated with an area that has an impact on your self-esteem. Feel free either to continue working on the same area or to switch to a new area on the Self-Esteem List (chapter 11, exercise 33). After listing the specific kinds of behavior associated with this new area, choose one and develop a recovery plan to modify it. Keep your plans small. If you did not complete your last plan, be especially careful to keep this next one even smaller, thus easier to complete. Record your plan below.

Feeling Exercise

Take time to do the Feeling Exercise as described in chapter one (page 15).

Journal

Take time to respond to the following questions in your journal:

1. When you were writing your short story about the child who discovers how to play, what parts were autobiographical?

2. What barriers still block the child within you from playing freely?

3. When you were watching children play, did any memories or feelings come up? Can you describe them?

4. What were your favorite games from as early as you can remember to age six?

5. What were your favorite games from ages seven through twelve?

6. What were your favorite games when you were a teenager?

7. What are your favorite games now?

8. What was it like to play the way a child does?

9. What was it like to ask someone else to play with you? If you felt afraid to ask someone, describe what your fears were.

10. What was it like to go to the toy store? Were there any toys, regardless of price, that you wished you could play with for a while? Which ones?

We encourage those of you who had a difficult time with the exercises in this chapter to give yourself other opportunities to explore your more playful nature. If necessary, this exercise can be completed over the next several months.

★ Recommendations

The playful, childlike side of your nature is encouraged by several books that you may never have read, or have forgotten. We cannot include all the possibilities and suggest you visit the children's section in your local bookstore.

Alice's Adventures in Wonderland, Lewis Carroll

The Cat in the Hat, Dr. Seuss

The Little Prince, Antoine de Saint-Exupéry

The Polar Express, Chris Van Allsburg

The Wizard of Oz, L. Frank Baum

Where The Wild Things Are, Maurice Sendak

The following films are recommended, either because of their absolute silliness or their captivating childlike qualities:

Duck Soup and *Animal Crackers*, with the Marx Brothers

The Gods Must Be Crazy, Warner Brothers

Fantasia, the Disney classic

Beauty and the Beast, Disney

The Never-Ending Story, Twentieth Century–Fox

The Muppets Go to Hollywood, by Jim Henson

Chapter Sixteen

Moving On

Our goal in writing this workbook has been to offer useful stepping-stones on the road to your recovery, not to provide final answers. This last chapter is designed to help you move on beyond this book—to the next stepping-stone on your journey. Two things tend to hinder ACoAs from moving on: unfinished business and difficulty saying good-bye.

Unfinished Business

On a personal level, few of us end up speaking as honestly to our parents as we could. Maybe you have tried to speak honestly and the reaction was so painful that you choose no longer to offer yourself up as a target. More often, it is simply fear that keeps ACoAs silent. You may be afraid that they will misunderstand you. You may fear that you will feel callous if you speak the truth. You may fear that you will feel more isolated if they push you further away.

Perhaps the best place to start is telling your parents that you still fear them. This may open the way to finishing some business. Pay attention to how your mother or father responds to your fear before deciding whether it is possible to proceed further. If they try to make you feel wrong or bad for being afraid, you may want to tell them that they are not making it easy for you to be honest. On the other hand, if further honesty seems too threatening, you may not want to say anything more than "How *is* the weather?"

It is more threatening to talk to your parents if they are still drinking or using drugs. Remember that intoxication is a pit of quicksand. Any path that leads into it sinks. The path of recovery may come right up to the edge, but it does not try to cross the pit. There are ways for you to follow your own recovery even if your parents continue to drink. But there are no ways for you to force your recovery into their lives if they are actively intoxicated. Their lives are closed to recovery when they are intoxicated; whatever your parents may say while intoxicated will probably be forgotten by the morning. If you have unfinished business with a parent, take care of it when they are sober. Otherwise, take care of yourself.

Do not assume that business with your parents must remain unfinished just because they are dead. The relationship between you and them remains alive, and potentially growing, as long as you still breathe. When my own father died, my heart was tightly closed to him. I was still reacting primarily out of my buried pain. If this hurt him at the time, I had no regrets. Today, I deeply regret the way I closed my heart. It certainly did *me* no good, and I know now that it caused him a lot of pain. If he were alive today, I know that I would contact him. I would try to talk to him more honestly than I was willing to for most of our lives together. Whether he would have been able to return my honesty is an unanswerable question. But it is a fact that my willingness to allow him back into my heart today, although accompanied by a lot of sadness that the fact that he is dead prevents this, also has ended some of the heartache I have lived with for much of my life. Don't get me wrong; I would still be scared if I were suddenly confronted with him living and breathing again. And I doubt that I would be quite as brave or honest as I imagine I might be. But neither would I be as closed as I once was. I'm clear that I benefit considerably by this greater openness and that the reservations that remain in me are harmful—and part of the unfinished business I still have with myself.

On a political level, there is a tremendous amount of unfinished business that faces all CoAs. The experiences you are still recovering from are being repeated today, in every city, town, and village across our country. Children of every race are still being confused and frightened by their drunken parents. Children in rich homes and children on the street, children in the suburbs and children in ghettos, children still in the womb and children born tonight, children in your neighborhood and your schools, children within walking distance, if not within earshot—children everywhere are still living through what you have known in your life.

As we described earlier, Entering Community means that recovery cannot happen in isolation from others. We need one another, and no one needs recovery more than children who are still trapped in their parents' quicksand. It is not enough for adult children of alcoholics to take care of their own recovery. You do have to take care of your own recovery first, just as the airlines tell you to put on your own oxygen mask before helping your children put theirs on. But if we take care of ourselves and then forget about others, we are not finished with the business at hand.

The Twelfth Step encourages us to continue recovery by giving it away through our example.* *Alcoholics Anonymous,* in the chapter "The Family Afterward," instructs us regarding remembering the plight of other children of alcoholics:

> This painful past may be of infinite value to other families still struggling with their problem. We think each family which has been relieved *owes* [italics added] something to those who have not. . . . Showing others who suffer how we were given help is the very thing which makes life seem so worthwhile to us now. Cling to the thought that, in God's hands, the dark past is the greatest possession you have—the key to life and happiness for others. With it you can avert death and misery for them. (p. 124)

Although your own child within needs attention, there are still nearly ten million children out there who need our attention as well. Ten million children under the age of eighteen are currently living with an addicted parent. Our business remains unfinished as long as they remain isolated and alone. Our souls are too connected to believe that healing can be complete without its being shared. Our recovery is too self-centered if we nurture the child within adequately but ignore the children without.

---

* "Having had a spiritual awakening as the result of these steps, we tried to carry this message to others, and to practice these principles in all our affairs."—Step Twelve.

There is a tremendous amount of unfinished business in our country regarding chemical dependence. A few years ago, when treatment for alcoholism and drug addiction reached its zenith, there were still precious few treatment programs for families and young children. Today, the availability of treatment for chemical dependence is rapidly shrinking. As a result, services for children are making little, if any, headway. The untreated children in chemically dependent families truly represent some of America's most unfinished business.

The exercises below suggest ways in which you can make this unfinished business your own. We believe that to ignore the unmet needs of children surrounding us is in direct conflict with the way of life called recovery. When each of us is ready, it becomes our responsibility to "carry the message to others," as we wish it had been carried to us.

Although Shakespeare wrote that "parting is such sweet sorrow," very few people from chemically dependent families taste much sweetness. Good-byes, endings, and partings are often difficult for ACoAs. So much has been lost in the past. You may have lost your parents—to early death, to divorce, or to the emotional oblivion that alcohol created for them. You may have felt abandoned so often that you lost your trust in this world. You may have lost friends as your family lost its self-respect. You may have lost opportunities as your family lost its status and money. We all have our own specific histories, but a common thread winding through most of them is the pain that comes with parting. The question facing groups, and you the reader, is how to bring your recovery into the current experience of loss, in order to have the least unfinished business preventing you from moving on.

Difficulty Saying Good-bye

Healthy ACoAs have learned to bring their recovery into saying good-byes by remaining emotionally present right up through the moments when the parting takes place. They remain aware of their experience, even though it feels uncomfortable. They do this not because they enjoy pain but because recovery means practicing Honesty, Honoring Feelings, and Entering Community, no matter *what* is happening.

When members of Genesis groups experience healthy good-byes, the moment is often very bittersweet. The bitterness is palpable. Tears sting their eyes. The grief is most profound when their current feelings open the floodgates for a spring of old tears that have been waiting to be shed for decades of earlier losses.

The sweet part of such parting is that it is shared. When you remain emotionally present during separation, the effect of the loss is quite different from that of other losses in your past. When you share the pain honestly, intimacy continues to grow right up until the moment you part. As a result, the feelings you are left with after separating are very different from those you experience when you go numb and leave emotionally before the actual separation.

We end the Genesis groups with the simple words "good-bye." We ask people to refrain from saying anything less (e.g., "bye-bye") or anything that denies the reality of parting ("See you later"). Even if members of the group intend to see one another later, their experience in the group is over. It can never be repeated. Even if they attended group sessions a second time, it would be a different experience. "Good-bye" acknowledges that this experience is over. By acknowledging that ending, and allowing yourself to have feelings about it, the decks get cleared. It becomes much easier to move on to the next experiences, which will replace what has been lost.

When we go through life dragging ungrieved losses like a thousand chains that stretch for miles into the past, only part of our energy is available to make new connections. We do not have an infinite supply of emotional energy, and it can be bound up by losses that remain ungrieved. Resolving their grief allows ACoAs to recover their vitality. And there is no better way to resolve grief than finding healthier ways to experience current losses.

As therapists, we are most aware of the bittersweet nature of parting when clients successfully end their individual therapy. By "successfully," we mean that they take the time to explore what we have meant to each other. We acknowledge that we have connected and had an impact on each other's lives that is permanent. There is a lifelong connection, and we are glad that it has been made. The saddest part of our job is that we work with people who need us only temporarily. The goal, from the beginning, is for them no longer to need us in the same way. Generally, clients would like us to remain a part of their lives after the early needs have been dealt with, but there comes a time when it is in their best interests for them to leave. There comes a time when it actually becomes harmful for them to continue relying upon us. We know this from the moment we meet them. But it still hurts when it is time for them to go.

We invite you to treat this book in the same way that we invite clients to treat us when they end their therapy. Put the book on the shelf, where it can always stay. The work you have done is a part of you now. You can share the book with others, but you do not need to. And it is best to be careful about whom you share it with. Let others buy their own book if they wish and work through it in their own way. If the time comes when you want to revisit the book, feel free to pull it down off the shelf and read whatever parts you wish to. It is likely that you will have the same experience piano students have when they go back and pick up an old piece that they struggled with once, only to find that the keys flow under their fingers with much less effort now.

This workbook provides just a few stepping-stones. You will move beyond it soon. It has been a privilege to support you for the moments that we could. But now it is time to say good-bye.

• • • • • • • • **EXERCISES** • • • • • • • •

> I remember how scared I was when I first came to this group. I was sure no one would understand what I went through in my family. Until I met you (smiling and looking around the room), I though for sure I had the worst childhood in the lot. Then as you all told your stories I thought, "My family was bad, but not that bad!" (Group laughter)
>
> After a couple of weeks I started thinking about some of the good things in my family. Now I feel like, well, for the most part my childhood was pretty bad and I feel sad about it—but I don't feel so alone.
>
> Gail

Recovery is often described as a commitment to "progress, not perfection." Undoubtedly you have not accomplished all that you hoped to in this workbook. But recovery directs attention more to what *has* been accomplished, not just to what remains to

be done. The first exercise below acknowledges the progress you
have made and uses this progress as the foundation for moving on
further.

**Exercise 48: Where
I Started**

1. Review your responses in chapter 1 to the questions
   about your hopes, your dreams, and your expectations
   for this workbook.

2. Use the journal to answer the following questions:

   • What reactions do you have today to reading your
     original hopes and expectations?

   • Which of them have been met?

   • Which haven't been met?

   • What progress did you make on the goals that were
     not met?

I didn't accomplish everything I wanted to, but I know
my expectations were pretty big. I wished my family
would get together again. I knew this was childish at the
time, but I secretly hoped that somehow my using this
workbook would magically cause my mother to stop
drinking.

                    Susan

3. Now flip through your entire journal, from chapters 1
   through 15 and mark entries that demonstrate progress.
   Your progress may be evident in any of the following:

   • reading and working in this workbook

   • reaching out to others

   • acknowledging your denial

   • visiting an Al-Anon/ACoA meeting

   • talking with a therapist about your alcoholic family

   • increasing words used in the feeling exercises

   • joining an ACoA group

   • understanding the characteristics of ACoAs that
     fit you

- understanding how these characteristics have been strengths
- writing or telling your story to another person
- increased awareness of your feelings
- expanding your emotional range
- greater recall of your childhood
- better understanding of how you survived your family
- better understanding of how and why you struggle for control in your life and relationships
- taking the first step in letting go of control
- increased awareness of your Committee
- increased understanding of how guilt and shame arose in your alcoholic family, and how they continue to affect your life
- awareness of the sadness and mourning you still carry from your childhood
- willingness to follow through with the mindfulness practice
- experimentation with being assertive
- exploration of the blessings and wounds within your spiritual history
- willingness to explore your playful nature
- changes in your friendships
- changes in your relationship to your parents
- changes in your relationships with your brothers and sisters
- changes in your relationship to a Higher Power
- changes in how you relate to yourself.

I have been dreading doing something like this. I just knew you were going to ask us about how we felt we've grown during the group. As soon as I started reviewing my journal, I could feel the judgmental part of me commenting on how I could have done more, how I could have worked on the exercises more thoroughly, how I could've gone to more Al-Anon meetings, et cetera.

But when I let those thoughts go and look at what I did accomplish, I feel pretty good. I'm getting much better at figuring out what I'm feeling at the moment. Before it used to take me a week to know what I was feeling, now I know within a minute or two. Not bad at all.

Susan

Exercise 49:
What's Ahead

Now that you've examined the progress made with this workbook, you can make an inventory of the changes to be worked on next and the resources you still have not fully used.

1. Copy the ten areas identified in your Self-Esteem List in a column in your journal. Record the next small step you can make in *each* one of the areas. Remember to chunk your steps down into easily attainable goals.

2. Check any of the following approaches that you have not yet used:

   - finding a therapist who understands the problems of ACoAs

   - being more honest with your therapist

   - looking at your own relationship to alcohol and drugs

   - attending more ACoA meetings

   - finding a sponsor

   - methodically working the Twelve Steps

   - reading more books and watching more movies listed in the Recommendations section

   - talking to your spiritual counselor, rabbi, priest, nun, or minister

   - reaching out to allies in your family

   - dealing with some of the compulsive behavior patterns that are hindering your recovery (spending, gambling, sex, drugs, alcohol, work, etc.)

I know I should get into individual therapy, but I'm just not ready. There's something about individual therapy that feels a little scary. I think I'm afraid of what I'll find out about myself. Right now, my next step is to go to more meetings and to finally get a sponsor.

Gail

Like many ACoAs, Gail is afraid not only of the intensity of one-on-one therapy but also the unknown of what lays hidden in her past. At the beginning of our group sessions, she had insisted that "I don't remember anything from my childhood, and nothing happened." By the end of the program she was acknowledging that fear kept her from looking any closer. That's progress. Whether her decision to use Twelve-Step meetings and a sponsor was still a way to avoid work that she needs to do in therapy, or whether it was a healthy way to pace her recovery, only time will tell.

Now that you have taken the time to acknowledge your unfinished business, we would like you to consider writing letters to your family.

We are not suggesting that you send the letters. We are only suggesting that you write each letter as an exercise in following through with articulating any unfinished business you might have.

Without intending to send it, write letters to the following:

Exercise 50: A Confidential Letter

- your alcoholic parent (whether alive or not)
- your codependent parent (whether alive or not)
- your brothers and sisters

Clearly and simply express what you have been holding back.

If you have difficulty organizing what you want to say, take a small step by focusing on just one incident, feeling, or event. Remember the exercise of focusing on a single kind of behavior and then chunking it down into something manageable. Keep it simple.

If, at some later point, you consider actually sending the letter, we encourage you to take time to assess all your reasons, and all the risks. This form of direct contact could be an important step in your recovery, but do not take this step without first getting the perspective of your group, therapist, sponsor, or friends.

Here's Susan's letter:

Dear Mom:

I don't know why you insist that our childhood "wasn't so bad." We've all talked to you about how difficult our life was because of your drinking. We've pleaded with you to get help. Your children are loving, good people, and yet you insist on putting us down.

Don't you remember how we suffered?

Let me tell you—We were always hungry, while you had money to buy booze. We were always wearing hand-me-downs from year to year—Mom . . . our clothes were never clean!

Do you remember when the lady from the Salvation Army brought us fresh clothes. I felt so ashamed. Maybe you can't remember; you were drunk when you got home.

Do you remember when you were so drunk you fell down the stairs and were knocked out. I was the oldest and I was only six. I held you and screamed at the top of my lungs 'til I was hoarse. Mrs. Beeman from next door heard me and called the police. They called an ambulance.

If you don't remember, ask the school. Ask your other children. Ask the minister at that church we used to go to.

These are facts that are not in dispute.

Mom. You are an alcoholic. Though all this has happened, I still have a place in my heart that loves you. That part pleads with you to get help; but I can't continue to visit or even talk with you on the phone when you're drunk. That's why I've hung up on you in the past. It has to stop.

Your daughter,
Susan

Susan never sent her letter to her mother, but the letter did have a powerful impact on her life. After writing it, Susan talked openly in the group about how she felt a huge weight lift from her soul. I remember noticing how she used the word *soul*. When I asked her about it, she said she still had the memory of what it felt like to have the burden weighing on her, but she no longer felt controlled by it.

"I know that I still want my mother to stop drinking," she said. "But for the first time I can remember, I feel that I can go on living even if she never gets sober. It would be sad, but I can live with it."

Exercise 51: Service

There are a wide variety of ways each of us can work toward bringing recovery to children of alcoholics. Some ways are intensely personal, such as talking to your alcoholic brother's daughter or a neighbor's child. Other ways are more organizational, such as writing letters to schools and newspapers or donating money. Use your creativity with the following exercise.

1. Use your journal to list at least ten ways in which you could serve children of alcoholics. We will give you a head start.

   • Suggest that your Al-Anon/ACoA meeting sponsor an Alateen Group

   • Become a member of NACoA (National Association for Children of Alcoholics, 11426 Rockville Pike, Suite 100, Rockville, MD 20852; [301] 468-0985, FAX [301] 468-0987)

   • Call a local school and ask what services they provide for CoAs.

Exercise 52: Anticipating the End

Respond to the following questions in your journal:

1. How does it feel to be at the end of the book? Describe the bitter aspects of ending the workbook as well as the sweet parts of finishing.

2. How does this compare with how you felt when you opened the first page many weeks ago?

You know, I do feel sad about ending this whole process. I know I'll miss some of you a whole lot more than I expected. I feel really good about what we've done together. . . . I feel different; not completely healed by any means, but I do feel better about myself. I feel less alone and safer talking with all of you than I have with any group in my life. I think that's something to celebrate!

Estella

Exercise 53: Saying Good-bye

In this chapter, we've identified some of the reasons that ACoAs have a hard time ending projects or saying good-bye in relationships. This exercise identifies those that apply to you.

1. List the ways in which you avoid saying good-bye, finding closure, and ending relationships in your life—both historically and currently.

Here's part of Estella's list:

1. I tend to leave others before they leave me.
2. I don't get close to people. I protect myself from pain by never getting close.
3. If someone at work leaves for a job somewhere else, I find a way to be out of town, sick, or away from the office the day of her going-away party so I don't have to say good-bye.
4. I say, "Let's not say good-bye, let's say 'See you later.'"

Like many ACoAs, Estella was adept at avoiding good-byes. She was well armored against feeling pain when anyone left her, or when she was leaving someone she cared about. This self-protection came at a high cost, because it pushed away the very things she craved—consolation, comfort, companionship, and intimacy.

2. Describe a specific good-bye that was particularly difficult to face.

3. If you have been left by someone without being able to say good-bye (perhaps because of his or her death), write a letter to say good-bye.

Exercise 52: Letting Us Know

During the course of using this workbook you have probably had thoughts, feelings, judgments, or reactions about it. This exercise gives you the opportunity to communicate these feelings. We welcome them all—from encouraging remarks to strong criticisms. You can write to us at the following address:

Timmen Cermak, M.D.

Jacques Rutzky, M.F.C.C.

Genesis Psychotherapy and Training Center

1325 Columbus Avenue

San Francisco, California 94133

Exercise 53: Ending

1. In order to address the importance of your completing the workbook, think of a personal ritual that would acknowledge and celebrate your success. The ritual could be any activity that has a symbolic meaning for you. For example:

   • going to an Al-Anon meeting

   • having a feast or special dinner

   • going for a walk in the woods

   • searching for a sacred object that would be a sign of your work and transformation

   • anything that has meaning for you (one of the authors is going to a baseball game to celebrate finishing the workbook).

Whatever you choose as a fitting ritual, it must be something that is a positive affirmation of your progress and not something that will cause you to have regrets later. For example, if you are a compulsive shopper it wouldn't be an affirming ritual for you to buy an expensive leather coat when you can't afford it. It doesn't

need to be something big and expensive, just something mean-
ingful.

> 2. Describe the ritual in detail in your journal.

> 3. Within the next month, carry out the ritual to acknowl-
>   edge your growth in recovery.

I decided I would take a weekend and go camping up in
Yosemite. I always love being out in nature, and it's a
treat for me. Mostly I go alone, but this time I think I'll
ask my lover if she wants to come. We've gotten closer in
the last few months.

> Sharon

Sharon's decision to take the initiative toward greater intimacy is a wonderful example of recovery.

Journal

If you have used your journal throughout this workbook, you
have developed a valuable recovery skill. We urge you to continue making weekly entries in the journal for at least the next
three months. This will help you watch the gradual changes this
workbook has set into motion, while simultaneously helping to
maintain the momentum of change. Journaling is a constant reminder that the final chapters of your life have not yet been
written.

We have faith that the more you understand and remember
the early chapters in your life, the less likely you are to repeat them.

That's progress.

That's recovery!

★ Recommendations

Three books may help with some unfinished business. If your
parents are still actively drinking, Vernon Johnson's *Intervention:
How to Help Someone Who Doesn't Want Help* can clarify what
you can, and cannot, do for them. ACoAs with children may

be helped by Patricia O'Gorman and Phil Oliver-Diaz's book, *Breaking the Cycle of Addiction: A Parent's Guide to Raising Healthy Kids*. And Claudia Black's *Double Duty* addresses several special topics, including issues for people of color, gays and lesbians, only children, chemically dependent ACoAs, etc.

Finally, an audiotape combining information, visualizations and exercises is available through Genesis (*A Time to Heal*, by Timmen Cermak) for those who wish to supplement this workbook further.

Appendix One

Guidelines for Peer Groups

Forming a Peer Group

Peer groups usually form when an inspired individual takes the initiative to reach out to others and organize a group. Many people put up notices at churches, synagogues, or local bulletin boards. Most Twelve-Step Programs develop an informal network for passing along information about groups that are forming.

We recommend being as clear as possible to prospective members about several things:

- the dates and times of meetings
- the kind of group you are forming, i.e., a peer group without a trained facilitator or therapist
- the focus of the group, i.e., adult children of alcoholics/drug abusers
- the use of this workbook as an integral part of the group
- the expectation that people will attend each meeting, with no more than two absences

One word of caution for the person organizing the peer group. Remember, getting the group together is not a license for you to be the authority once the meetings start. It may be difficult to sit back and be an equal member after having invested energy in starting the group. Nevertheless, you'll probably find your experience more rewarding if you can do so.

If you find yourself being bossy, controlling, and acting like a therapist, you might want to explore your own need for control within the group and ask group members how they feel about your taking on this role.

General Group Guidelines

1. Meet regularly (preferably weekly or every other week) at the same time in order to assure consistency for the group. Start on time, and end on time. Of course, anyone can be sick or have to be out of town on business; we have found, however, that more than two absences tend to disrupt the continuity of the group.

2. Keep groups no larger than ten people and no smaller than five. A gathering of more than ten tends to limit the intimacy and amount of time available to share. A group smaller than five tends to be too vulnerable to absences and loss of momentum.

3. An hour-and-a-half-long meeting is sufficient. Less time limits the number of people who can share. Longer than an hour and a half often creates more intensity than people can handle in a single sitting.

4. Announce absences (vacations, business trips, etc.) at least two weeks in advance. This gives group members a chance to adjust to the loss of a group member and share feelings about a group member's upcoming absence while that person is there.

5. Sharing personal experience is encouraged on the basis of willingness rather than demand. If members feel forced or coerced to share, some of them will feel intruded upon. We encourage you to permit silence and offer the option of sharing as each individual feels comfortable. It's always okay to "pass" on any question from the workbook or from another group member.

6. There should be an explicit agreement among members prohibiting physical violence, threats, or verbal or emotional abuse among group members. This is not to be confused with expressing strong feelings. But if a member makes threatening comments or gestures, it is important for the group not to let these actions slide by without comment. Not commenting is the same as keeping silent in an alcoholic family. Commenting on the problematic behavior helps break the group denial and reestablishes trust and safety in the group. If the individual becomes antagonized and the group polarizes around the abusive behavior, we recommend that the group consider bringing in a trained therapist/consultant to help process the impasse.

7. We recommend that group members abstain from using alcohol/drugs for twenty-four hours prior to and after the group meeting. Whether your drinking is overtly problematic or not, having a single beer after group to cope with or numb your feelings is incompatible with recovery. If you spend the time and energy to uncover and explore your feelings about growing up in an alcoholic family, numbing out at the end of the day is like taking one step forward and two steps back.

8. The inclusion or exclusion of cross-talk (speaking directly and personally to another group member either in response to something said or in directing a response to the group member) should be openly discussed and a consensus reached to promote the group's comfort and safety. In a new group, many members find it safer to put off cross-talk until everyone knows one another better and the likelihood of being offended or hurt by direct communication is minimized. Keep in mind that as the group develops a sense of cohesion and safety, the tolerance for cross-talk may grow as well.

9. Homework is encouraged but not mandatory. We have always felt that people must decide about completing the exercises based on their individual needs to pace themselves. In this way, the work is done with a sense of personal motivation and will have more meaning for the individual. Choice is always preferable to coercion.

10. Everyone should read the workbook Preface, Introduction, chapter 1, and the Peer Group Suggestion for Week One in preparation for the first meeting.

Suggestions for Discussion

The exercises for each chapter are designed to prepare you for meetings. We suggest that you allow enough time at each meeting to discuss your experience with these exercises. In addition, the following chapter-by-chapter suggestions will help organize your discussions.

Meeting One: Breaking the Silence

When the group gathers for the first meeting, we recommend that you begin with short (one-minute) personal introductions that answer the question "Why am I here?" Keeping the introductions short gives everyone a chance to say something almost immediately.

When all members have had a chance to introduce themselves and as time permits, you can share your thoughts and feelings about the following questions:

- What are your expectations, hopes, or fears for the group?
- Does anyone in your family know about your participation in a group like this?
- Does anyone in the group feel a kind of disloyalty in talking about the alcoholism in the family?
- How did your family enforce the rule not to talk?

Meeting Two: Our Common Ground

All groups go through an awkward stage of deciding just how meetings will begin. Some get off the ground when one person has the courage to begin talking. In order to make the best use of the time available, facilitate discussions, and relieve the tension of getting started, some groups create a ritual of giving each person an opportunity to take a minute to check in with the group about how they're feeling at that moment and whether they have any thoughts or feelings left over from the previous week. Whatever format your group chooses, we urge you to strive for a consensus.

Sometimes there are awkward silences before and after an individual's sharing. Although some group members find the silences intolerable and tense, others welcome the respite to begin formulating their own thoughts. If you notice one or more group members relieving the silence on a regular basis, you may want to explore both your feelings and those of the other group members about the silence being broached.

We suggest that you begin week two with a group exercise (using a chalkboard, if available) to list the characteristics of adult children of alcoholics that the members of the group most identify with. This can then be a visual reference for discussing the following topics:

- What characteristics do you identify with in your childhood?
- What characteristics do you identify with in your present life?

Meeting Three: Remembering the Past

Following any check-in or leftovers from last week, week three has one focus:

- Each person shares his or her story of being an adult child of an alcoholic.

Although it is highly unlikely that anyone will have enough time to tell her whole life's story, each person should share what seems most important. It is best if people can speak with as few interruptions as possible. The purpose is not to discuss your history but to tell it and have it listened to. If the group runs out of time and some people haven't spoken, the group can decide whether to continue sharing stories the following week. If there is any leftover time you might share what it was like to do the family genogram.

**Meeting Four:
Welcoming Feelings**

We organize a group's discussion of feelings by inviting people to share *feeling words* from their own workbook lists while one group member writes them on a chalkboard. Inviting everyone in the group to share means that those who are ready have the opportunity to do so and those who feel unsafe do not feel coerced.

By sharing feelings lists, the group can begin to explore how their emotions have been constricted, blocked, or held back. If you have the time, and the level of safety in the group is high enough, you can begin talking about those feelings that you are most reluctant to acknowledge to the rest of the group.

**Meeting Five:
Survival**

This week is often difficult for many group members. People are more likely to forget to come, call in sick, or suddenly become too busy to make the meeting. These difficulties all reflect the extreme fear and caution many ACoAs have about remembering the past, experiencing old feelings, and being too vulnerable to others. When group members discuss the Home Exercise (#15), we make it clear that people are free to share nothing, to share only the safer parts of their story, or to share everything.

We recommend that the group share and discuss the following questions:

- What was it like to do the Home Exercise?
- Which coping strategies discussed in the chapter did you use to survive during childhood?
- Which of these strategies do you still employ today?
- Which have you used here in the group?

This week's group session tends to evoke powerful memories. Just listening to the personal stories of other ACoAs, especially when physical, sexual or emotional abuse was present, brings up a lot of buried feelings. It is important to remember that the focus is not only on the past but also on the sense of companionship that develops in the group as each person's feelings are shared. Most ACoAs find little difficulty identifying with one another, even when dramatic painful events were absent from their own alcoholic family, because the *feelings* that each experienced have so much in common.

The sixth meeting explores the ACoA characteristic of compulsively needing to be in control—of yourself, of others, of relationships, and even of many external events that are beyond our control. We recommend that the group explore the following questions:

Meeting Six: Control

- What are some of the ways you and your family tried to control the alcoholic and his/her drinking?
- What are some of the ways you try to control yourself and others today?
- What are some of the subtle ways in which you have tried to exert control over the group or certain individuals in the group?

Regardless of the definition of the codependence that each group member brings to the group, most ACoAs identify with the experience of giving up parts of themselves to get someone to like them, for the survival of the family, or for no apparent reason at all. For the meeting on codependence, we urge the group to raise the following questions:

Meeting Seven: Codependence

- What does it feel like when you are being codependent?
- In what ways have you been codependent with your alcoholic family?
- In what ways have you been codependent within this group?

Group members are sometimes surprised to learn that a member has been codependent with them; and sometimes they are surprised to learn that everyone already knew. In either case, it is important to be gentle with one another as you begin lifting the veil from the truth about what has been going on below the surface of your interactions with one another.

Meeting Eight:
Anger

The group session on anger is usually intense. Frequently group members will cope with the tension during the session by joking or intellectualizing. We do not try to stop this from happening, because it keeps things safer. But we do help people examine their feelings underneath the joking and intellectualizing.

For this group we use the chalkboard and work together to create a Group Anger Graph. This helps some members who had difficulty with the exercise develop a larger repertoire of anger words. We encourage group members to focus on the following questions:

- What makes your feelings of anger hard to express to others?
- What makes feelings of anger hard to receive from others?
- What feelings on the Group Anger Graph have people felt *while in the group*?
- If these feelings have been felt, why have they not been expressed?

This session is often pivotal in helping the group develop a sense of cohesiveness. Enough safety has usually developed so that people can begin acknowledging some irritation with each other and to explore together the reasons this has gone unexpressed.

Meeting Nine:
Shame

This group session can be difficult. Allow yourselves to go slowly as you focus on the shame that many ACoAs carry from childhood—shame about your alcoholic family, and about your own inability to fix the family. We recommend discussing the following questions:

- How does each person experience shame?
- What things about your alcoholic family cause you shame?
- In what ways did shame lead you to neglect your own best interests in your alcoholic family?
- Are there people *you* have hurt?

This meeting often takes on the power of a confessional, where "sins" are met with compassion and understanding. The respect and confidentiality of the group provide an almost sacred place for each member to talk about skeletons hidden away in their closets.

This meeting explores your feelings of grief and loss. The goal is to:

Meeting Ten: Mourning

- explore individual and group *barriers* to mourning
- identify the actual feelings of loss, grief, and sadness that you experienced growing up in an alcoholic family

You may find many other feelings coming up along with the sadness. Some people find anger and rage as well; others find loneliness and emptiness. We recommend that you take time to acknowledge all these feelings.

This group focuses on sharing personal experience with individual and group psychotherapy, Twelve-Step Programs, spiritual practices, and other avenues to healing. We encourage you to organize your discussion around the following questions:

Meeting Eleven: Healing

- What stage of recovery most describes you? Why?
- Which tools have most helped your recovery? How?
- Which tools have not been helpful? Why not?
- Which of the healing forces do you most need to activate— Honesty, Welcoming Feelings, or Entering Community?

One pitfall that groups consistently encounter when discussing their own healing occurs when members preach so much about the benefit of their own experience that a power struggle develops around a given recovery tool. We encourage each of you to speak from a personal perspective that avoids criticism, judgments, and salesmanship.

In addition, discuss your experience with the Recovery Planning Exercise.

- What area of self-esteem did you choose to work on?
- What task did you set for yourself?
- Do the other group members think this task was an effective and manageable way to reach your goal?
- Were you able to accomplish your task?
- If you did not accomplish your task, why not?

We suggest that you make Meeting Eleven longer than the others, in order to give everyone enough time to discuss the Recovery Planning Exercise. Include some discussion of the Recovery Planning Exercise in each meeting from this point on.

Meeting Twelve:
Honesty

Some groups have begun the discussion of honesty by doing the Mindfulness Exercise (#34) together for the first twenty minutes of their meeting. Whether you choose to bring the meditation experience into the group or not, sharing your experience about this exercise is very useful.

- What difficulties did you experience with the Mindfulness Exercise?
- If you did experience moments when your mind quieted, describe this experience.

In addition, discussions of the Committee can be very valuable.

- Describe your experience with the Committee.
- Can you identify any of the voices in your Committee?
- What things trigger the Committee or turn up the volume of its voice?
- What things turn the volume down?

Meeting Thirteen:
Honoring Feelings

This session provides an opportunity to discuss the concept of assertiveness as we have presented it in this chapter. Share your experience with the workbook exercises, and air your positive and painful experiences with being assertive in your life.

- What are your fears about being assertive?
- How does being unassertive affect your life?
- In what ways have you failed to be assertive in the group?

Meeting Fourteen:
Entering Community

In this group we focus on the experiences that members have had in their spiritual growth and development. Difficulties in this discussion occur when members begin to quote Al-Anon literature and Scripture, use jargon, or intellectualize rather than personalize the nature of the spiritual experience in recovery. We encourage you to strive toward more personal self-revelation by discussing the following:

- How did your family relate to spirituality and religion?
- What spiritual wounds have you suffered?
- What experiences of transcendence have you had? When are they most likely to occur?

At the end of this session, group members sometimes hold hands in a circle for a few minutes before leaving.

Meeting Fifteen: Play and Spontaneity

In this meeting we like to play, not just talk about playing. We suggest that each group member come with his or her own suggestion about a playful activity for the meeting. Don't be afraid to push all the chairs to the side of the room and sit on the floor in order to have enough room. Randomly select which group member goes first, second, third, etc., and then let yourselves be led into whatever play that person suggests. *It is critically important for each of you to monitor your own comfort level—and to hold back from doing anything that you don't want to do.* We offer the following suggestions for play, but we strongly encourage you not to limit yourself by this list.

- Music and dancing
- Charades or Pictionary
- Mimicking animals
- Making up a story and switching storytellers randomly
- Sharing the illustrations of your fairy tale

Toward the end of the group, give yourselves time to discuss the following:

- What feelings made you reluctant to play?
- What was your experience with visiting the playground?
- Do a "Show and Tell" with the toy you bought yourself.
- What does it feel like when you *do* give yourself over to play?

The final task for this meeting is to agree jointly on how you would like to celebrate your last session. Frequently groups suggest bringing food and drinks (nonalcoholic), small gifts, or cards.

Meeting Sixteen: Moving On

This meeting focuses on identifying unfinished business (which can involve either negative or positive feelings), saying good-bye, and celebrating the group with the ritual chosen last week.

Sharing unfinished business can be a risk for people who decide to reveal thoughts and feelings that they have held back. Each individual has to decide whether it's worth holding on to something or talking about it openly. We bring no pressure to bear to encourage people one way or the other because it is an individual risk, and we discourage cross-talk unless it is invited. We suggest the following framework for sharing unfinished business:

- State your unfinished business (e.g., telling a group member that you were hurt by something she said three weeks ago, but hid your anger—or thanking someone for a kindness he showed you earlier).
- Tell the person whether you want her reaction or not.
- If you are invited to respond, don't speak unless you can say something that is neither attacking nor defensive. You might just express regret for how someone else feels or describe the impact it has on you to learn about the unfinished business.

People often have a tremendous welling up of feelings before this group meeting. Before proceeding, take time to do the following:

- Tell others about the feelings you had during the week about the group's ending.
- Describe the impact this group is having on you.
- Acknowledge the feelings you are having right at the moment.

After sharing these final feelings about the group, treat yourselves to whatever ritual your group chose to celebrate itself.

Finally, to facilitate the group's last good-byes, set aside fifteen minutes at the very end. Gather into a circle facing inward. One by one, each member should move around the circle, pause in front of each person for a few moments, then simply say "good-bye."

Pay close attention to your feelings as you say, and hear, the good-byes.

When everyone has completed the circle, the group is disbanded.

Feelings List

Accepting: open, receptive, responsive, understanding, approving, compliant, sympathetic, tolerant

Admired: looked up to, important, respected, venerated, valued, honored, praised, prized, appreciated, cherished, delighted, adored, idolized, revered, worshipped, treasured

Alive: vibrant, bubbly, animated, effervescent, buoyant, invigorated, active, dynamic, spirited, strong, vivacious, energized, exhilarated, vital, orgasmic

Alone: isolated, cut off, abandoned, ostracized, left out, lonely, lonesome, alienated, detached, removed, secluded, neglected, apart, severed, unwelcome

Angry: furious, resentful, fuming, seething, hostile, hateful, indignant, bitter, combative, militant, violent, cross, feisty, upset, ferocious, fierce, savage, vicious, cranky, grouchy, aggravated, incensed, irate, mad, injured, wrathful, enraged, irritated, antagonistic, infuriated, burning

Appreciative: fortunate, lucky, thankful, grateful, indebted

Attractive: lovely, handsome, beautiful, pretty, admired, gorgeous, stunning, sensational, alluring, desirable, erotic, exciting, becoming, pleasing, radiant, charming, foxy, luscious

Bad: naughty, worthless, inferior, terrible, disgusting, unappealing, immoral, disturbing, tough, mean, rough, evil, rotten, putrid, sour, defective, inadequate, corrupt, malevolent, malignant, menacing, unpleasant, fraudulent, immoral, Machiavellian, vile, wicked

Beautiful: attractive, handsome, gorgeous, glorious, delightful, good, magnificent, terrific, wonderful, alluring, comely, lovely, luscious

Bored: disinterested, dull, numb, disconnected

Bothered: pestered, annoyed, troubled, imposed upon, burdened, intruded on, afflicted, disturbed, intimidated, oppressed, upset, worried, antagonized, bugged, distressed, disturbed, hassled, stressed, aggravated, exasperated, frazzled, incensed, miffed, peeved, riled, vexed, harried

Burdened: endured, put-up with, tolerated, in the way, encumbered, imposed upon, bothered, afflicted, distressed, hurt, aggrieved, depressed, dejected, disheartened, weighed down, hampered, hindered, oppressed, overdone, overloaded, taxed, disturbed, daunted, fazed

Calm: at peace, satisfied, peaceful, composed, comfortable, tranquil, serene, quiet, safe, sustained, detached, steady, balanced, quiet, subdued, appeased, assuaged, lulled, pacified, placated, soothed, coolheaded, passive, casual, collected, demure, gentle, placid, poised, relaxed, restful, sedate, still, unflappable, untroubled

Cold: distant, apart, callous, indifferent, aloof, lukewarm, apart, uncaring, disinterested, unloving, lifeless, frigid, inhibited, passionless, repressed, restrained, reticent, unemotional, coldhearted, impassive

Comfortable: cozy, warm, at peace, agreeable, soft, contented, comfy, cushy, homey, secure, snug

Concerned: caring, interested, attentive, sympathetic, understanding, solicitous, involved, committed, dedicated, afraid, aghast, anxious, apprehensive, fearful, frightened, nervous, paranoid, disturbed, affected, bothered, distressed

Confident: adequate, competent, assured, capable, poised, secure, brazen, cocksure, positive, sure, optimistic, hopeful, upbeat, assertive, aggressive, driven, insistent, pushy

Confused: mixed-up, wasted, dispirited, stricken, unreasonable, dizzy, foggy, misguided, heady, unfeeling, ambivalent, bewildered, incoherent, lighthearted, dazed, fuzzy, unclear, confounded, baffled, jumbled, boggled, befuddled, distracted, perplexed

Cordial: welcoming, friendly, hospitable, warm, polite, amiable, affable, approachable, genial, gracious, likable, pleasant, serene, civilized, courteous, decent

Dead: numb, dull, vacuous, unfeeling, unavailable, cold, shut off, spiritless, forgotten, lost, inanimate, inert, lifeless, ancient, obsolete, extinct, old, outdated, passé, worn, bleak, desolate, drab, dreary

Delighted: enchanted, bewitched, amused, captivated, excited, wonderful, marvelous, tingly, alive, pleased, glad, ecstatic, elated, overjoyed, thrilled, tickled, satisfied, contented

Defeated: discouraged, failing, weak, hopeless, wasted, resigned, submissive, overpowered, conquered, exasperated, overwhelmed, dispirited, disoriented, sad, deflated, overcome, crushed, distraught, subdued, beaten, clobbered, dejected, depressed, whipped, drowned, outdone, bested, downed, outmaneuvered, outsmarted

Disappointed: let down, discouraged, disillusioned, disenchanted, dissatisfied, failed, frustrated

Disgusted: repelled, immoral, repugnant, sickened

Disinterested: indifferent, bored, unconcerned, aloof, cool, dispassionate, unconnected, blasé, careless, composed, detached, diffident, distant, nonchalant, remote, reserved, withdrawn

Embarrassed: mortified, shamed, ashamed, befuddled, flustered, rattled, ruffled, belittled, debased, defiled, degraded, deprecated, abashed, chagrined, humiliated

Enlightened: enriched, fulfilled, at peace, calmed, balanced, harmonious, clear, tranquil, alive, whole, spiritually alive, complete, joyful, lucid

Excited: enthusiastic, eager, elated, ecstatic, animated, thrilled, energized, alive, delighted, vibrant, explosive, kinetic, exuberant, orgasmic, happy, ebullient, euphoric, exhilarated, intoxicated, stimulated, agitated, frantic, frenzied, passionate, aroused, roused, stirred, activated, charged, electrified, energized, turned on, sparked, motivated

Feminine: beautiful, needed, receptive, loved, wanted, cared for, desirable, vibrant, flexible, soft, strong, lovely, graceful, intuitive, expansive, empathetic, productive, ladylike, gentle, nurturing

Free: childlike, expressive, unencumbered, outgoing, uninhibited, light, liberated, emancipated, unbound, unchained, clear, exonerated, vindicated, unattached, uncommitted, uninvolved, loose, unconfined, uncontrolled

Frightened: scared, afraid, horrified, cautious, terrified, fearful, deleterious, ominous, unknown, cold, harmful, anxious, aghast, apprehensive, concerned, nervous, paranoid, worried, intimidated, alarmed, terrorized, panicked, shocked, spooked, startled

Frustrated: trapped, cornered, caged, censored, appeased, discouraged, inhibited, displeased, irritated, mad, pissed off, stuck, disappointed, thwarted, foiled, confounded, aggravated, encumbered, halted, hampered, repressed, restrained, slowed, throttled

Guilty: sad, grief-stricken, indebted, sorry, ashamed, condemned

Happy: pleased, joyful, jubilant, delighted, enchanted, cheerful, delirious, ecstatic, intoxicated, transported, contented, thrilled, overjoyed, giddy, gay, engaging, well wishing, lucky, ebullient, elated, euphoric, excited, exhilarated, bright, exuberant

Hostile: angry, resentful, furious, hurtful, dangerous, curt, frightening, harmful, sarcastic, catty, spiteful, nasty, belligerent

Hurt: upset, harmed, pained, sad, injured, recoiled, wounded, bruised, lacerated, mangled, depressed, damaged, abused, blemished, marred, despairing, agonized, sore

Inferior: inadequate, unworthy, less than, diminished, subordinate, deficient, defective, insufficient, wretched, despicable, low, little, meager, shabby, flawed, imperfect, lousy, mediocre, paltry, second-rate

Insecure: unloved, uncared for, unwanted, unwelcome, vulnerable, uncertain, off balance, unsafe, anxious, fearful, nervous, precarious, threatened, unstable, unsure

Interested: stimulated, fascinated, curious, engaged, enthusiastic, enchanted, attracted, absorbed, engrossed, amused, aroused, attracted, excited, intrigued, seduced, stirred, tantalized

Inspired: impressed, uplifted, transported, enlightened, fulfilled, energized, motivated, kinetic, delighted, encouraged, animated, brightened, enlivened, incited, excited, aroused, electrified, instigated, prodded, provoked, spurred

Jealous: envious, desiring, green, insecure, resentful, covetous, suspicious, bitter

Left Out: unwanted, unloved, rejected, abandoned, ignored, disconnected, discarded, undesirable, unwelcome, deserted, depraved, desolate, forsaken, dumped, cast off, disenfranchised, disowned, ditched, jilted, spurned

Loved: cared for, loving, affectionate, supported, accepted, secure, trusted, wanted, safe, protected, enamored, considered, desired, adored, respected, beloved, cherished, esteemed, precious, revered, treasured, worshiped, admired, doted on, idolized, appreciated, coveted

Manipulated: managed, used, placated, maneuvered, imposed upon, exploited, misused, taken advantage of, controlled, handled, groped, commanded, swayed

Masculine: virile, needed, alive, protective, masterful, purposeful, handsome, capable, strong, muscular, brave, courageous, macho, potent

Needed: wanted, loved, cared for, indispensable, vital, trusted

Optimistic: outgoing, gregarious, enthusiastic, hopeful, positive, affirmative, confident, promising, upbeat

Passive: weak, unenergetic, unmoving, withdrawn, static, coy, unassertive, apathetic, indifferent, languid, peaceful, calm, nonaggressive, inactive, inert, stagnant, laid-back, immobile, motionless, acquiescent, compliant, docile, meek, mild, asleep, dormant

Positive: sure, right, active, decisive, forthright, charged, affirmative, optimistic, brazen, certain, confident, exuberant, buoyant, cheerful, helpful, constructive, favorable, fruitful, productive, useful, worthwhile, definite, emphatic, unequivocal, vested, assertive, authentic

Put Down: overworked, picked on, pressured, labored, burdened, enslaved, censored, subdued, humiliated, criticized, condemned, accused, blamed, scolded, disgraced, belittled, cast down, defiled, deflated, degraded, demeaned, deprecated, derogated, devalued, embarrassed

Receptive: responsive, open, accepting, taken in, understood, amiable, congenial, charitable, lenient, patient, consenting, tolerant

Refreshed: renewed, revitalized, replenished, restored, rejuvenated, revived

Resistant: resentful, fighting, acting out, stubborn, subversive, restrained, held back, negative, obtuse, withdrawn, withholding, contained, tight, pulled back, distracted, opposed, defiant, constrained

Restless: uneasy, nervous, tense, agitated, distressed, disturbed, distracted, sleepless, anxious, edgy, fidgety, impatient, troubled, uncomfortable, uptight, worried, antsy, high-strung, irritable, jittery, jumpy, moody, shaky, skittish

Rich: prosperous, wealthy, successful, fulfilled, complete, quantity, full, comfortable, generous, sumptuous

Romantic: sentimental, thoughtful, tender, amorous, loving, intimate, affectionate, caring, devoted, enamored, fond

Sad: depressed, blue, maudlin, sorrowful, heartbroken, grim, dour, sour, woeful, gloomy, despondent, hopeless, melancholy, somber, sorry

Satisfied: pleased, proud, triumphant, fulfilled, m-m-m good, full, filled, sated, saturated, quenched, satiated, appeased, comforted, indulged, pampered, spoiled

Sensitive: tender, responsive, delicate, hypervigilant, hurt, caring, concerned, attentive, intuitive, touchy, sore, irritated, unstable, perceptive, keen, shrewd

Sexy: sensuous, luscious, voluptuous, seductive, luxurious, erotic, lustful, horny, attractive, stimulating, passionate, lewd, hot, amorous, turned on

Shocked: numb, shaken, stunned, dead, paralyzed, immobilized, stressed, disturbed, taken aback, dazed, stupefied, jarred, jolted, jostled, rattled, shook, startled, mazed, dazed, horrified, offended, outraged, overwhelmed, terrified, unnerved, petrified, panicked, frightened, alarmed, intimidated

Sincere: earnest, honest, real, genuine, heartfelt, open

Stifled: blocked, squashed, held back, squeezed, suppressed, overpowered, crushed, defeated, overwhelmed, suffocated, asphyxiated, choked, constricted, gagged, smothered, strangled, censored, inhibited, quelled, quieted, restrained, subdued

Superficial: shallow, flimsy, ignorant, narrow-minded, lightweight, empty, hypocritical, insincere, hollow, vacant

Superior: greater, excellent, one-up, cocky, self-righteous, better than, higher, superb

Supported: sustained, encouraged, understood, validated, persuaded, relieved, comforted, consoled, solaced, uplifted, bolstered, fortified, nurtured

Surprised: amazed, astonished, flabbergasted, annoyed, irritated, taken aback, knocked off, astounded, awed, confounded, dazzled, dumbfounded, stunned

Sympathetic: pitying, empathetic, tactful, caring, understanding

Talented: gifted, purposeful, productive, intelligent, poised, genius, successful, capable, creative, skilled, merciful, tolerant, affable, compassionate, considerate

Tired: weary, exhausted, dispirited, drowsy, lethargic, sleepy, dull, worn out, beat, burned out, bushed, fatigued, drained

Trusting: accepted, loved, responsible, intimate, close, safe, gullible, believing

Uncomfortable: uneasy, fidgety, ill at ease, irritated, restless, restricted, cramped, queasy, tense, uptight, worried, troubled

Understood: cared for, loved, considered, appreciated, acknowledged, heard, known, recognized, seen, accepted

Unfeeling: uncaring, uncared for, unloved, numb, dead, confused, disoriented, heartless, undemonstrative, cold, impassive, dull, phlegmatic, reserved, stoic, unaffected, unemotional, unmoved, untouched, callous, brutal, compassionless, hardened, mean, malicious, unsympathetic

Upset: troubled, bothered, restless, agitated, shaken, uptight, frantic, emotional, hysterical, irritated, unbalanced, disturbed, wild, perturbed, pissed off, annoyed, distressed, worried, fussed, concerned, affected, fazed, intimidated, agitated, flustered, ruffled, unsettled, bugged, hassled, exasperated, miffed, antagonized, incensed

Victorious: triumphant, successful

Vulnerable: weak, helpless, threatened, tormented, insecure, nervous, uncertain, defenseless, dependent, disarmed, exposed, powerless, unprotected

Wanted: considered, cared for, loved, included, desired, needed, valued, chosen, envied, lusted after, longed for, pined over, thirsted after

Wild: impetuous, frantic, hysterical, impulsive, out of control, vibrant, alive, energetic, unbridled, free, reckless, unrestrained, frenzied, furious, liberated, licentious, loose, unbridled

Bibliography

Al-Anon Faces Alcoholism. New York: Al-Anon Family Group Headquarters, Inc., 1984.

Al-Anon's Twelve Steps and Twelve Traditions. New York: Al-Anon Family Group Headquarters, Inc., 1981.

Alcoholics Anonymous. New York: Alcoholics Anonymous World Services, Inc., 1976.

Blueprint for Progress: Al-Anon's Fourth Step Inventory. New York: Al-Anon Family Group Headquarters, Inc., 1976.

One Day at a Time in Al-Anon. New York: Al-Anon Family Group Headquarters, Inc., 1981.

The 12 Steps for Adult Children. San Diego: Recovery Publications, 1987.

Aftel, Mandy, and Robin Lakoff. *When Talk is Not Cheap or How to Find the Right Therapist When You Don't Know Where to Begin*. New York: Warner Books, 1985.

Aliki. *Feelings*. New York: Mulberry Books, 1986.

Baum, Frank L. *The Wizard of Oz*. New York: Ballantine Books, 1986.

Beattie, Melodie. *Co-dependent No More*. New York: Harper/ Hazelden, 1987.

Black, Claudia. *Double Duty*. New York: Ballantine Books, 1990.

————. *It Will Never Happen To Me*. New York: Ballantine Books, 1987.

Bowden, Julie, and Herbert Gravitz. *Genesis: Spirituality in Recovery from Childhood Traumas*. Deerfield Beach, FL: Health Communications, Inc., 1988.

―――――. *A Guide to Recovery for Adult Children of Alcoholics*. Holmes Beach, FL: Learning Publications, Inc., 1985.

Bradshaw, John. *Healing the Shame that Binds You*. Deerfield Beach, FL: Health Communications, Inc., 1988.

Brooks, Cathleen. *The Secret Everyone Knows*. San Diego: Operation Cork, 1981.

Brown, Stephanie. *Safe Passage: Recovery for Adult Children of Alcoholics*. New York: John Wiley & Sons, Inc., 1992.

Carroll, Lewis. *Alice's Adventures in Wonderland*. New York: Bantam, 1985.

Cermak, Timmen. *Diagnosing and Treating Co-dependence*. Minneapolis: Johnson Institute Books, 1986.

―――――. *A Primer for Adult Children of Alcoholics*. Deerfield Beach, FL: Health Communications, Inc., 1989.

―――――. *A Time to Heal*. Los Angeles: Jeremy Tarcher, Inc., 1988.

Colgrove, Melba, et al. *How to Survive the Loss of a Love*. New York: Bantam, 1984.

de Saint-Exupéry, Antoine. *The Little Prince*. San Diego: Harcourt Brace, 1982.

Dillard, Annie. *Pilgrim at Tinker Creek*. New York: Harper's Magazine Press, 1974.

Fossum, Merle, and Marilyn Mason. *Facing Shame: Families in Recovery*. New York: W. W. Norton & Company, 1986.

Fox, Matthew, ed. *Western Spirituality: Historical Roots, Ecumenical Routes*. Santa Fe: Bear & Co., 1981.

Gelles, Richard, and Murray Strauss. *Intimate Violence: The Causes & Consequences of Abuse in the American Family*. New York: Touchstone Books, 1989.

Gil, Eliana. *Outgrowing the Pain*. New York: Dell, 1988.

Goldstein, Joseph. *The Experience of Insight: A Simple and Direct Guide to Buddhist Meditation*. Boston: Shambala, 1987.

Goodwin, Donald. *Is Alcoholism Hereditary?* New York: Ballantine Books, 1988.

Hanh, Thich Nhat. *Being Peace*. Berkeley: Parallax Press, 1987.

Haught, John F. *What Is Religion? An Introduction.* Mahwah, NJ: Paulist Press, 1970.

Hesse, Hermann. *Siddhartha.* New York: Bantam, 1981.

Hubbard, Woodleigh. *C Is for Curious: An ABC of Feelings.* San Francisco: Chronicle Books, 1990.

Johnson, Vernon. *I'll Quit Tomorrow.* New York: Harper & Row, 1980.

————. *Intervention: How to Help Someone Who Doesn't Want Help.* Minneapolis: Johnson Institute Books, 1986.

Kübler-Ross, Elisabeth. *On Death and Dying.* New York: Macmillan, 1969.

Kushner, Harold. *When Bad Things Happen to Good People.* New York: Schocken, 1987.

————. *Who Needs God.* New York: Summit Books, 1989.

Larsen, Earnie. *From Anger to Forgiveness.* New York: Ballantine Books, 1992.

Le Carré, John. *A Perfect Spy.* New York: Bantam, 1988.

Lerner, Harriet G., *The Dance of Anger.* New York: Harper & Row, 1985.

McGoldrick, Monica, and Randy Gerson. *Genograms in Family Assessment.* New York: Norton, 1985.

Mellody, Pia. *Facing Co-dependence.* New York: Harper & Row, 1989.

Merton, Thomas. *No Man Is an Island.* New York: Walker, 1986.

Miller, Alice. *The Drama of the Gifted Child.* New York: Basic Books, Harper Colophon Books, 1979.

Mowat, Farley. *Woman in the Mists.* New York: Warner Books, 1987.

Norwood, Robin. *Women Who Love Too Much.* Los Angeles: Jeremy P. Tarcher, Inc., 1985.

O'Gorman, Patricia, and Phil Oliver-Diaz. *Breaking the Cycle of Addiction: A Parent's Guide to Raising Healthy Kids.* Deerfield Beach, FL: Health Communications, Inc., 1987.

Scales, Cynthia. *Potato Chips for Breakfast.* Rockaway, NJ: Quotidian, 1986.

Schellenbaum, Peter. *How to Say No to the One You Love,* translated by Boris Matthews. Pittsburgh: Chiron Publishing, 1987.

Sendak, Maurice. *Where the Wild Things Are.* New York: Harper & Row, 1963.

Seuss, Dr. *The Cat in the Hat.* New York: Random House, 1985.

Shah, Idries. *The Way of the Sufi.* New York: Dutton, 1969.

Smith, Manuel. *When I Say No I Feel Guilty.* New York: Bantam, 1985.

Somers, Suzanne. *Keeping Secrets.* New York: Warner, 1988.

_____. *Wednesday's Children.* New York: Putnam/Healing Vision Publishing, 1992.

Suzuki, Shunryu. *Zen Mind, Beginner's Mind.* New York: Weatherhill, 1970.

Tart, Charles. *Waking Up: Overcoming the Obstacles to Human Potential.* Boston: Shambala, 1987.

Van Allsburg, Chris. *The Polar Express.* Boston: Houghton Mifflin, 1985.

Wegscheider-Cruse, Sharon. *Another Chance: Hope and Health for the Alcoholic Family.* Palo Alto, CA: Science & Behavior Books, 1981.

Whitfield, Charles. *Healing the Child Within.* Deerfield Beach, FL: Health Communications, Inc., 1987.

Wholey, Dennis. *Becoming Your Own Parent.* New York: Doubleday, 1988.

_____. *The Courage to Change.* Boston: Houghton Mifflin, 1984.

Woititz, Janet. *Adult Children of Alcoholics.* Deerfield Beach, FL: Health Communications, Inc., 1983.

_____. *A Struggle for Intimacy.* Deerfield Beach, FL: Health Communications, Inc., 1985.

Wolff, Tobias. *This Boy's Life: A Memoir.* New York: Harper & Row, 1989.

Wolin, Steven, and Sybil Wolin. *The Resilient Self.* New York: Villard Books, 1993.

Zybert, Richard. *Notebook on Time.* San Francisco: Marginal Press, 1981.

Discover more of yourself with Inner Work Books.

The following Inner Work Books are part of a series that explores psyche and spirit through writing, visualization, ritual, and imagination.

The Artist's Way: A Spiritual Path to Higher Creativity　　　　BY JULIA CAMERON

At a Journal Workshop (revised edition): *Writing to Access the Power of the Unconscious and Evoke Creative Ability*　　　　BY IRA PROGOFF, PH.D.

The Family Patterns Workbook: Breaking Free of Your Past and Creating a Life of Your Own　　　　BY CAROLYN FOSTER

Following Your Path: Using Myths, Symbols, and Images to Explore Your Inner Life　　　　BY ALEXANDRA COLLINS DICKERMAN

The Inner Child Workbook: What to Do with Your Past When It Just Won't Go Away　　　　BY CATHRYN TAYLOR, M.F.C.C.

A Journey Through Your Childhood: A Write-in Guide for Reliving Your Past, Clarifying Your Present, and Charting Your Future　　　　BY CHRISTOPHER BIFFLE

Pain and Possibility: Writing Your Way Through Personal Crisis　　　　BY GABRIELE RICO

The Path of the Everyday Hero: Drawing on the Power of Myth to Meet Life's Most Important Challenges　　　　BY LORNA CATFORD, PH.D., AND MICHAEL RAY, PH.D.

Personal Mythology: Using Ritual, Dreams, and Imagination to Discover Your Inner Story　　　　BY DAVID FEINSTEIN, PH.D., AND STANLEY KRIPPNER, PH.D.

The Possible Human: A Course in Extending Your Physical, Mental, and Creative Abilities　　　　BY JEAN HOUSTON

The Search for the Beloved: Journeys in Mythology and Sacred Psychology　　　　BY JEAN HOUSTON

Smart Love: A Codependence Recovery Program Based on Relationship Addiction Support Groups　　　　BY JODY HAYES

A Time to Heal Workbook: Stepping-stones to Recovery for Adult Children of Alcoholics　　　　BY TIMMEN L. CERMAK, M.D., AND JACQUES RUTZKY, M.F.C.C.

True Partners: A Workbook for Building a Lasting Intimate Relationship　　　　BY TINA B. TESSINA, PH.D., AND RILEY K. SMITH, M.A.

Your Mythic Journey: Finding Meaning in Your Life Through Writing and Storytelling　　　　BY SAM KEEN AND ANNE VALLEY-FOX

To order call 1-800-788-6262 or send your order to:

Jeremy P. Tarcher, Inc.
Mail Order Department
The Putnam Berkley Group, Inc.
390 Murray Hill Parkway
East Rutherford, NJ 07073-2185

	Title	ISBN	Price
_____	The Artist's Way	0-87477-694-5	$12.95
_____	At a Journal Workshop	0-87477-638-4	$15.95
_____	The Family Patterns Workbook	0-87477-711-9	$13.95
_____	Following Your Path	0-87477-687-2	$14.95
_____	The Inner Child Workbook	0-87477-635-X	$12.95
_____	A Journey Through Your Childhood	0-87477-499-3	$12.95
_____	Pain and Possibility	0-87477-571-X	$12.95
_____	The Path of the Everyday Hero	0-87477-630-9	$12.95
_____	Personal Mythology	0-87477-484-5	$10.95
_____	The Possible Human	0-87477-218-4	$13.95
_____	The Search for the Beloved	0-87477-476-4	$13.95
_____	Smart Love	0-87477-472-1	$ 9.95
_____	A Time to Heal Workbook	0-87477-745-3	$14.95
_____	True Partners	0-87477-727-5	$13.95
_____	Your Mythic Journey	0-87477-543-4	$ 9.95

Subtotal $_____

Shipping and handling* $_____

Sales tax (CA, NJ, NY, PA, VA) $_____

Total amount due $_____

Payable in U.S. funds (no cash orders accepted). $15.00 minimum for credit card orders.

* Shipping and handling: $2.50 for one book, $0.75 for each additional book, not to exceed $6.25.

Enclosed is my ☐ check ☐ money order

Please charge my ☐ Visa ☐ MasterCard ☐ American Express

Card # _____ Expiration date _____

Signature as on credit card _____

Daytime phone number _____

Name _____

Address _____

City _____ State _____ Zip _____

Please allow six weeks for delivery. Prices subject to change without notice.

Source key **IWB**